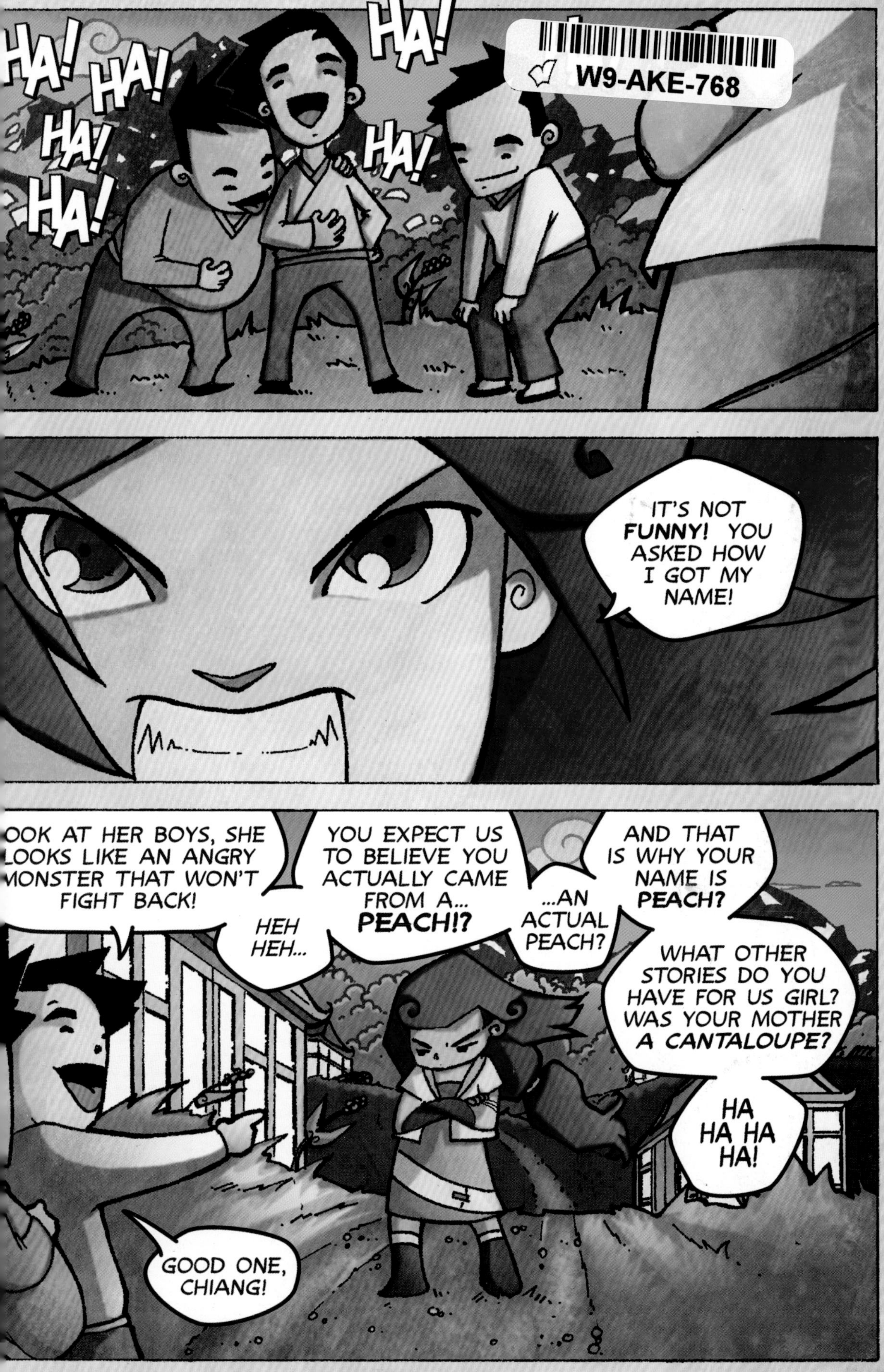
HA! HA! HA! HA! HA! HA!
IT'S NOT FUNNY! YOU ASKED HOW I GOT MY NAME!
OOK AT HER BOYS, SHE LOOKS LIKE AN ANGRY MONSTER THAT WON'T FIGHT BACK!
HEH HEH...
YOU EXPECT US TO BELIEVE YOU ACTUALLY CAME FROM A... PEACH!?
...AN ACTUAL PEACH?
AND THAT IS WHY YOUR NAME IS PEACH?
WHAT OTHER STORIES DO YOU HAVE FOR US GIRL? WAS YOUR MOTHER A CANTALOUPE?
HA HA HA HA!
GOOD ONE, CHIANG!

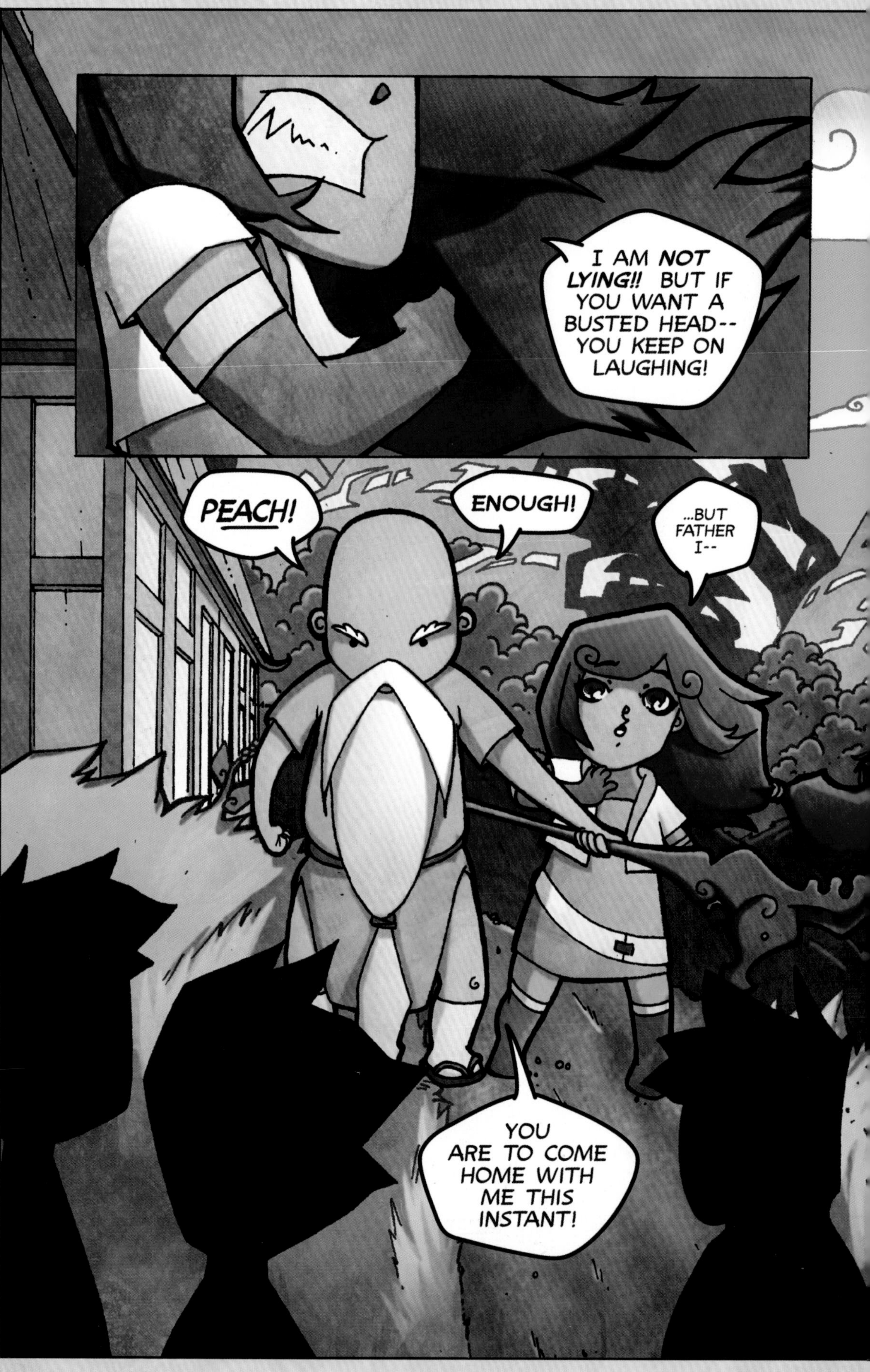
I AM NOT LYING!! BUT IF YOU WANT A BUSTED HEAD-- YOU KEEP ON LAUGHING!
PEACH!
ENOUGH!
...BUT FATHER I--
YOU ARE TO COME HOME WITH ME THIS INSTANT!

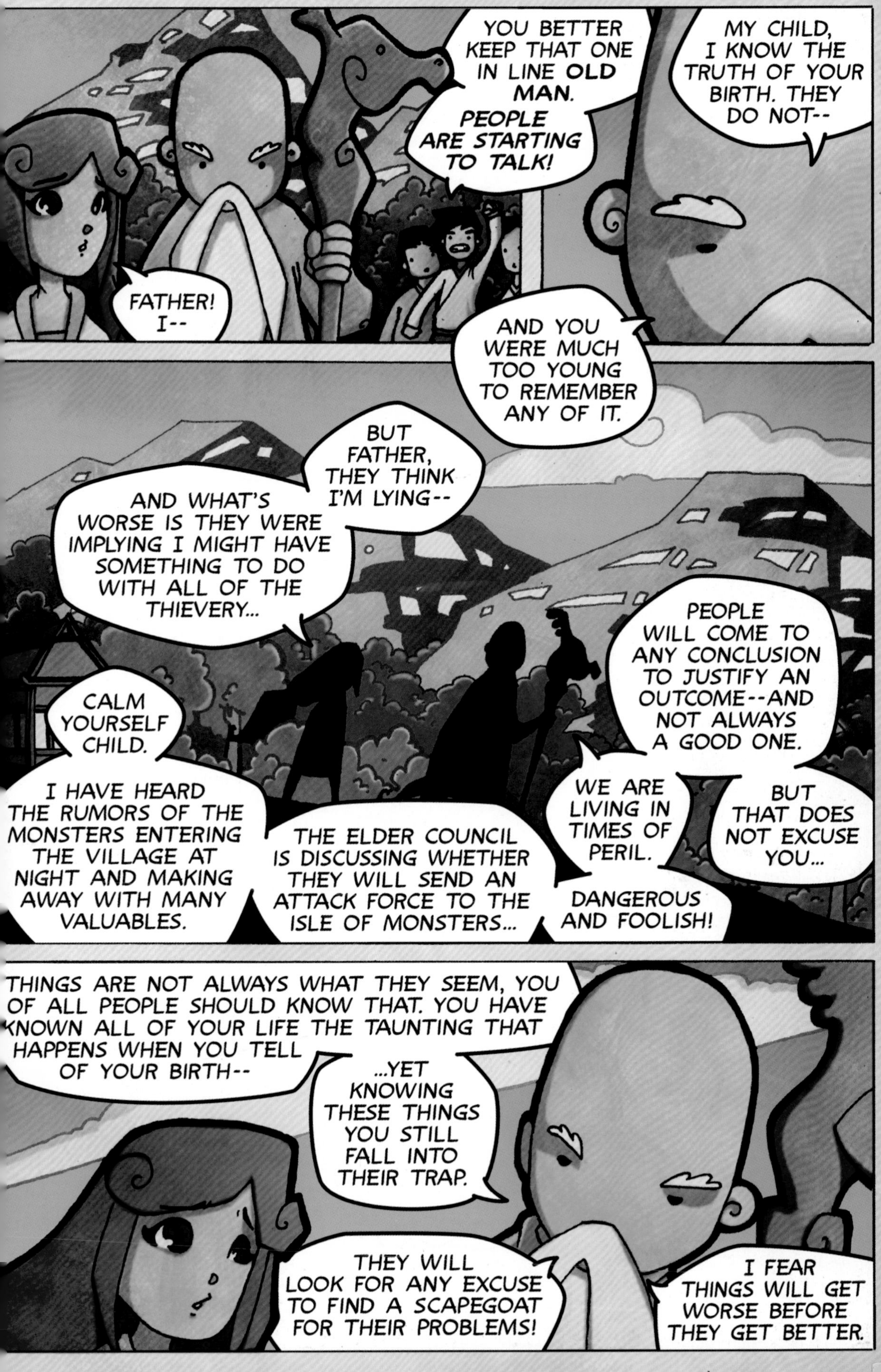
YOU BETTER KEEP THAT ONE IN LINE OLD MAN.
PEOPLE ARE STARTING TO TALK!
FATHER! I--
MY CHILD, I KNOW THE TRUTH OF YOUR BIRTH. THEY DO NOT--
AND YOU WERE MUCH TOO YOUNG TO REMEMBER ANY OF IT.
BUT FATHER, THEY THINK I'M LYING--
AND WHAT'S WORSE IS THEY WERE IMPLYING I MIGHT HAVE SOMETHING TO DO WITH ALL OF THE THIEVERY...
CALM YOURSELF CHILD.
I HAVE HEARD THE RUMORS OF THE MONSTERS ENTERING THE VILLAGE AT NIGHT AND MAKING AWAY WITH MANY VALUABLES.
THE ELDER COUNCIL IS DISCUSSING WHETHER THEY WILL SEND AN ATTACK FORCE TO THE ISLE OF MONSTERS...
PEOPLE WILL COME TO ANY CONCLUSION TO JUSTIFY AN OUTCOME--AND NOT ALWAYS A GOOD ONE.
WE ARE LIVING IN TIMES OF PERIL.
DANGEROUS AND FOOLISH!
BUT THAT DOES NOT EXCUSE YOU...
THINGS ARE NOT ALWAYS WHAT THEY SEEM, YOU OF ALL PEOPLE SHOULD KNOW THAT. YOU HAVE KNOWN ALL OF YOUR LIFE THE TAUNTING THAT HAPPENS WHEN YOU TELL OF YOUR BIRTH--
...YET KNOWING THESE THINGS YOU STILL FALL INTO THEIR TRAP.
THEY WILL LOOK FOR ANY EXCUSE TO FIND A SCAPEGOAT FOR THEIR PROBLEMS!
I FEAR THINGS WILL GET WORSE BEFORE THEY GET BETTER.

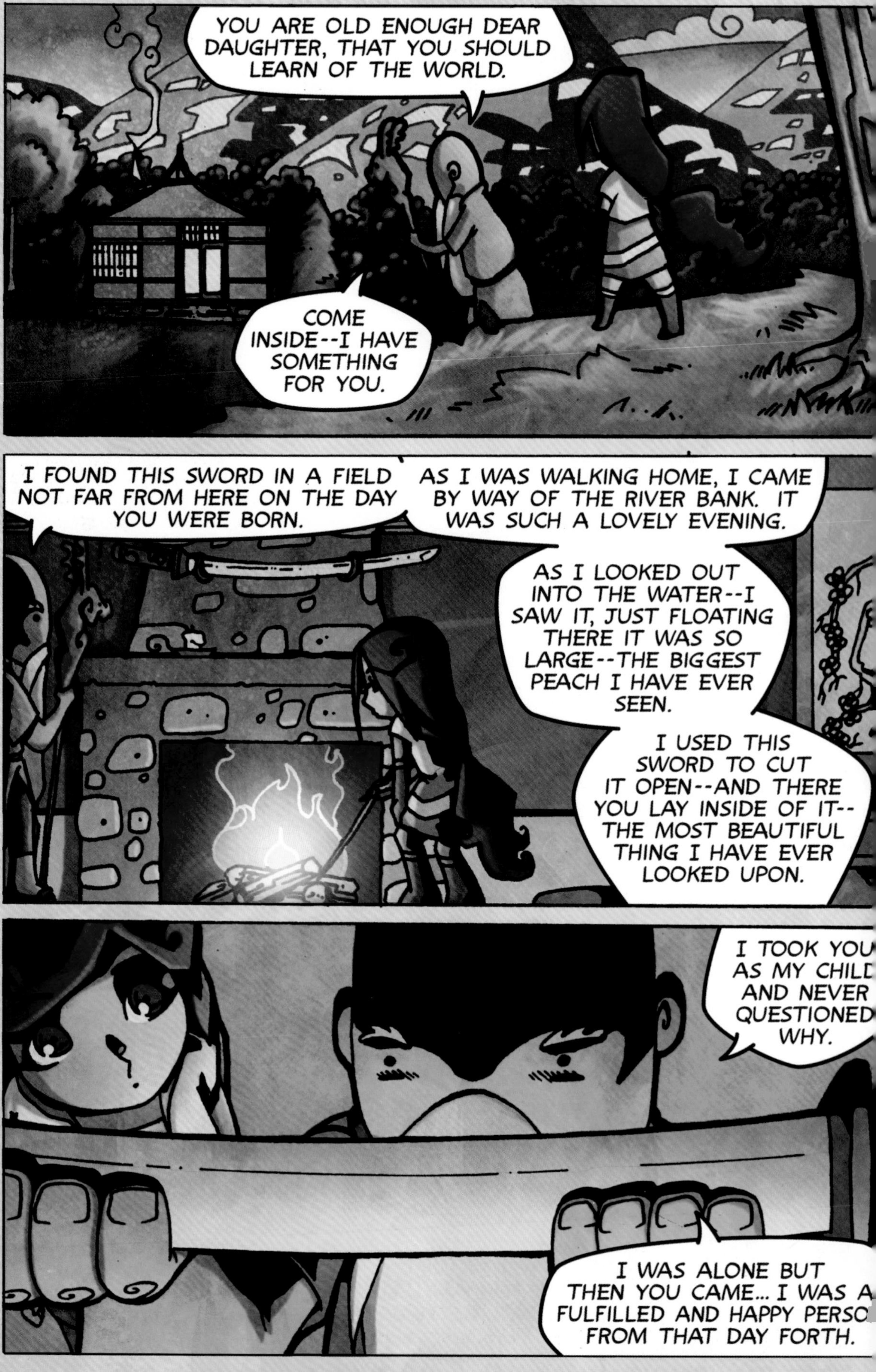
YOU ARE OLD ENOUGH DEAR DAUGHTER, THAT YOU SHOULD LEARN OF THE WORLD.
COME INSIDE--I HAVE SOMETHING FOR YOU.
I FOUND THIS SWORD IN A FIELD NOT FAR FROM HERE ON THE DAY YOU WERE BORN.
AS I WAS WALKING HOME, I CAME BY WAY OF THE RIVER BANK. IT WAS SUCH A LOVELY EVENING.
AS I LOOKED OUT INTO THE WATER--I SAW IT, JUST FLOATING THERE IT WAS SO LARGE--THE BIGGEST PEACH I HAVE EVER SEEN.
I USED THIS SWORD TO CUT IT OPEN--AND THERE YOU LAY INSIDE OF IT--THE MOST BEAUTIFUL THING I HAVE EVER LOOKED UPON.
I TOOK YOU AS MY CHILD AND NEVER QUESTIONED WHY.
I WAS ALONE BUT THEN YOU CAME... I WAS A FULFILLED AND HAPPY PERSO FROM THAT DAY FORTH.

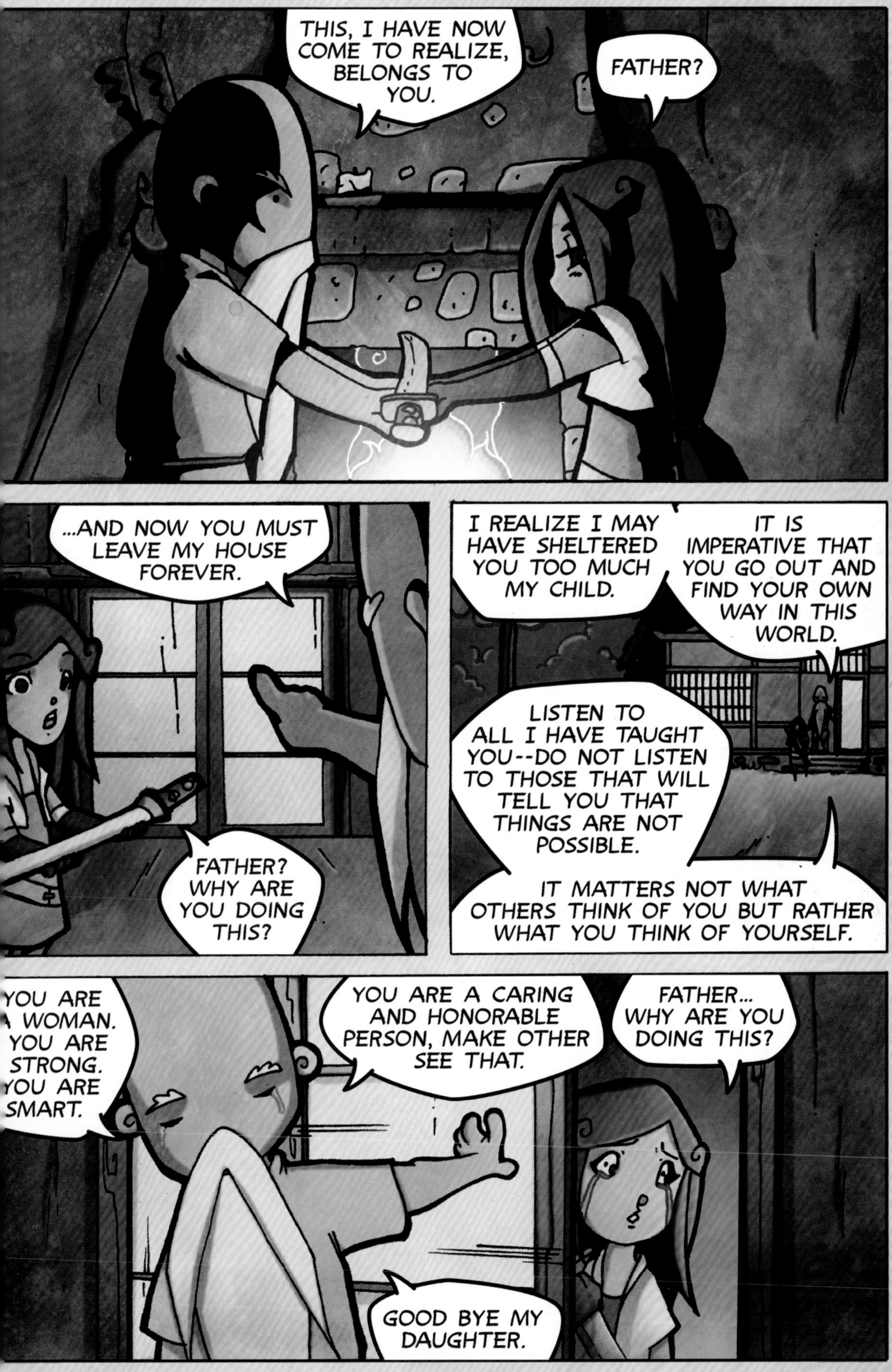
THIS, I HAVE NOW COME TO REALIZE, BELONGS TO YOU.
FATHER?
...AND NOW YOU MUST LEAVE MY HOUSE FOREVER.
FATHER? WHY ARE YOU DOING THIS?
I REALIZE I MAY HAVE SHELTERED YOU TOO MUCH MY CHILD.
IT IS IMPERATIVE THAT YOU GO OUT AND FIND YOUR OWN WAY IN THIS WORLD.
LISTEN TO ALL I HAVE TAUGHT YOU--DO NOT LISTEN TO THOSE THAT WILL TELL YOU THAT THINGS ARE NOT POSSIBLE.
IT MATTERS NOT WHAT OTHERS THINK OF YOU BUT RATHER WHAT YOU THINK OF YOURSELF.
YOU ARE A WOMAN. YOU ARE STRONG. YOU ARE SMART.
YOU ARE A CARING AND HONORABLE PERSON, MAKE OTHER SEE THAT.
FATHER... WHY ARE YOU DOING THIS?
GOOD BYE MY DAUGHTER.

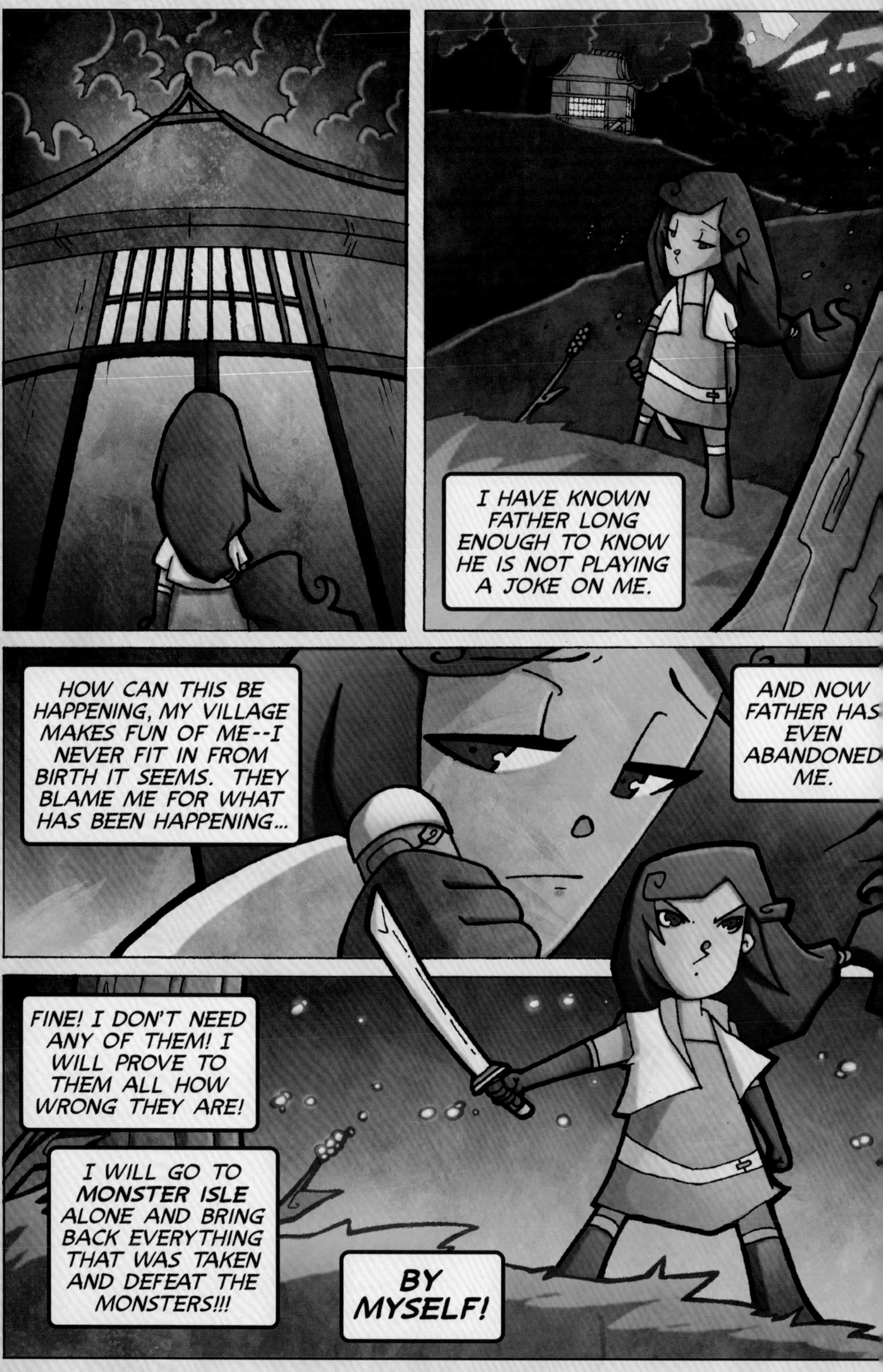
I HAVE KNOWN FATHER LONG ENOUGH TO KNOW HE IS NOT PLAYING A JOKE ON ME.
HOW CAN THIS BE HAPPENING, MY VILLAGE MAKES FUN OF ME--I NEVER FIT IN FROM BIRTH IT SEEMS. THEY BLAME ME FOR WHAT HAS BEEN HAPPENING...
AND NOW FATHER HAS EVEN ABANDONED ME.
FINE! I DON'T NEED ANY OF THEM! I WILL PROVE TO THEM ALL HOW WRONG THEY ARE!
I WILL GO TO MONSTER ISLE ALONE AND BRING BACK EVERYTHING THAT WAS TAKEN AND DEFEAT THE MONSTERS!!!
BY MYSELF!

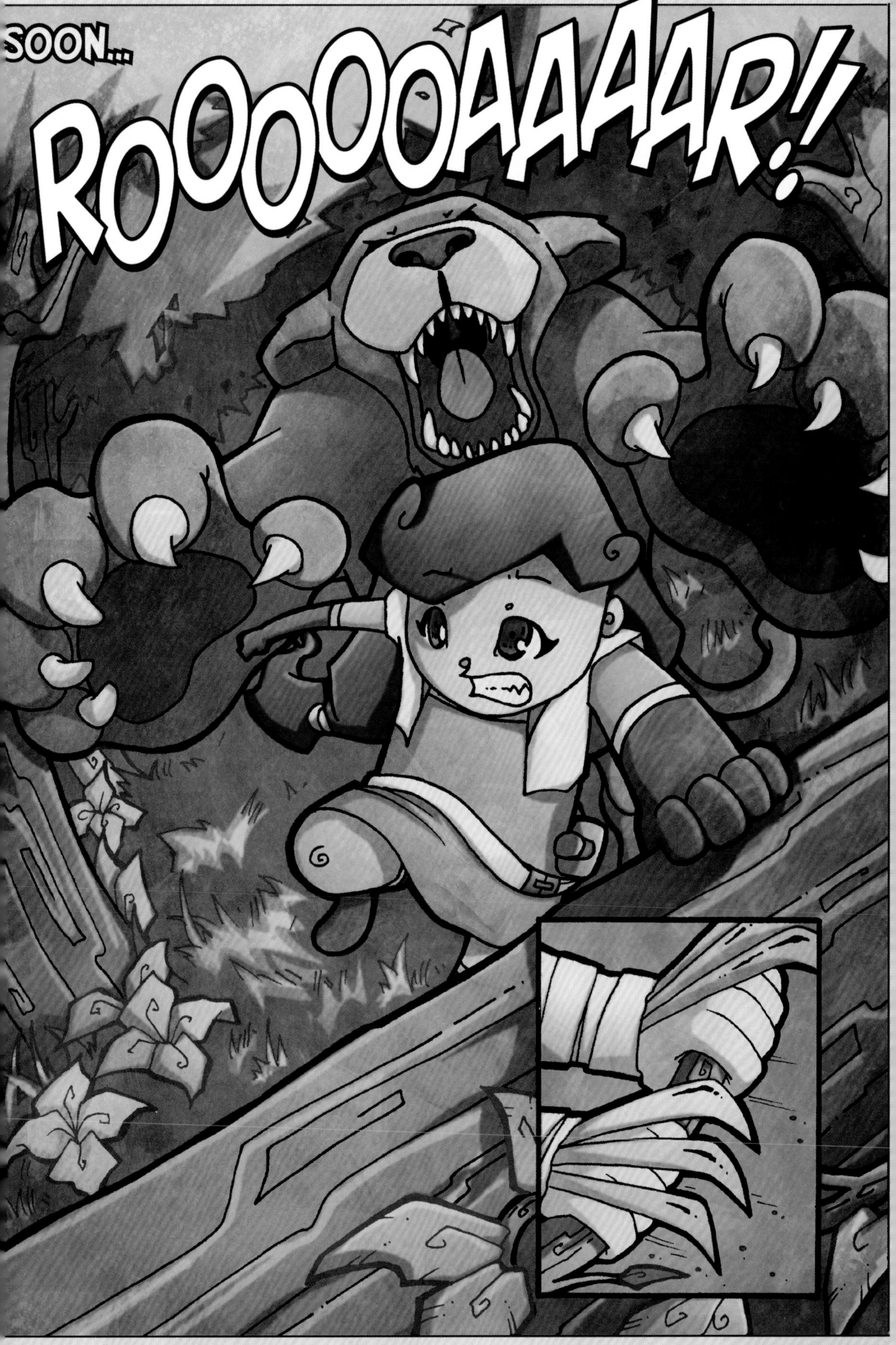
SOON...
ROOOOOAAAAR!!

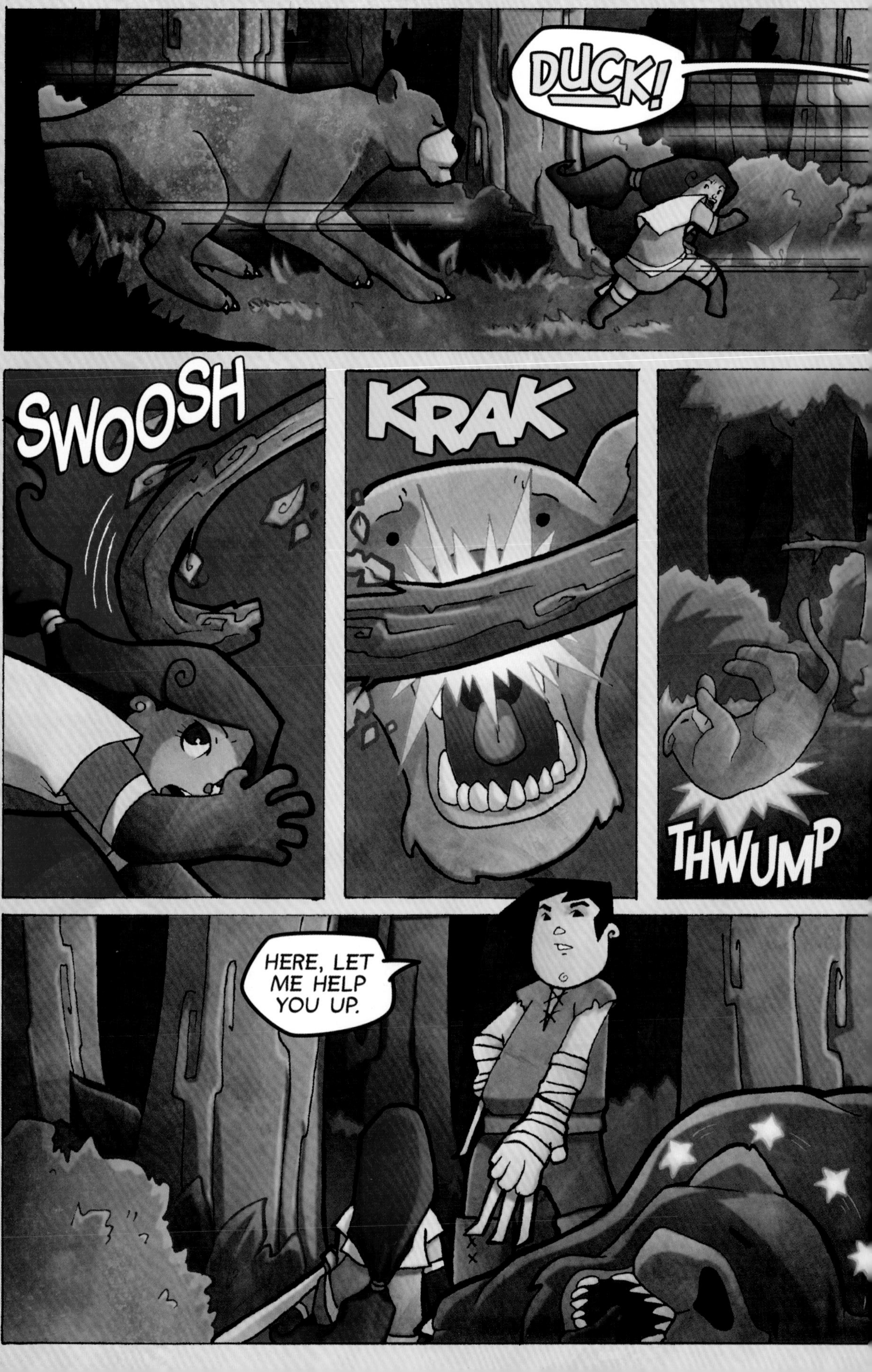
DUCK!
SWOOSH
KRAK
THWUMP
HERE, LET ME HELP YOU UP.

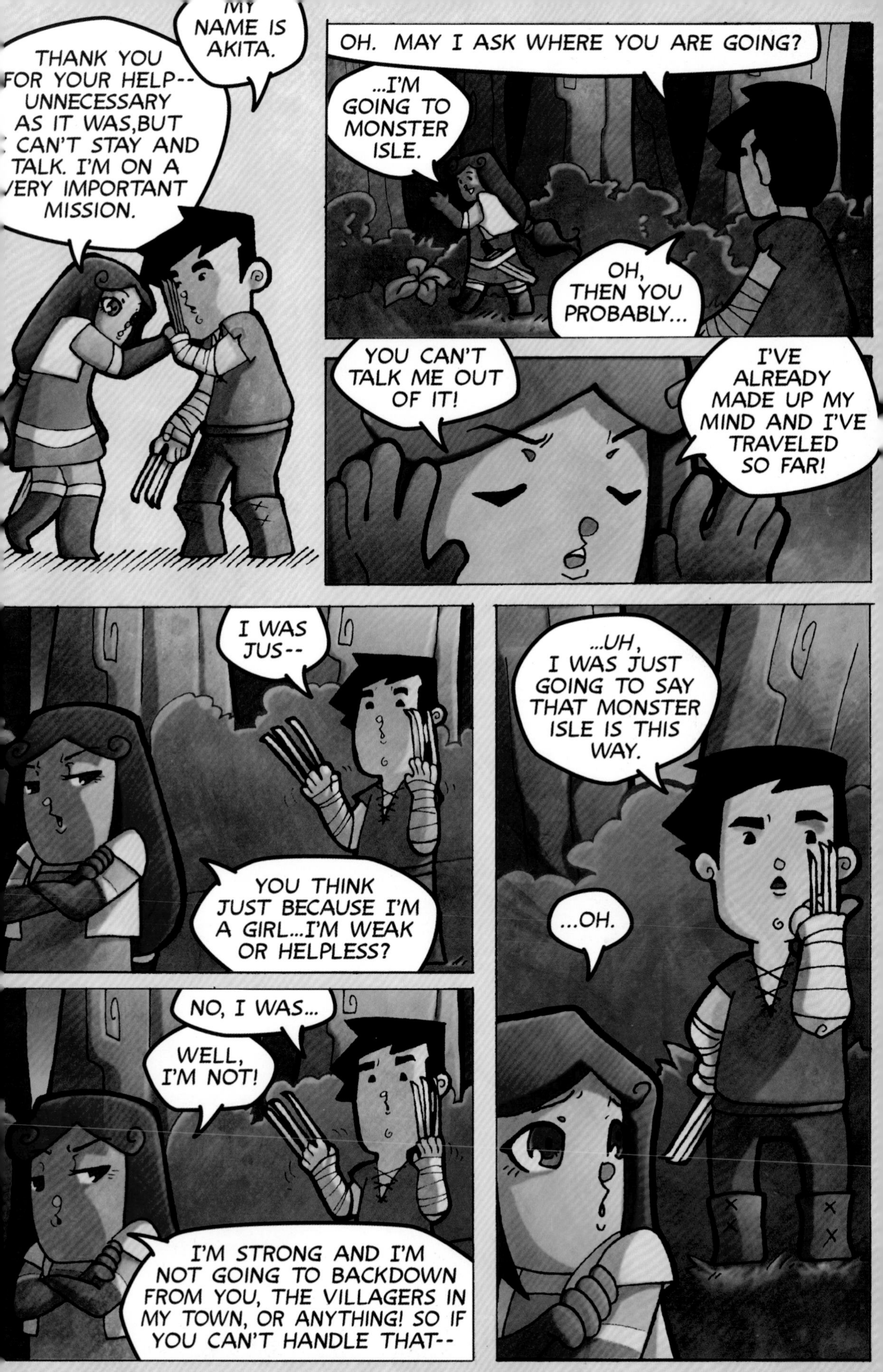
THANK YOU FOR YOUR HELP-- UNNECESSARY AS IT WAS,BUT CAN'T STAY AND TALK. I'M ON A ERY IMPORTANT MISSION.
MY NAME IS AKITA.
OH. MAY I ASK WHERE YOU ARE GOING?
...I'M GOING TO MONSTER ISLE.
OH, THEN YOU PROBABLY...
YOU CAN'T TALK ME OUT OF IT!
I'VE ALREADY MADE UP MY MIND AND I'VE TRAVELED SO FAR!
I WAS JUS--
YOU THINK JUST BECAUSE I'M A GIRL...I'M WEAK OR HELPLESS?
NO, I WAS...
WELL, I'M NOT!
I'M STRONG AND I'M NOT GOING TO BACKDOWN FROM YOU, THE VILLAGERS IN MY TOWN, OR ANYTHING! SO IF YOU CAN'T HANDLE THAT--
...UH, I WAS JUST GOING TO SAY THAT MONSTER ISLE IS THIS WAY.
...OH.

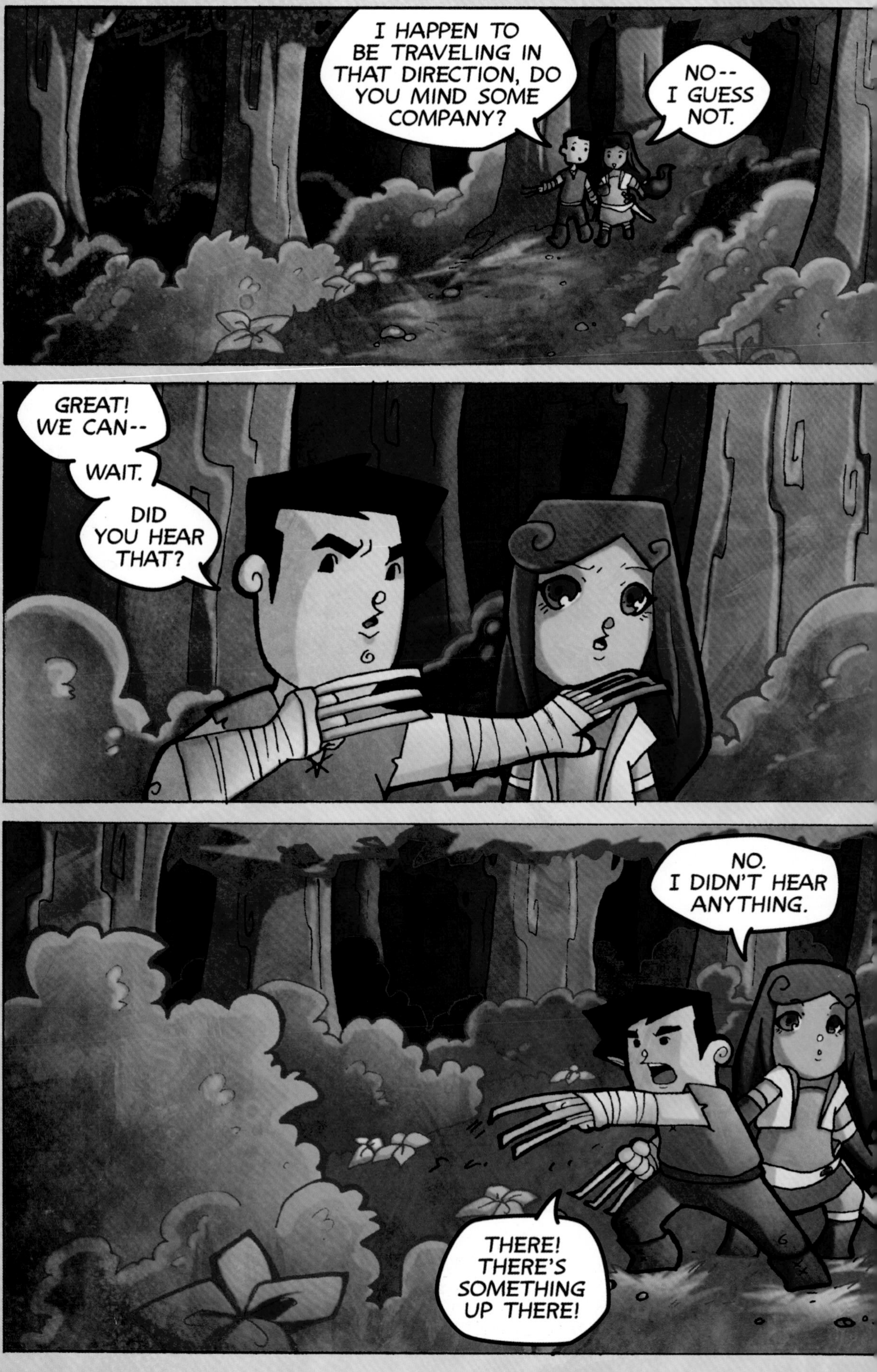
I HAPPEN TO BE TRAVELING IN THAT DIRECTION, DO YOU MIND SOME COMPANY?
NO-- I GUESS NOT.
GREAT! WE CAN--
WAIT.
DID YOU HEAR THAT?
NO. I DIDN'T HEAR ANYTHING.
THERE! THERE'S SOMETHING UP THERE!

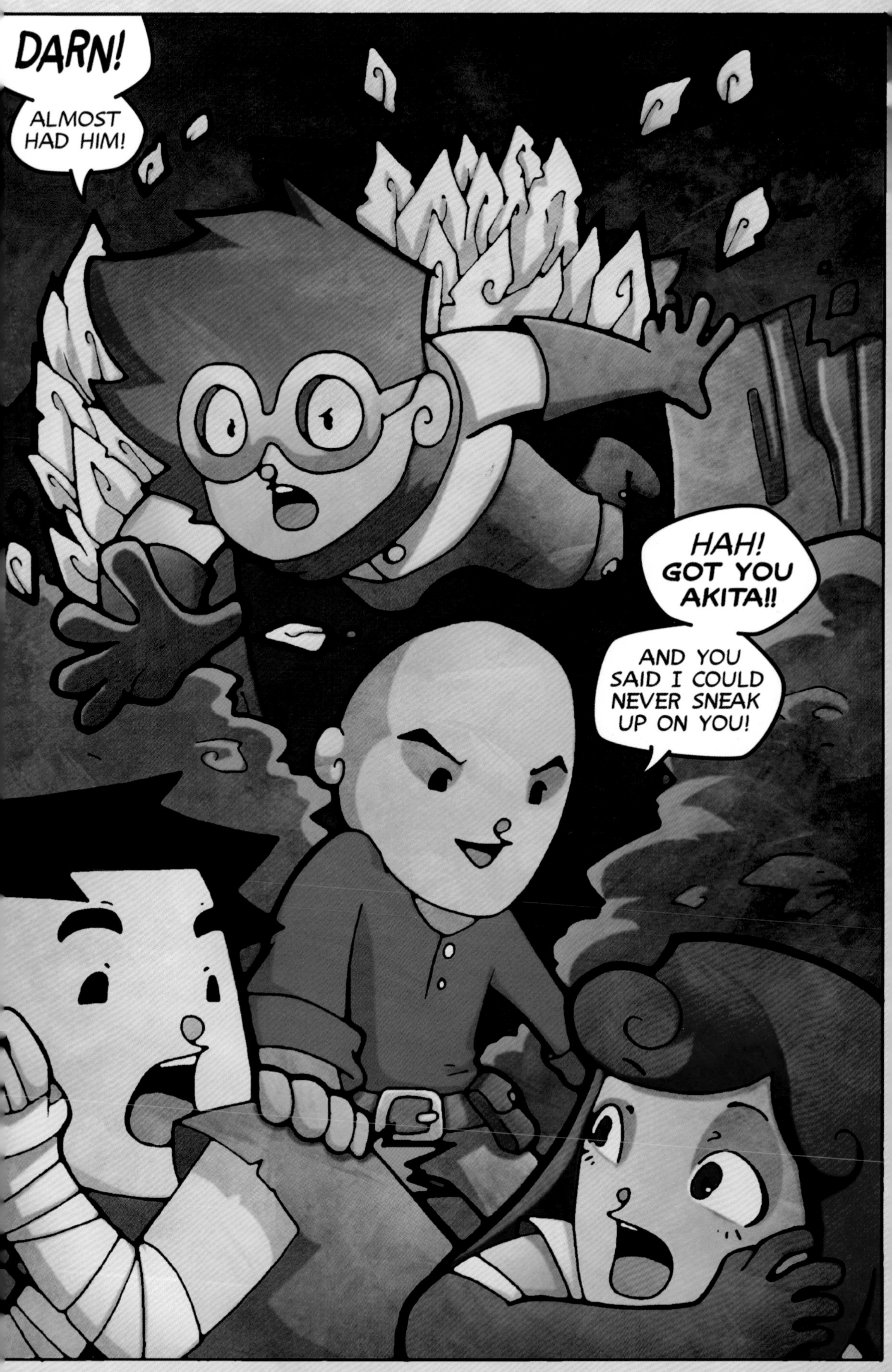
DARN!
ALMOST HAD HIM!
HAH! GOT YOU AKITA!!
AND YOU SAID I COULD NEVER SNEAK UP ON YOU!

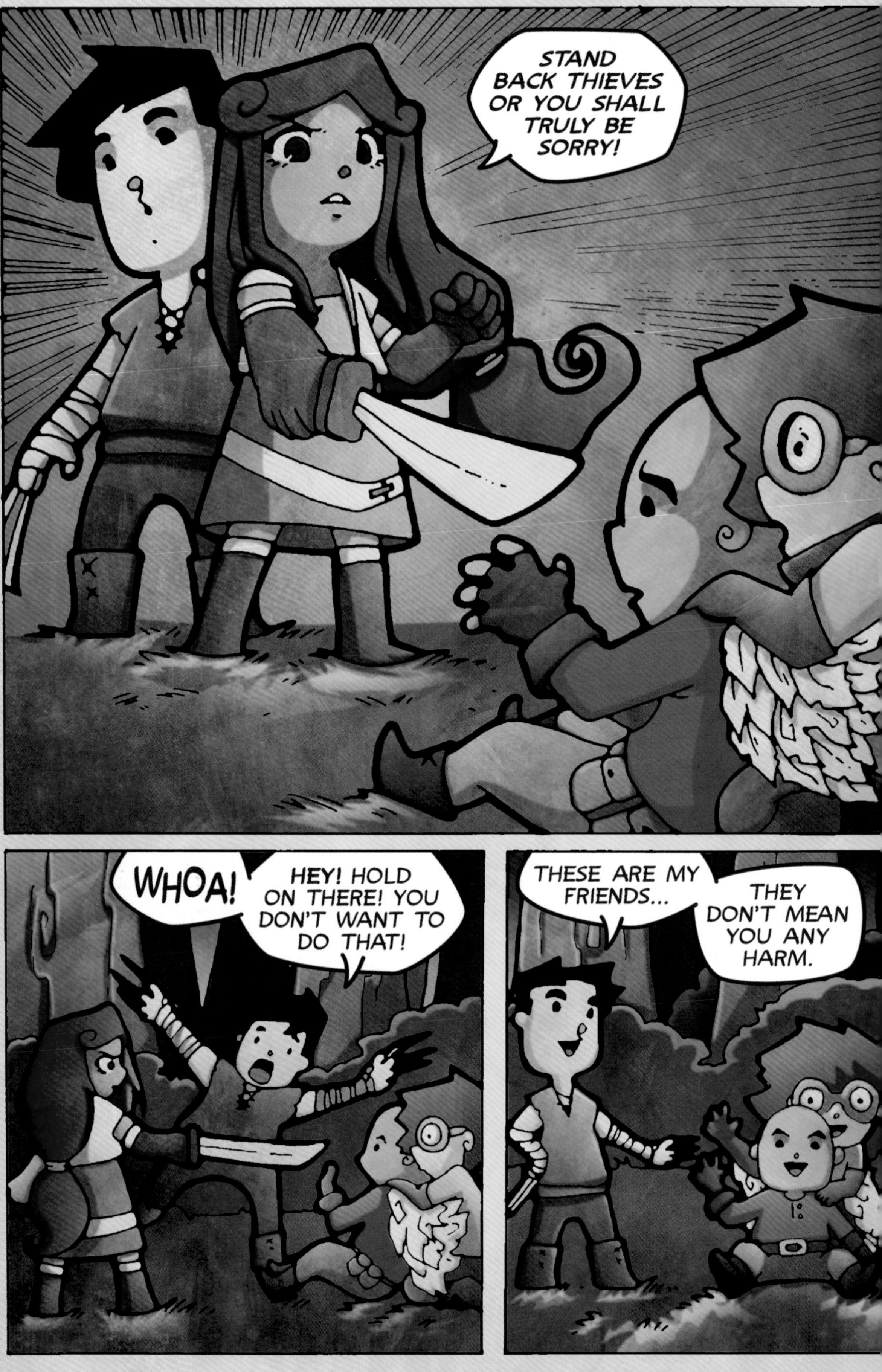
STAND BACK THIEVES OR YOU SHALL TRULY BE SORRY!
WHOA!
HEY! HOLD ON THERE! YOU DON'T WANT TO DO THAT!
THESE ARE MY FRIENDS...
THEY DON'T MEAN YOU ANY HARM.

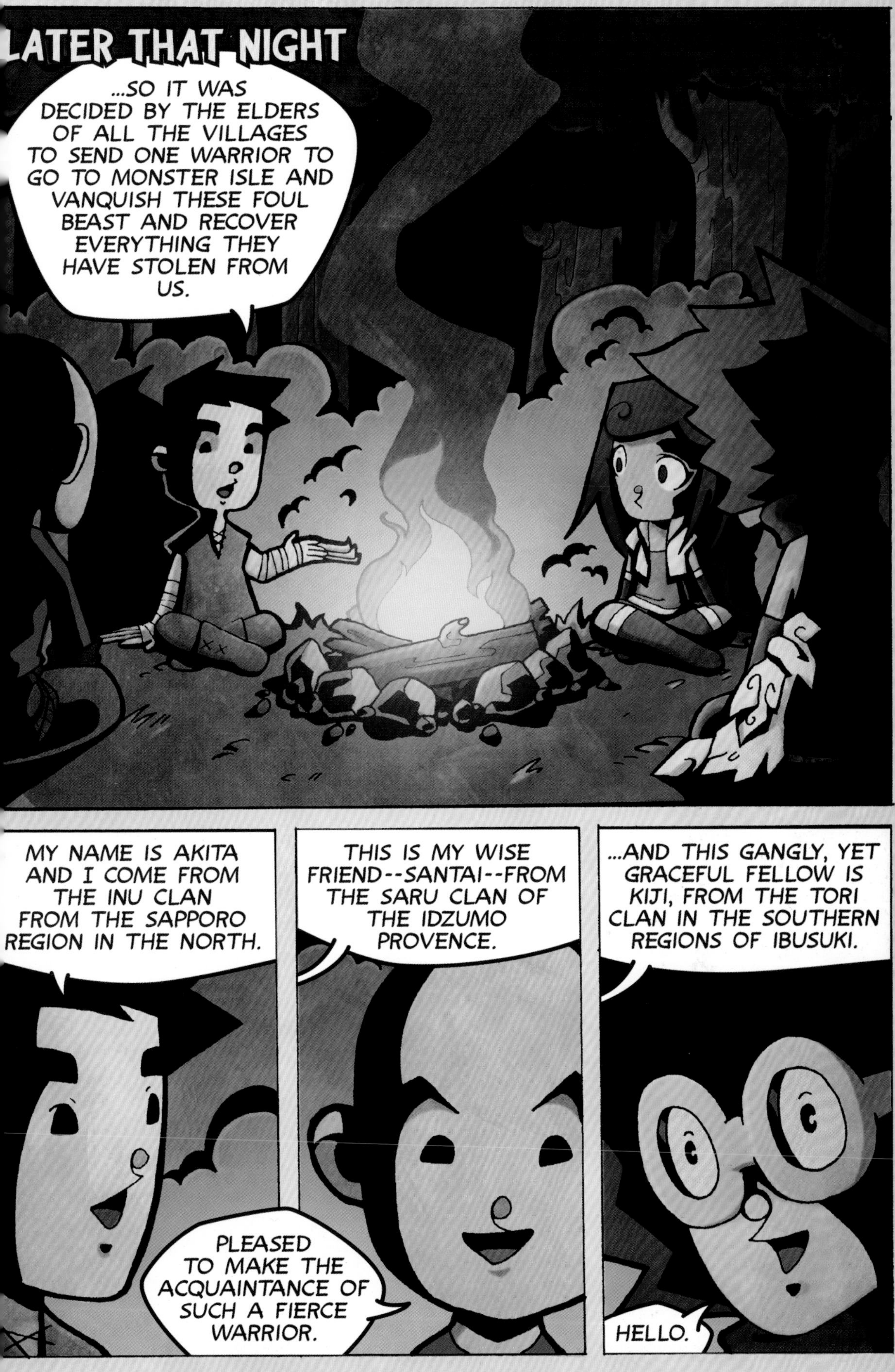
LATER THAT NIGHT
...SO IT WAS DECIDED BY THE ELDERS OF ALL THE VILLAGES TO SEND ONE WARRIOR TO GO TO MONSTER ISLE AND VANQUISH THESE FOUL BEAST AND RECOVER EVERYTHING THEY HAVE STOLEN FROM US.
MY NAME IS AKITA AND I COME FROM THE INU CLAN FROM THE SAPPORO REGION IN THE NORTH.
THIS IS MY WISE FRIEND--SANTAI--FROM THE SARU CLAN OF THE IDZUMO PROVENCE.
PLEASED TO MAKE THE ACQUAINTANCE OF SUCH A FIERCE WARRIOR.
...AND THIS GANGLY, YET GRACEFUL FELLOW IS KIJI, FROM THE TORI CLAN IN THE SOUTHERN REGIONS OF IBUSUKI.
HELLO.

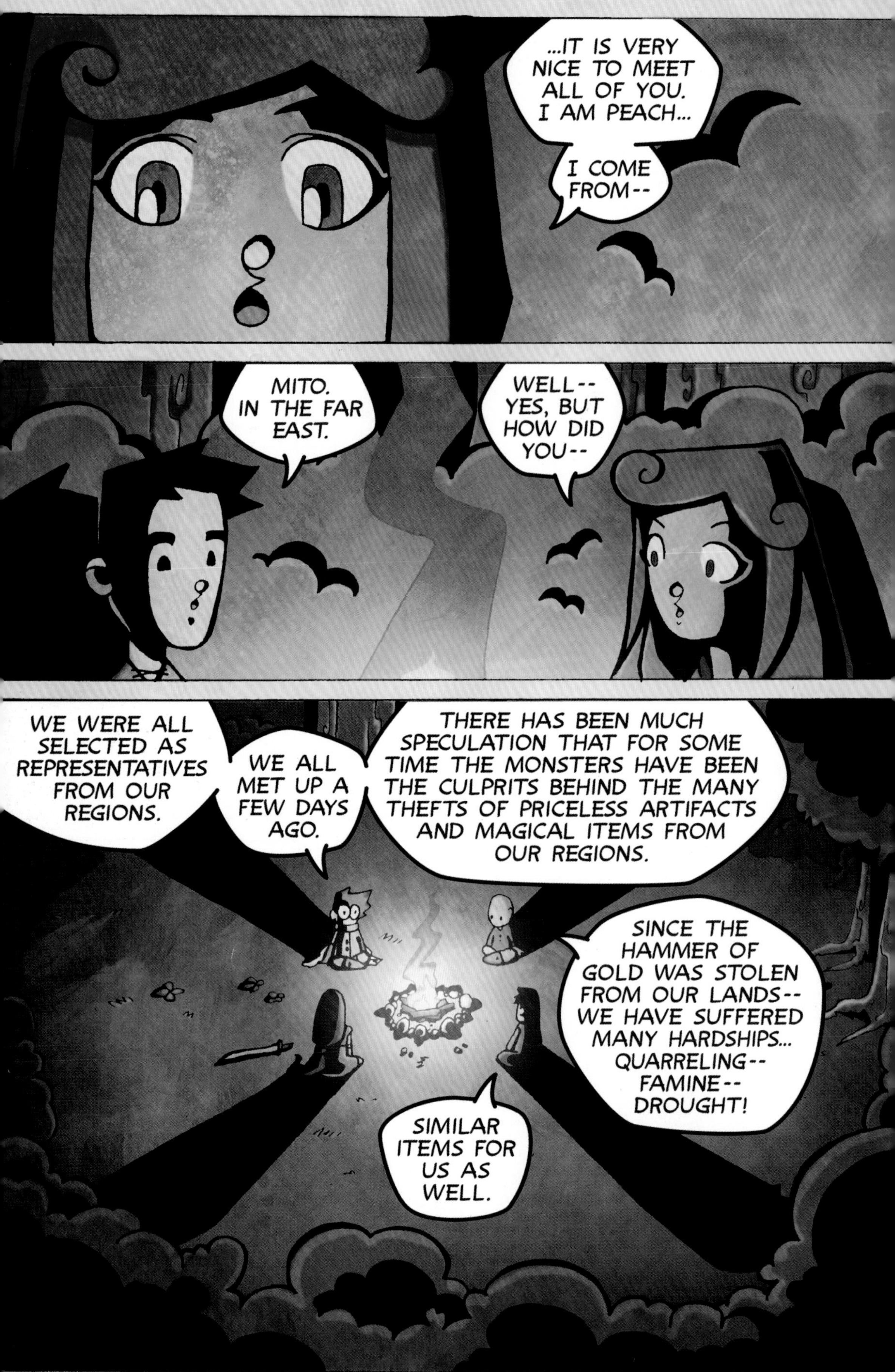
...IT IS VERY NICE TO MEET ALL OF YOU. I AM PEACH...
I COME FROM--
MITO. IN THE FAR EAST.
WELL--YES, BUT HOW DID YOU--
WE WERE ALL SELECTED AS REPRESENTATIVES FROM OUR REGIONS.
WE ALL MET UP A FEW DAYS AGO.
THERE HAS BEEN MUCH SPECULATION THAT FOR SOME TIME THE MONSTERS HAVE BEEN THE CULPRITS BEHIND THE MANY THEFTS OF PRICELESS ARTIFACTS AND MAGICAL ITEMS FROM OUR REGIONS.
SINCE THE HAMMER OF GOLD WAS STOLEN FROM OUR LANDS--WE HAVE SUFFERED MANY HARDSHIPS... QUARRELING--FAMINE--DROUGHT!
SIMILAR ITEMS FOR US AS WELL.

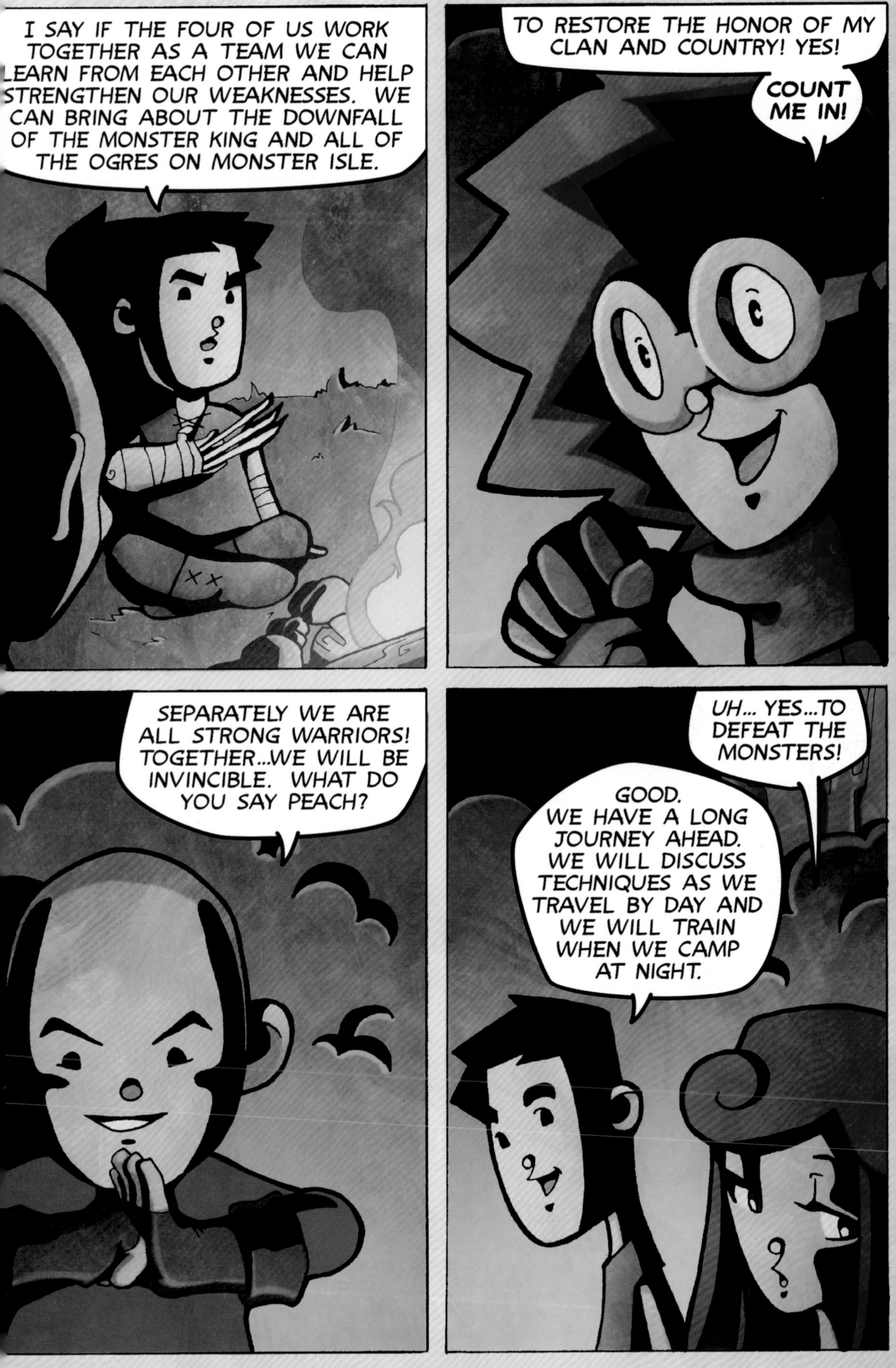
I SAY IF THE FOUR OF US WORK TOGETHER AS A TEAM WE CAN LEARN FROM EACH OTHER AND HELP STRENGTHEN OUR WEAKNESSES. WE CAN BRING ABOUT THE DOWNFALL OF THE MONSTER KING AND ALL OF THE OGRES ON MONSTER ISLE.
TO RESTORE THE HONOR OF MY CLAN AND COUNTRY! YES!
COUNT ME IN!
SEPARATELY WE ARE ALL STRONG WARRIORS! TOGETHER...WE WILL BE INVINCIBLE. WHAT DO YOU SAY PEACH?
UH... YES...TO DEFEAT THE MONSTERS!
GOOD. WE HAVE A LONG JOURNEY AHEAD. WE WILL DISCUSS TECHNIQUES AS WE TRAVEL BY DAY AND WE WILL TRAIN WHEN WE CAMP AT NIGHT.

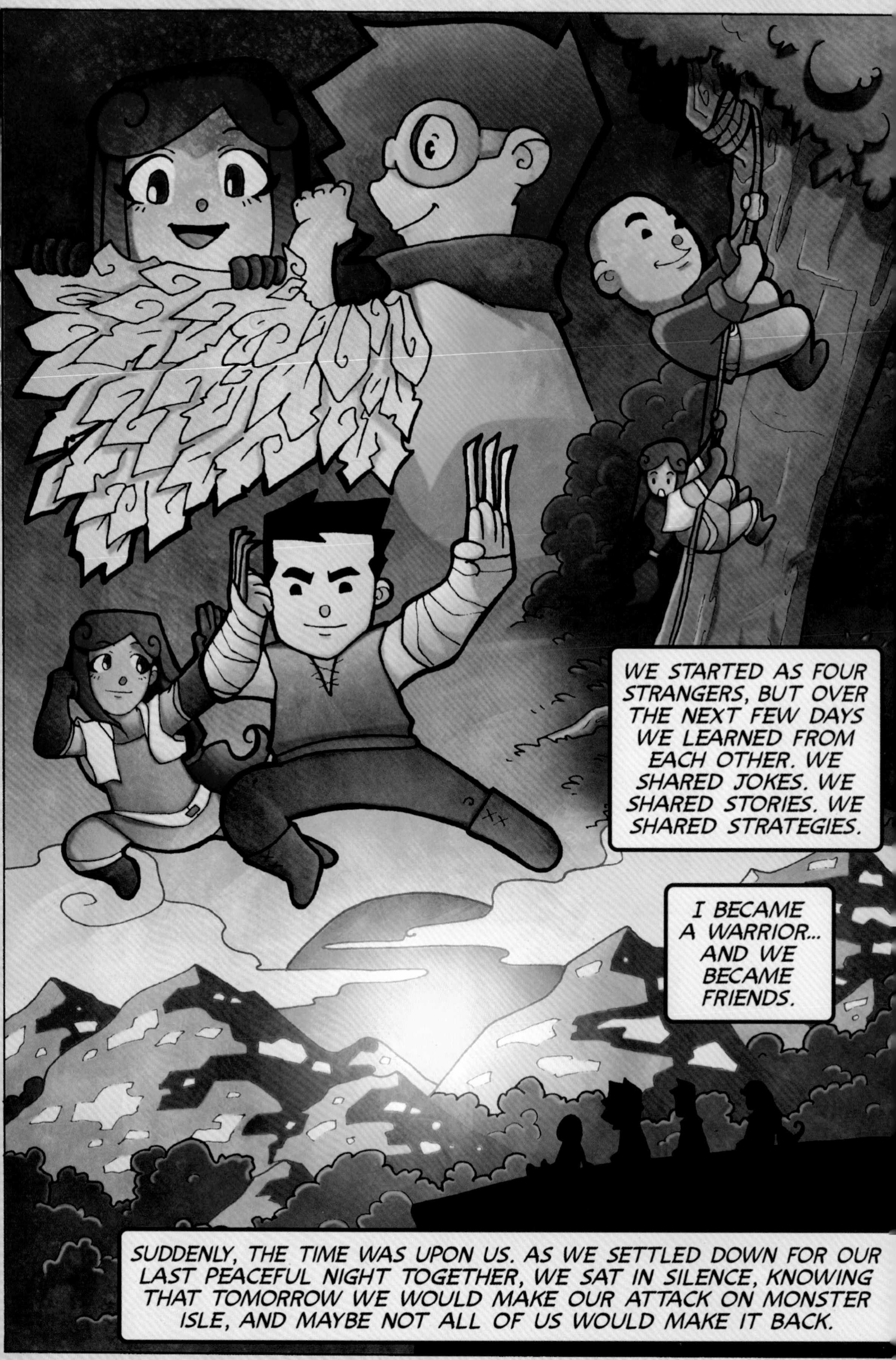
WE STARTED AS FOUR STRANGERS, BUT OVER THE NEXT FEW DAYS WE LEARNED FROM EACH OTHER. WE SHARED JOKES. WE SHARED STORIES. WE SHARED STRATEGIES.
I BECAME A WARRIOR... AND WE BECAME FRIENDS.
SUDDENLY, THE TIME WAS UPON US. AS WE SETTLED DOWN FOR OUR LAST PEACEFUL NIGHT TOGETHER, WE SAT IN SILENCE, KNOWING THAT TOMORROW WE WOULD MAKE OUR ATTACK ON MONSTER ISLE, AND MAYBE NOT ALL OF US WOULD MAKE IT BACK.

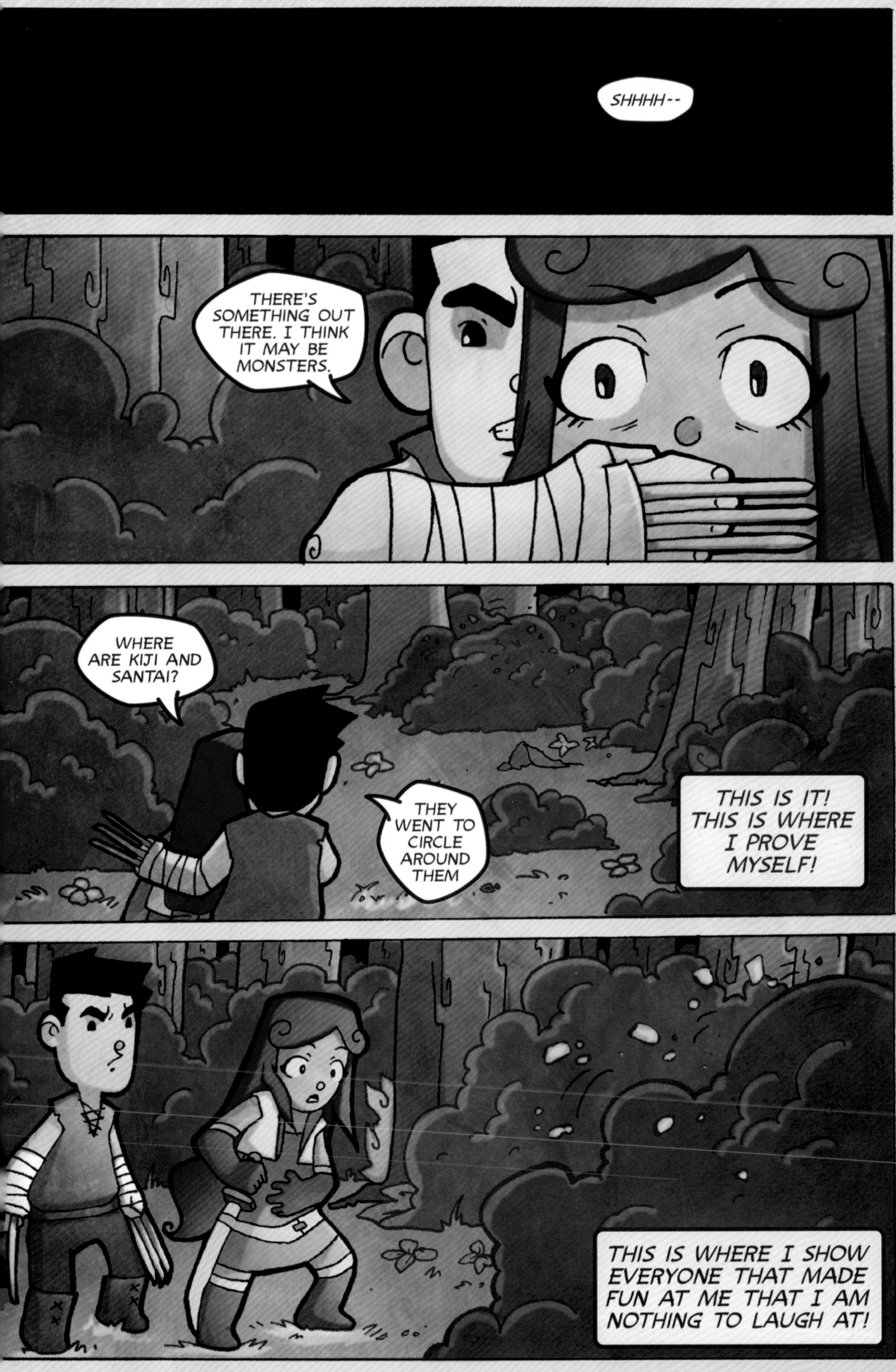
SHHHH--
THERE'S SOMETHING OUT THERE. I THINK IT MAY BE MONSTERS.
WHERE ARE KIJI AND SANTAI?
THEY WENT TO CIRCLE AROUND THEM
THIS IS IT! THIS IS WHERE I PROVE MYSELF!
THIS IS WHERE I SHOW EVERYONE THAT MADE FUN AT ME THAT I AM NOTHING TO LAUGH AT!

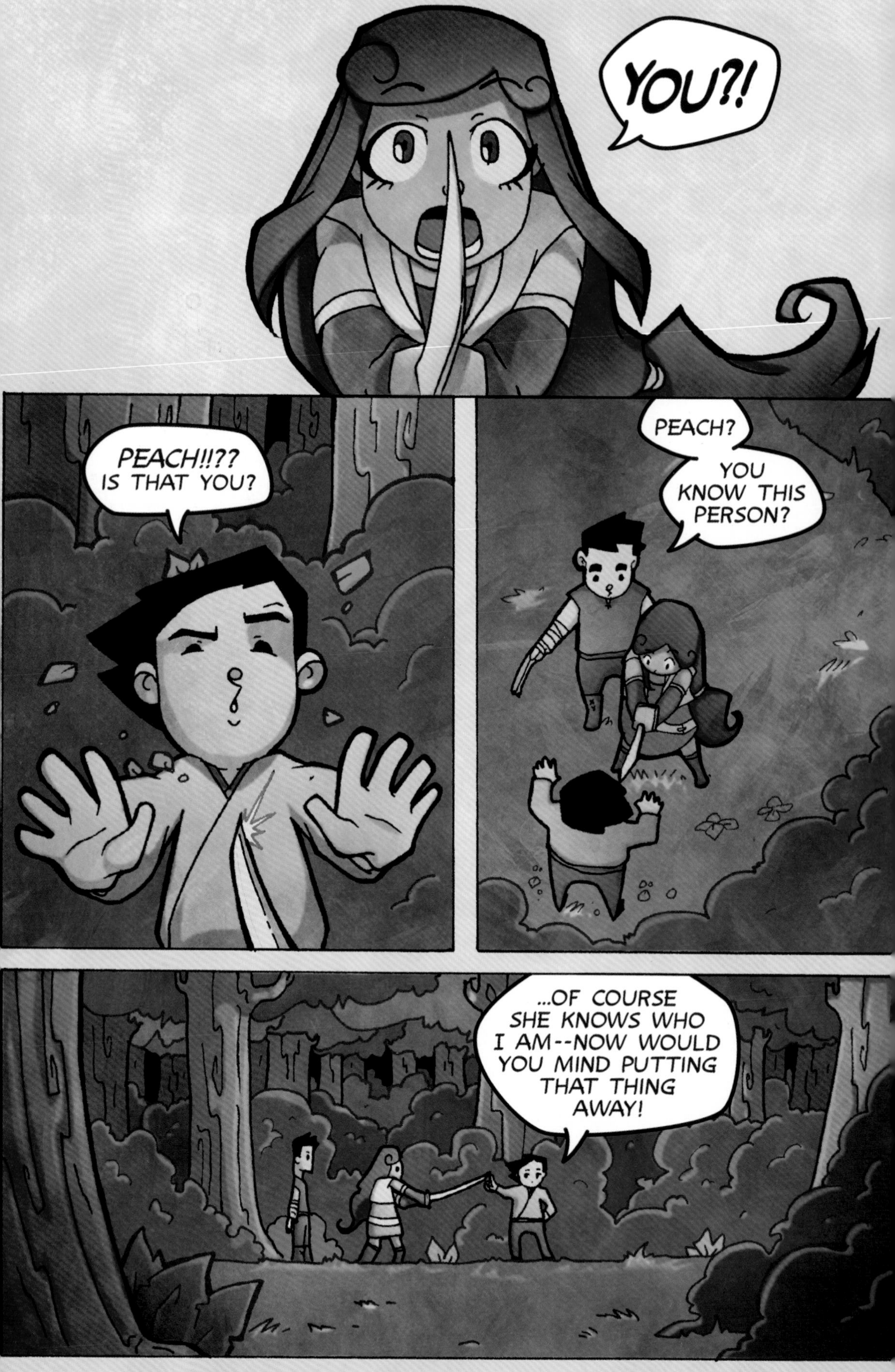
YOU?!
PEACH!!?? IS THAT YOU?
PEACH?
YOU KNOW THIS PERSON?
...OF COURSE SHE KNOWS WHO I AM--NOW WOULD YOU MIND PUTTING THAT THING AWAY!

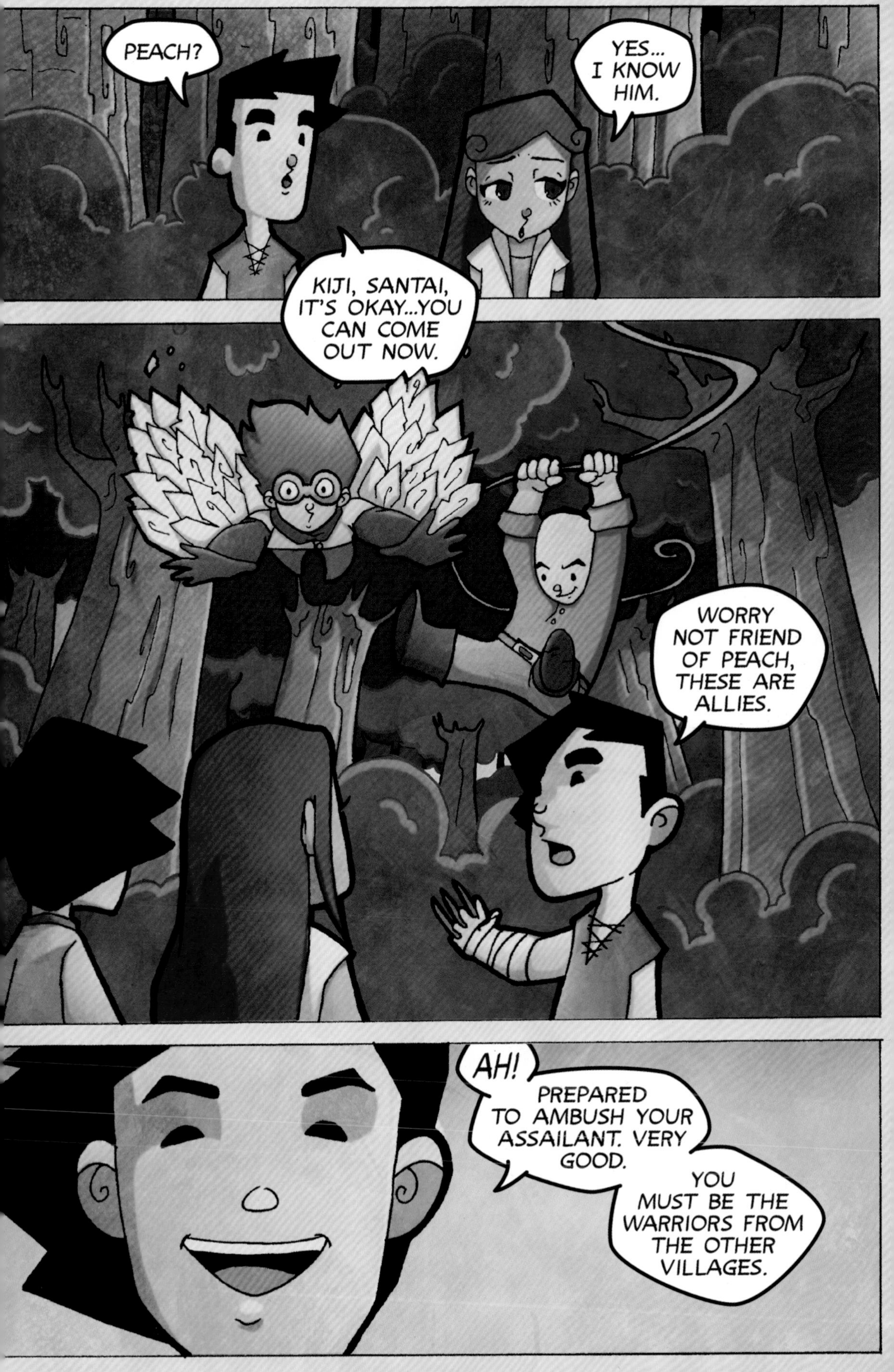
PEACH?
YES... I KNOW HIM.
KIJI, SANTAI, IT'S OKAY...YOU CAN COME OUT NOW.
WORRY NOT FRIEND OF PEACH, THESE ARE ALLIES.
AH!
PREPARED TO AMBUSH YOUR ASSAILANT. VERY GOOD.
YOU MUST BE THE WARRIORS FROM THE OTHER VILLAGES.

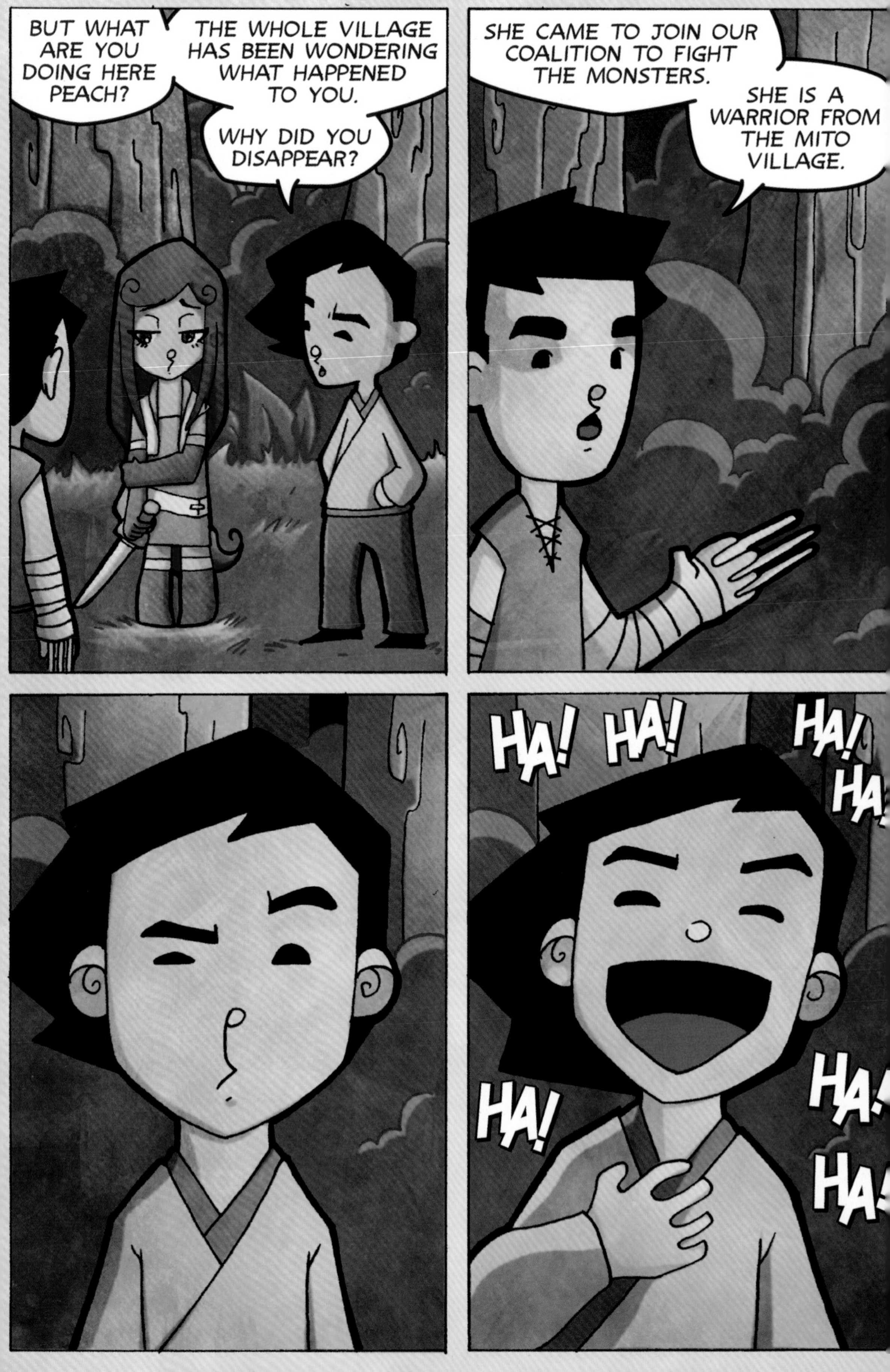
BUT WHAT ARE YOU DOING HERE PEACH?
THE WHOLE VILLAGE HAS BEEN WONDERING WHAT HAPPENED TO YOU.
WHY DID YOU DISAPPEAR?
SHE CAME TO JOIN OUR COALITION TO FIGHT THE MONSTERS.
SHE IS A WARRIOR FROM THE MITO VILLAGE.
HA! HA!
HA!
HA!
HA!
HA!
HA!

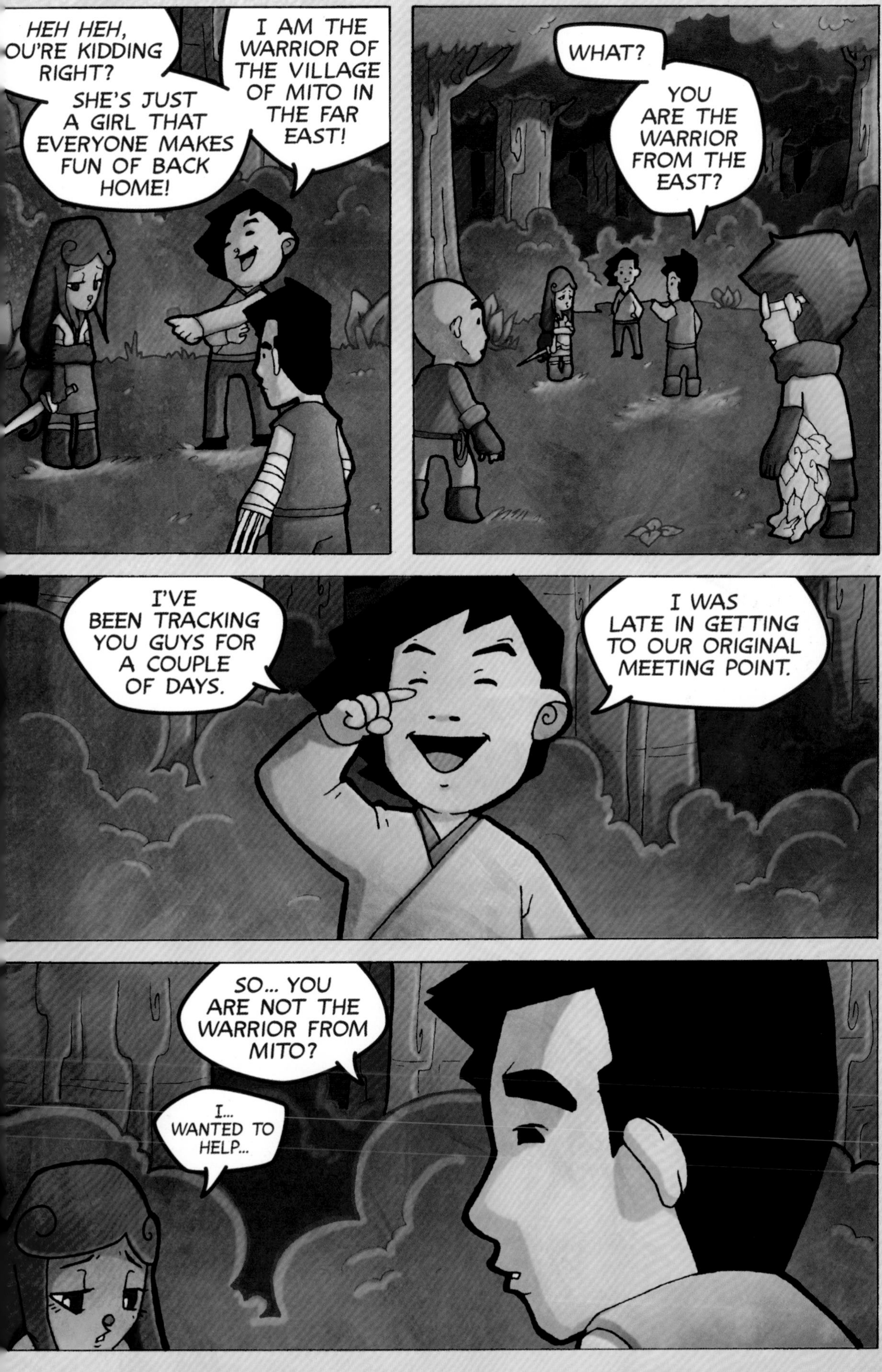
HEH HEH, OU'RE KIDDING RIGHT?
SHE'S JUST A GIRL THAT EVERYONE MAKES FUN OF BACK HOME!
I AM THE WARRIOR OF THE VILLAGE OF MITO IN THE FAR EAST!
WHAT?
YOU ARE THE WARRIOR FROM THE EAST?
I'VE BEEN TRACKING YOU GUYS FOR A COUPLE OF DAYS.
I WAS LATE IN GETTING TO OUR ORIGINAL MEETING POINT.
SO... YOU ARE NOT THE WARRIOR FROM MITO?
I... WANTED TO HELP...

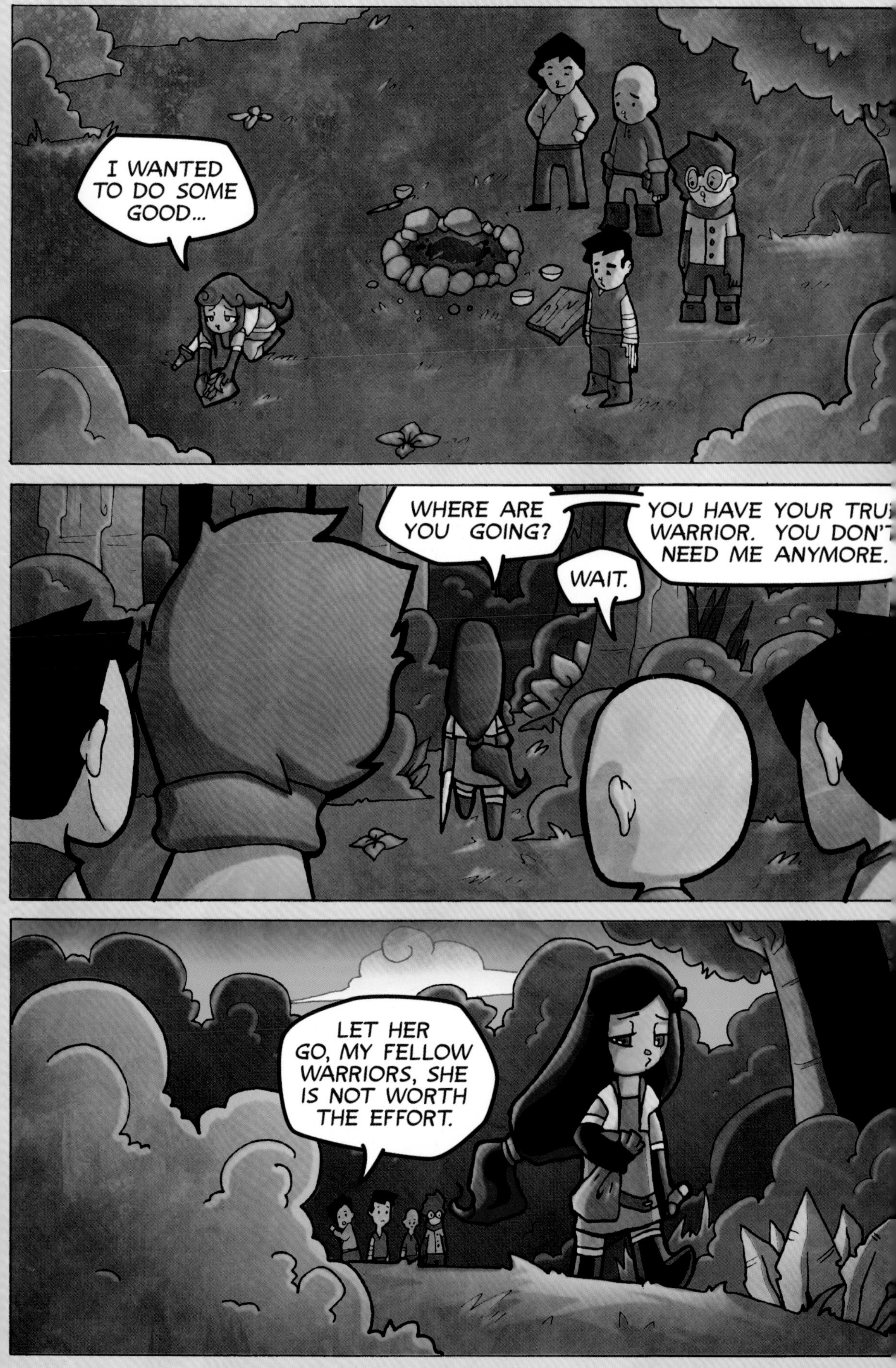
I WANTED TO DO SOME GOOD...
WHERE ARE YOU GOING?
YOU HAVE YOUR TRU
WARRIOR. YOU DON'
NEED ME ANYMORE.
WAIT.
LET HER GO, MY FELLOW WARRIORS, SHE IS NOT WORTH THE EFFORT.

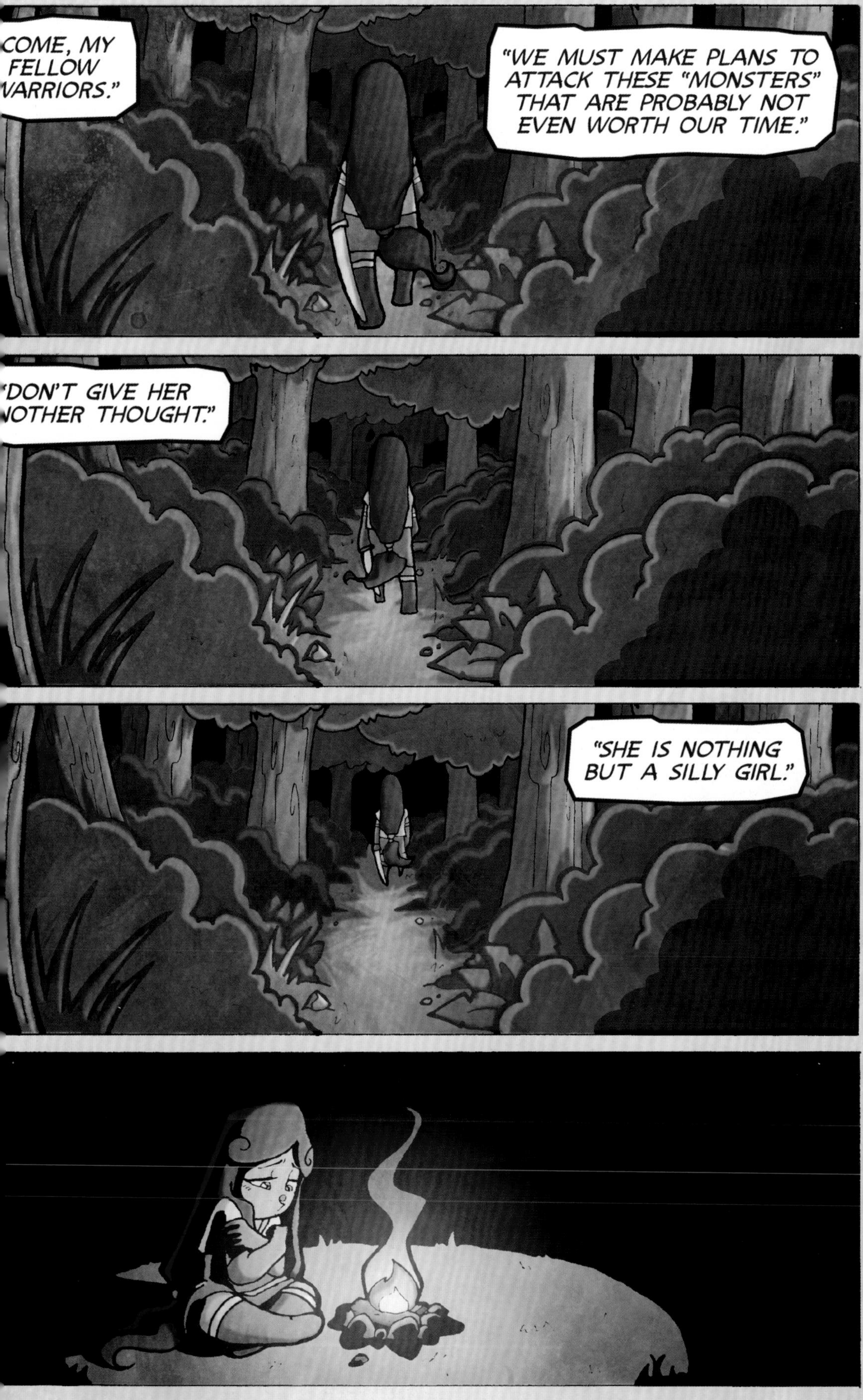
COME, MY FELLOW
"WE MUST MAKE PLANS TO ATTACK THESE "MONSTERS" THAT ARE PROBABLY NOT EVEN WORTH OUR TIME."
DON'T GIVE HER THOUGHT."
"SHE IS NOTHING BUT A SILLY GIRL."

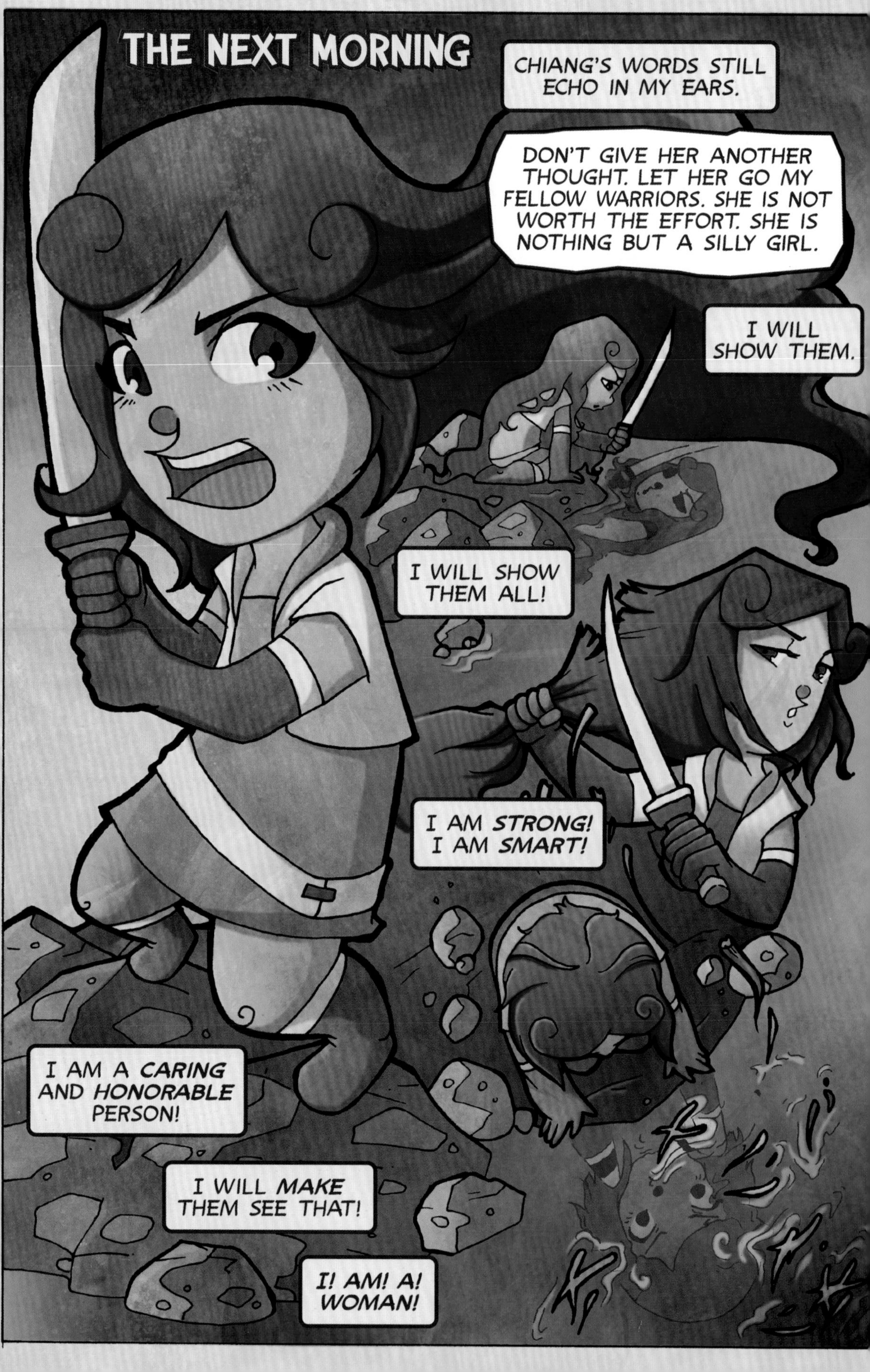
THE NEXT MORNING
CHIANG'S WORDS STILL ECHO IN MY EARS.
DON'T GIVE HER ANOTHER THOUGHT. LET HER GO MY FELLOW WARRIORS. SHE IS NOT WORTH THE EFFORT. SHE IS NOTHING BUT A SILLY GIRL.
I WILL SHOW THEM.
I WILL SHOW THEM ALL!
I AM *STRONG!* I AM *SMART!*
I AM A *CARING* AND *HONORABLE* PERSON!
I WILL *MAKE* THEM SEE THAT!
I! AM! A! WOMAN!

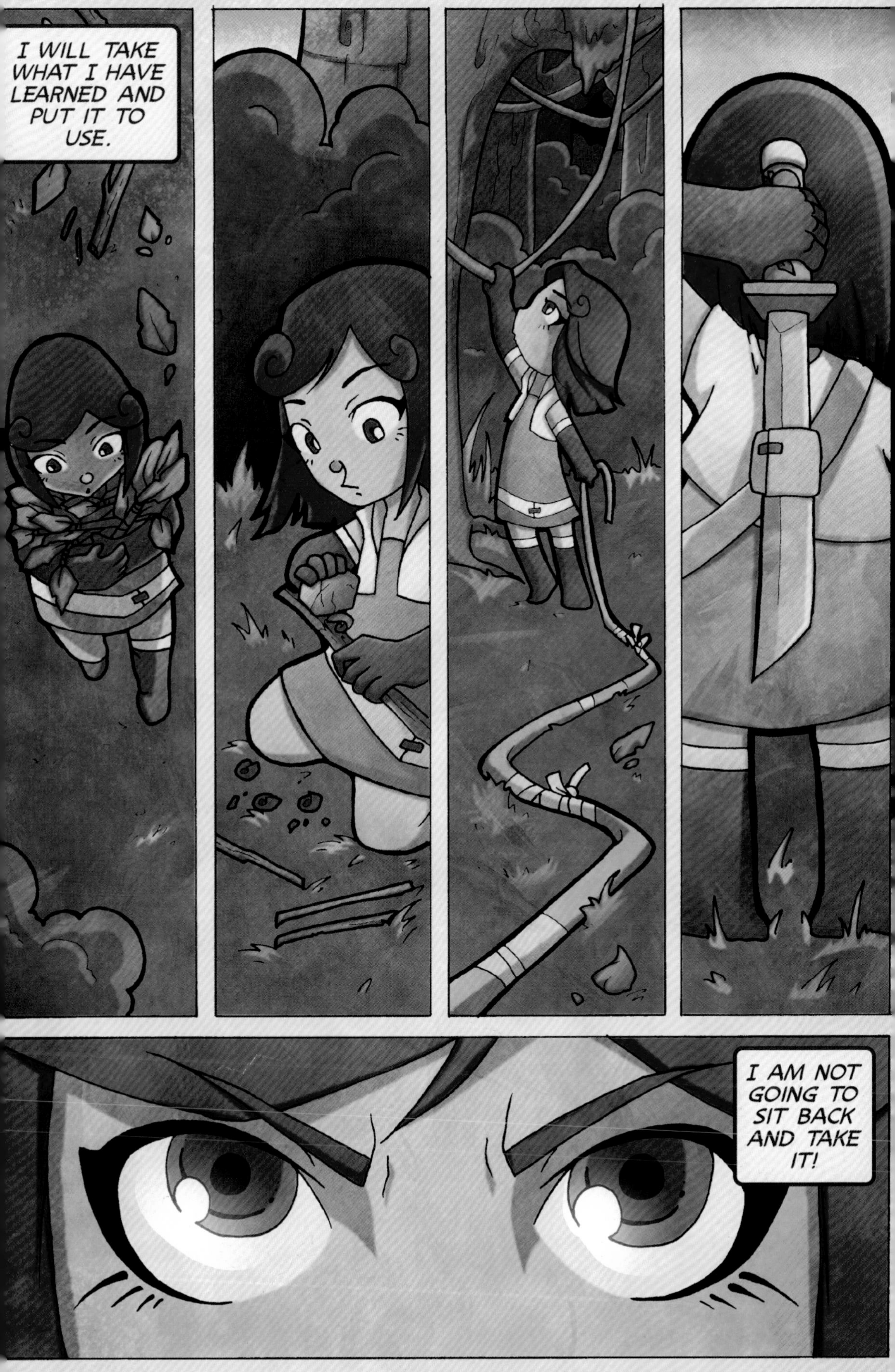
I WILL TAKE WHAT I HAVE LEARNED AND PUT IT TO USE.
I AM NOT GOING TO SIT BACK AND TAKE IT!

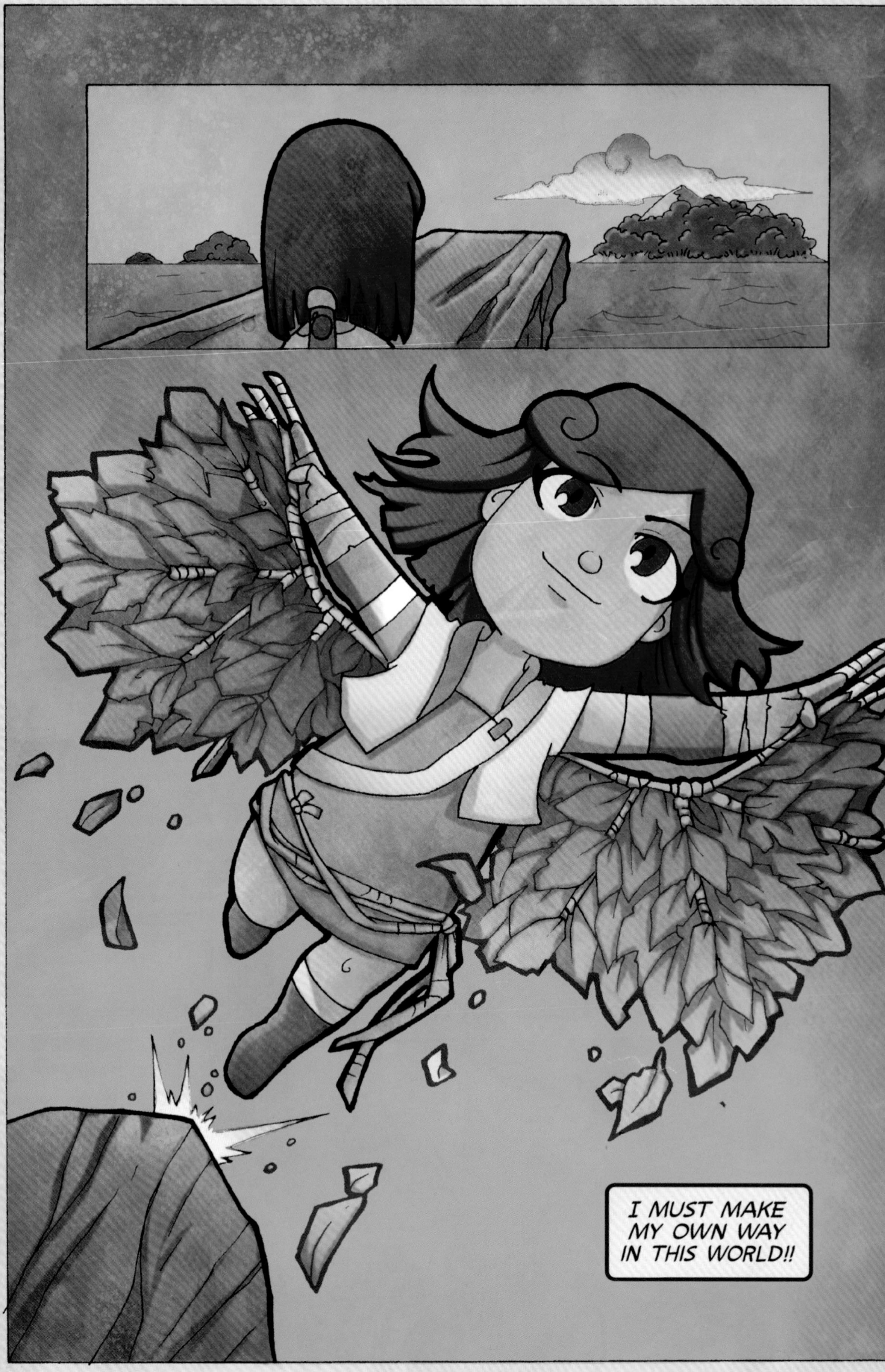
I MUST MAKE MY OWN WAY IN THIS WORLD!!

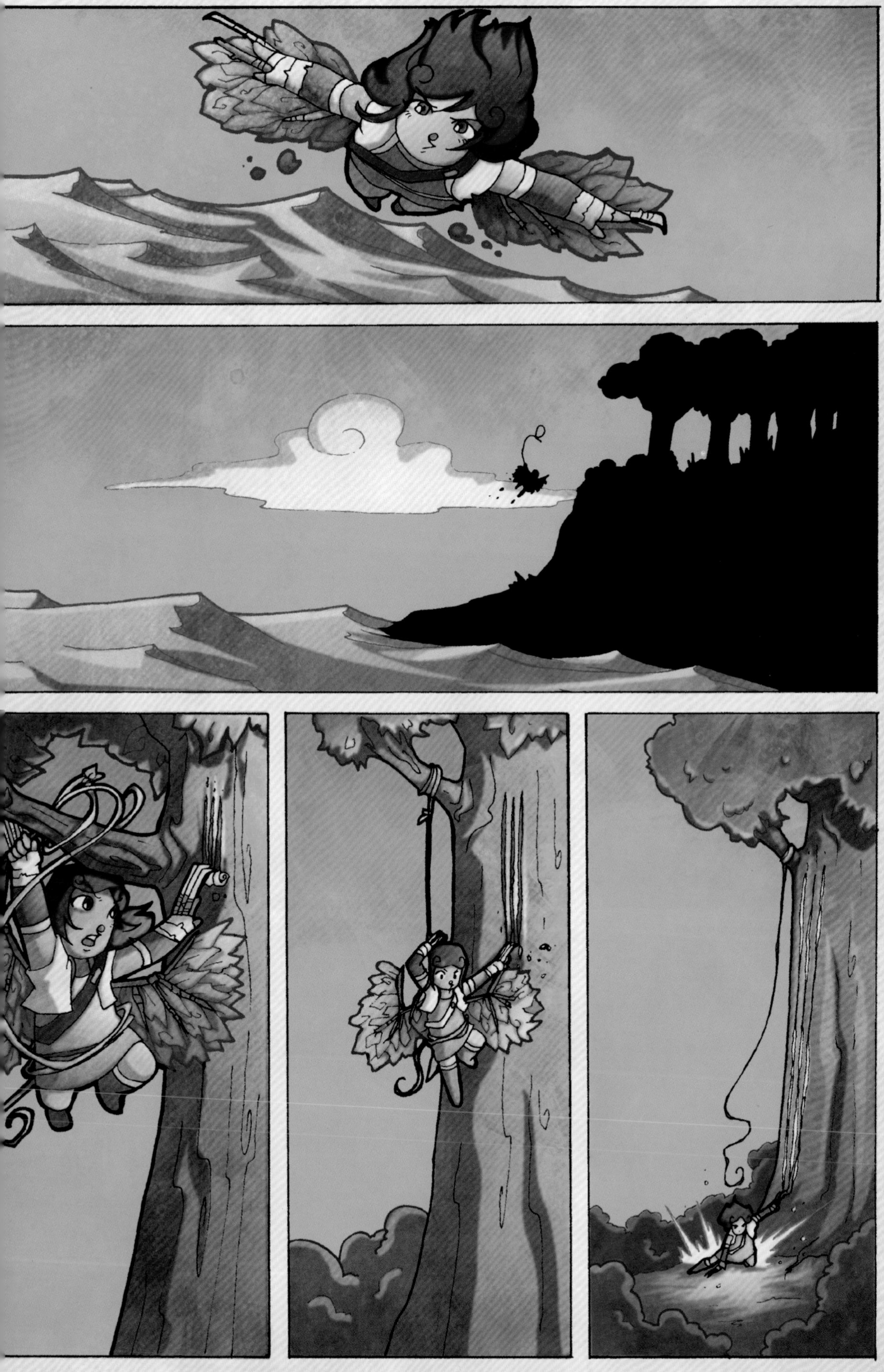

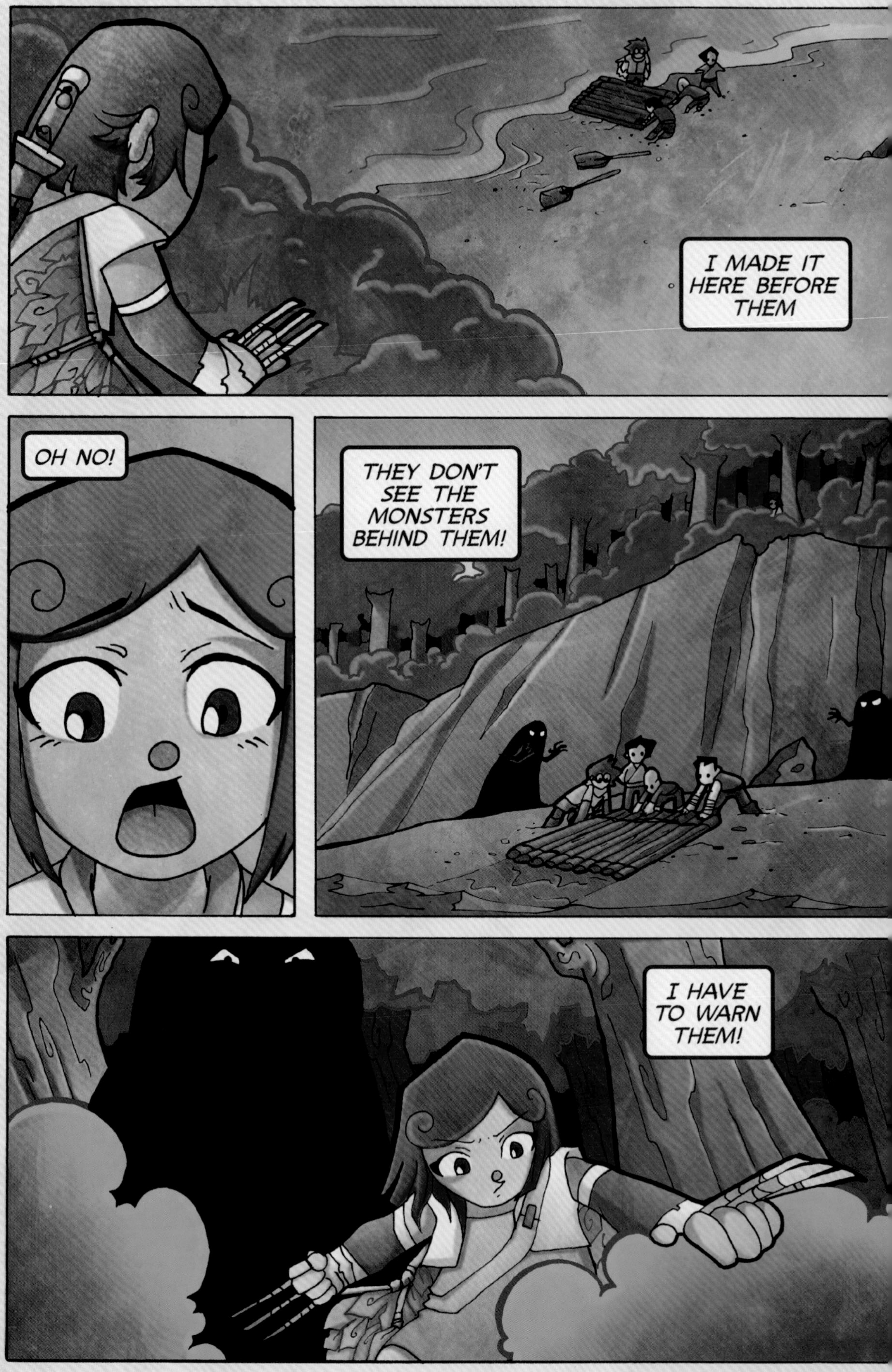
I MADE IT HERE BEFORE THEM
OH NO!
THEY DON'T SEE THE MONSTERS BEHIND THEM!
I HAVE TO WARN THEM!

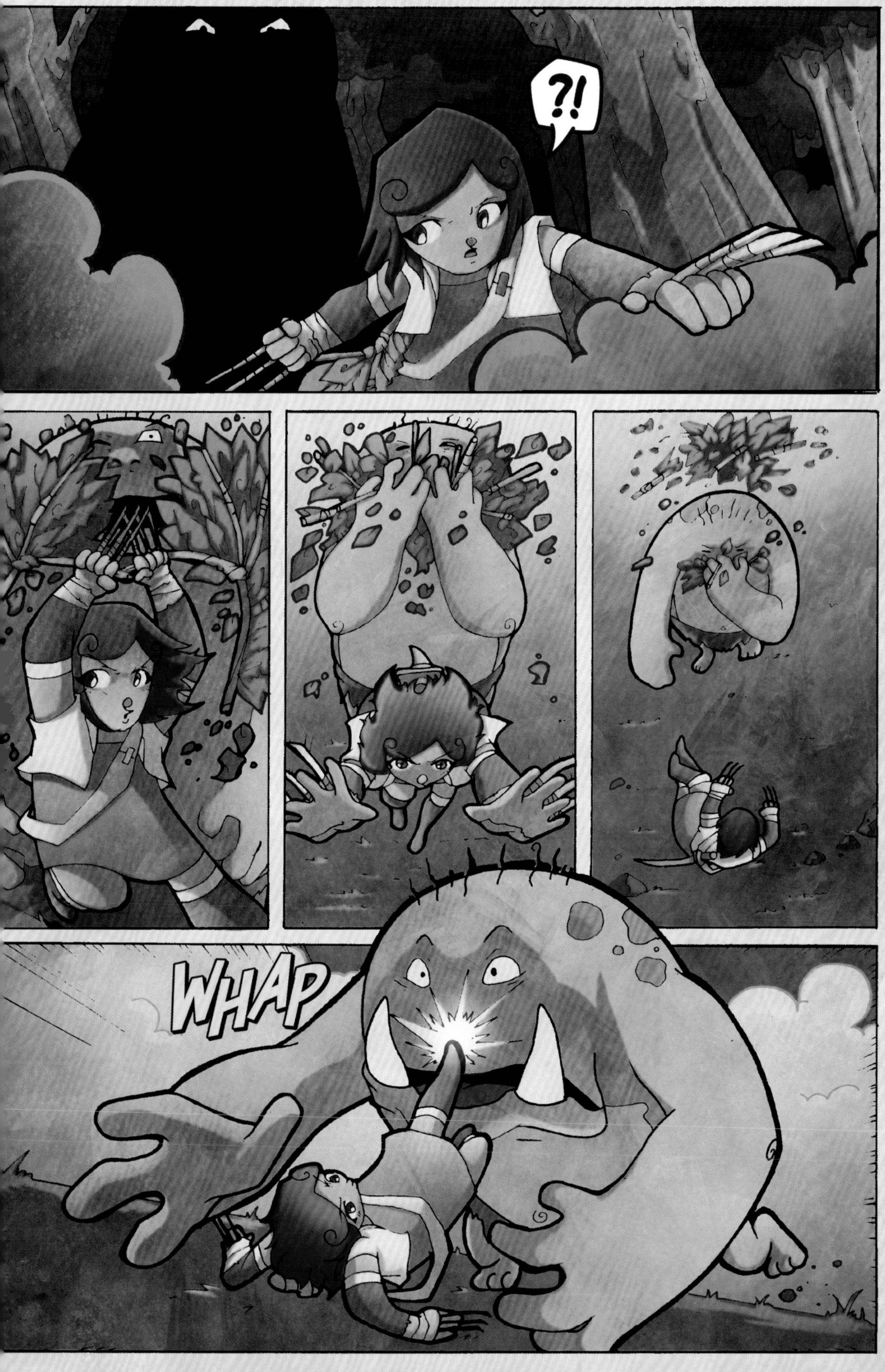
?!
WHAP

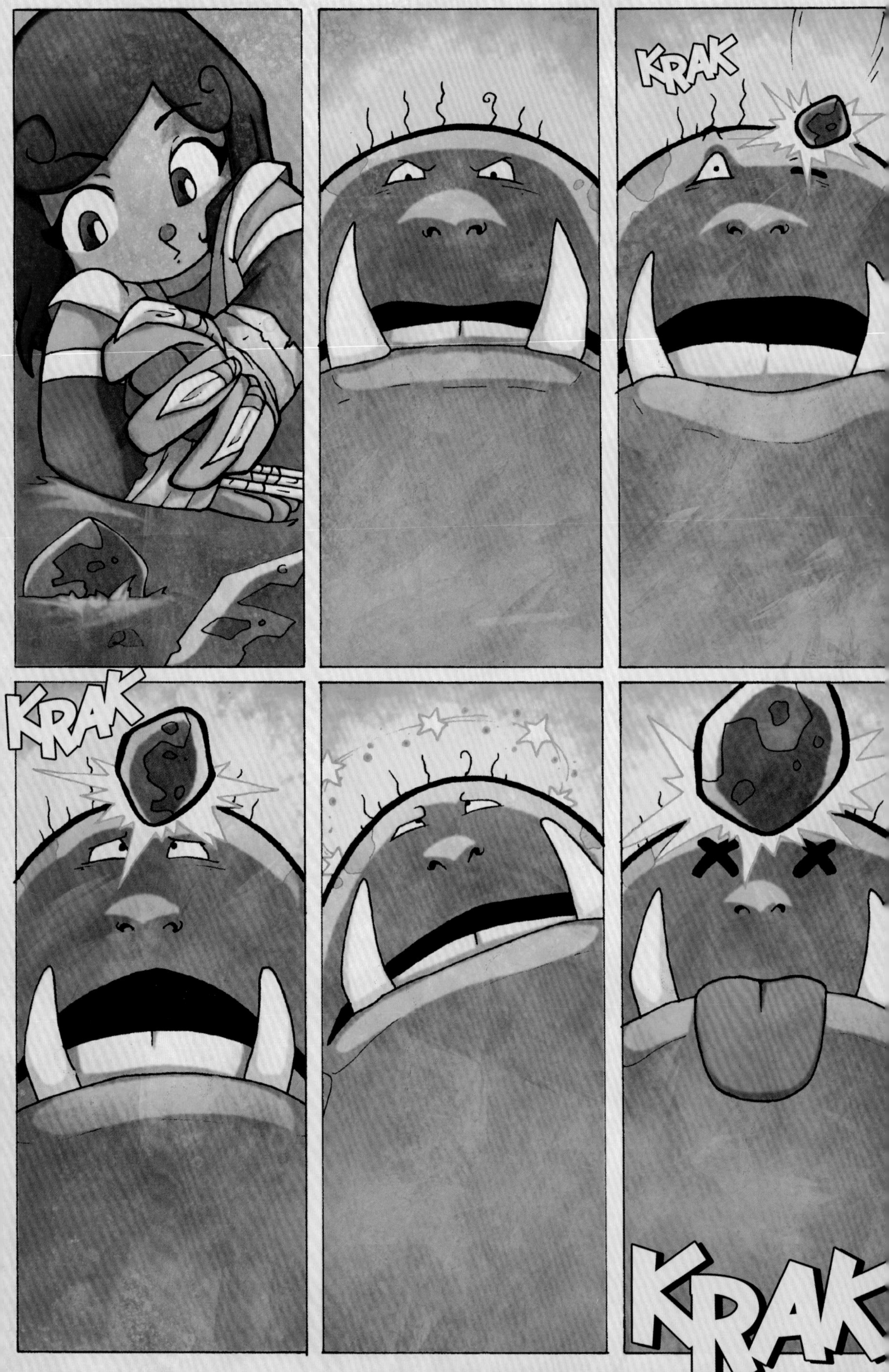
KRAK
KRAK
KRAK

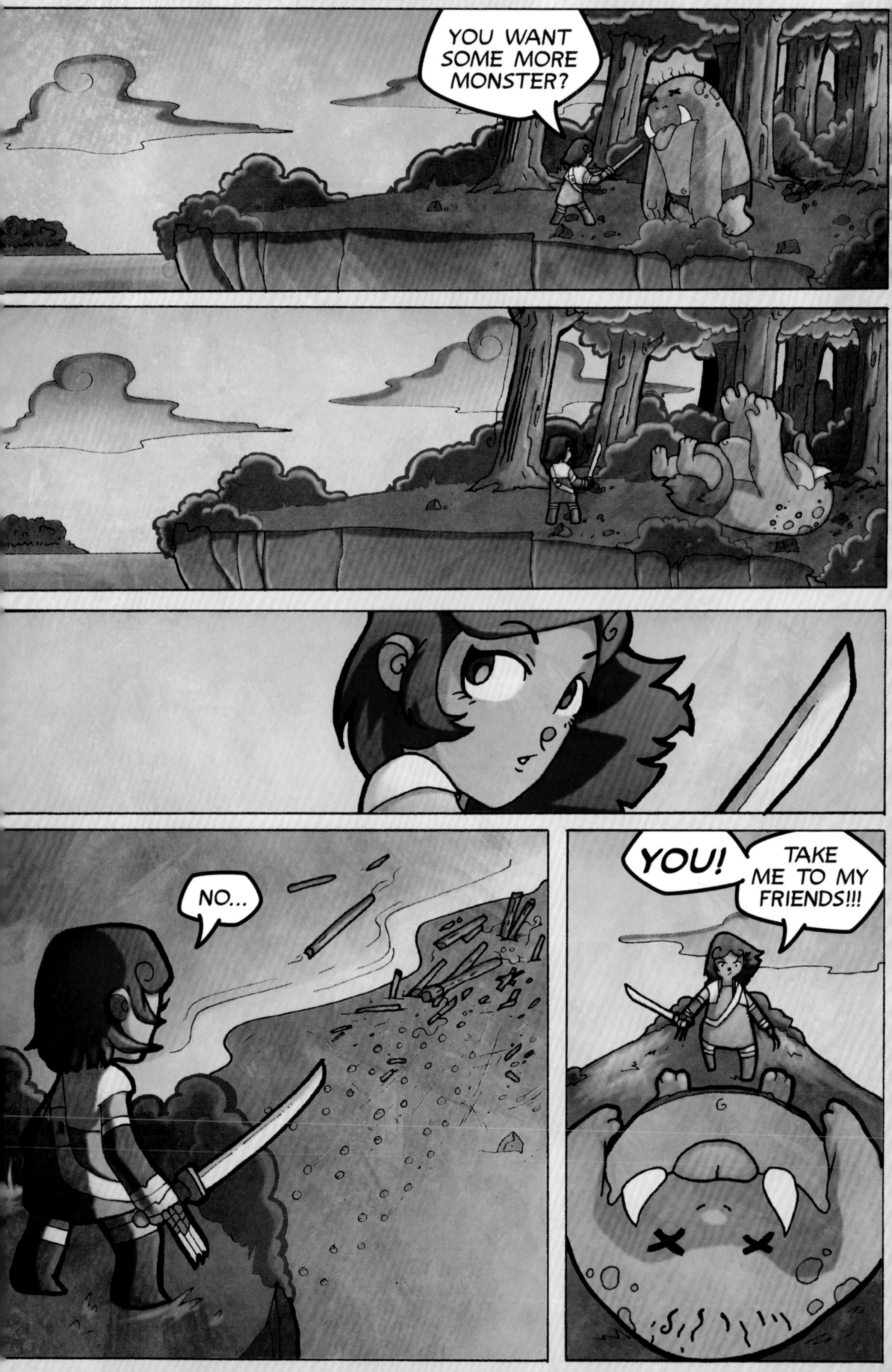
YOU WANT SOME MORE MONSTER?
NO...
YOU!
TAKE ME TO MY FRIENDS!!!

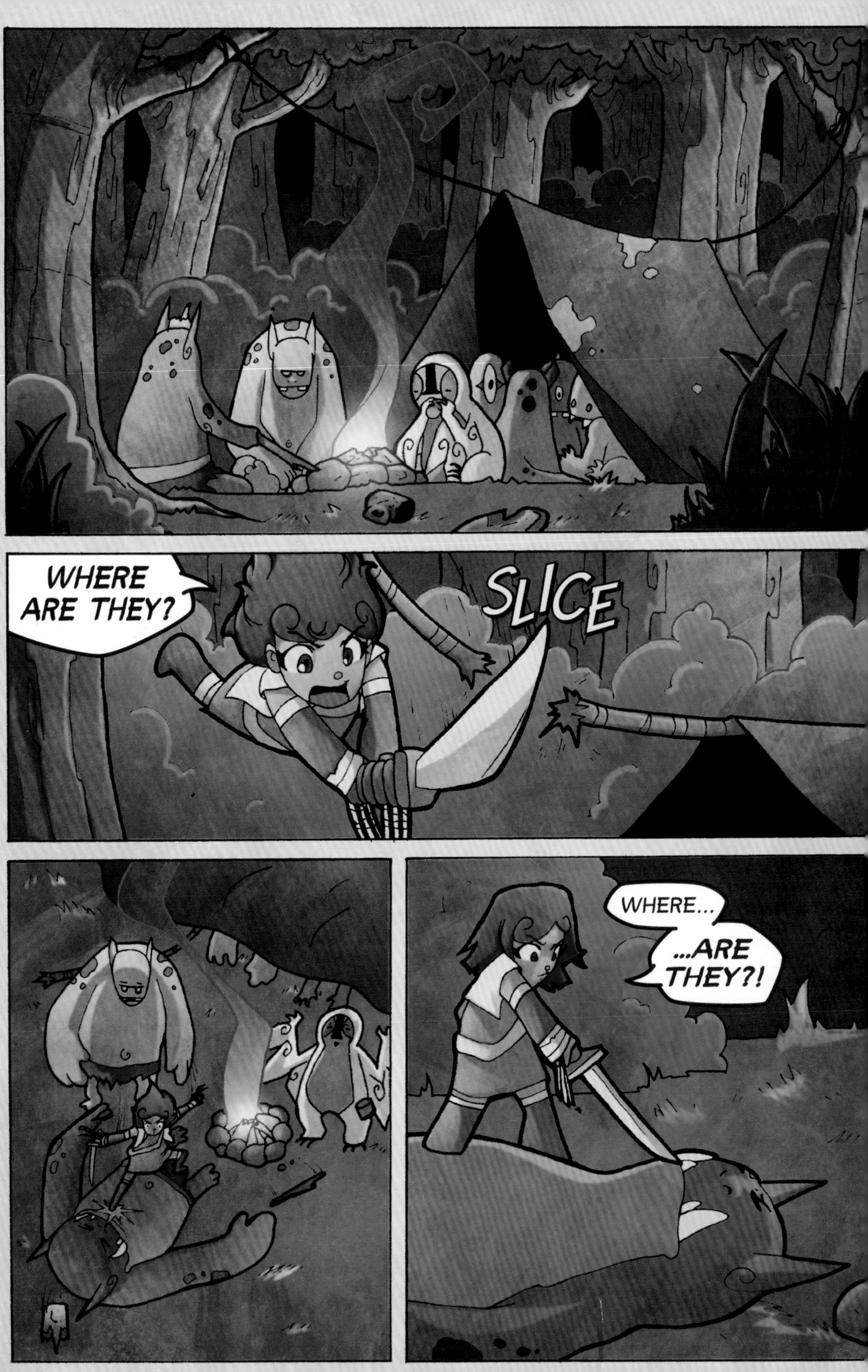
WHERE ARE THEY?
SLICE
WHERE...
...ARE THEY?!

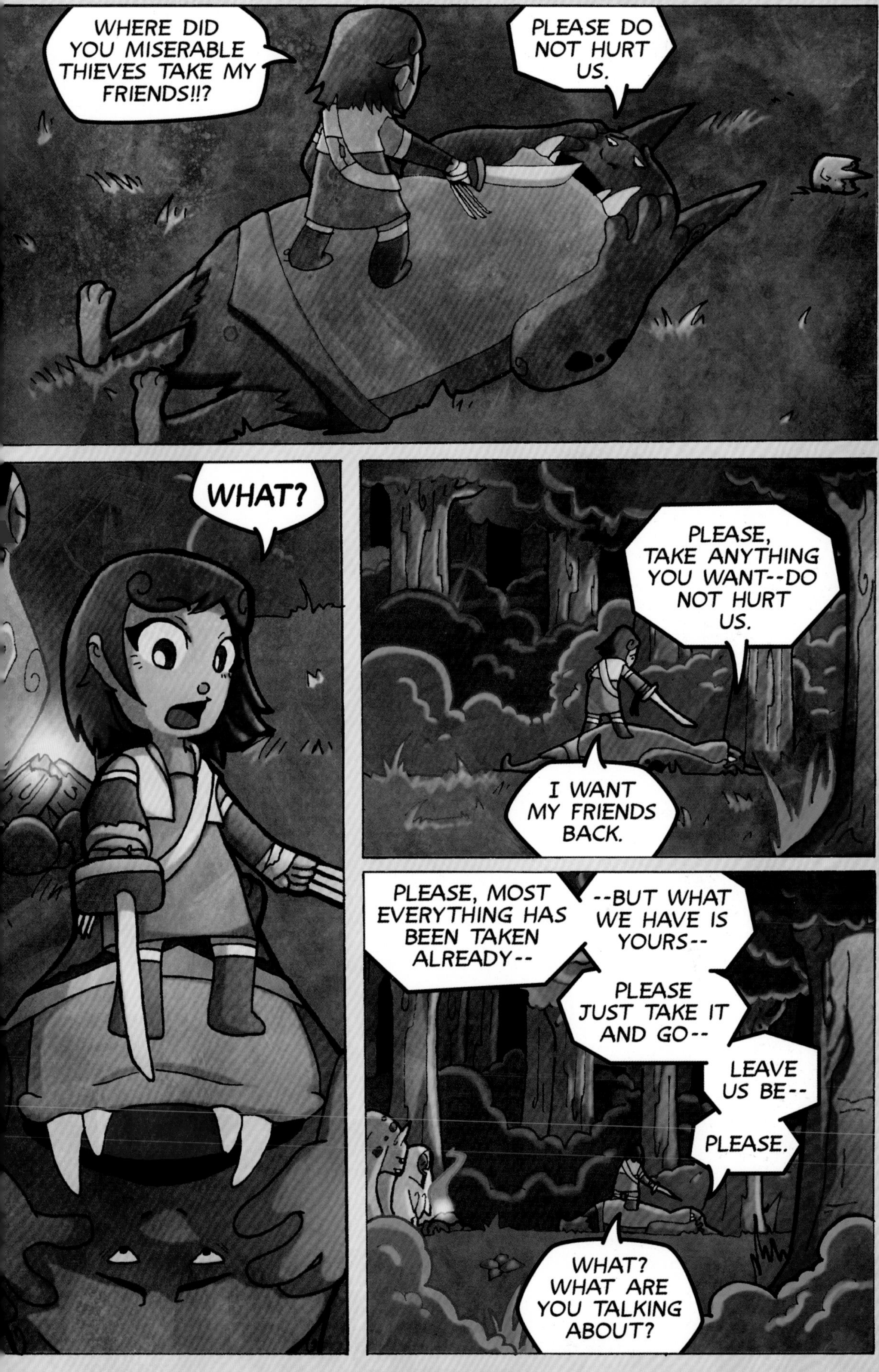
WHERE DID YOU MISERABLE THIEVES TAKE MY FRIENDS!!?
PLEASE DO NOT HURT US.
WHAT?
PLEASE, TAKE ANYTHING YOU WANT--DO NOT HURT US.
I WANT MY FRIENDS BACK.
PLEASE, MOST EVERYTHING HAS BEEN TAKEN ALREADY--
--BUT WHAT WE HAVE IS YOURS--
PLEASE JUST TAKE IT AND GO--
LEAVE US BE--
PLEASE.
WHAT? WHAT ARE YOU TALKING ABOUT?

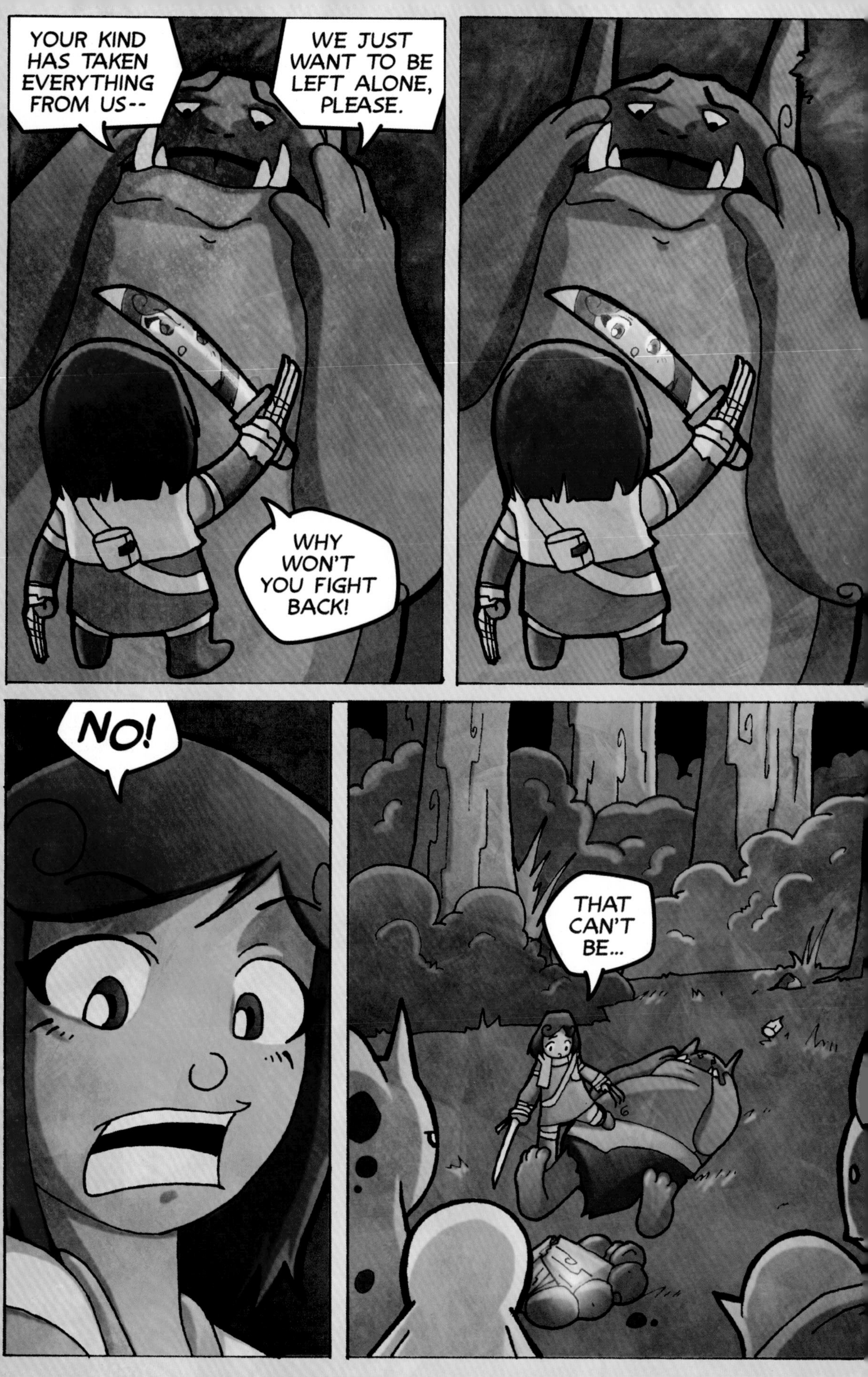
YOUR KIND HAS TAKEN EVERYTHING FROM US--
WE JUST WANT TO BE LEFT ALONE, PLEASE.
WHY WON'T YOU FIGHT BACK!
NO!
THAT CAN'T BE...

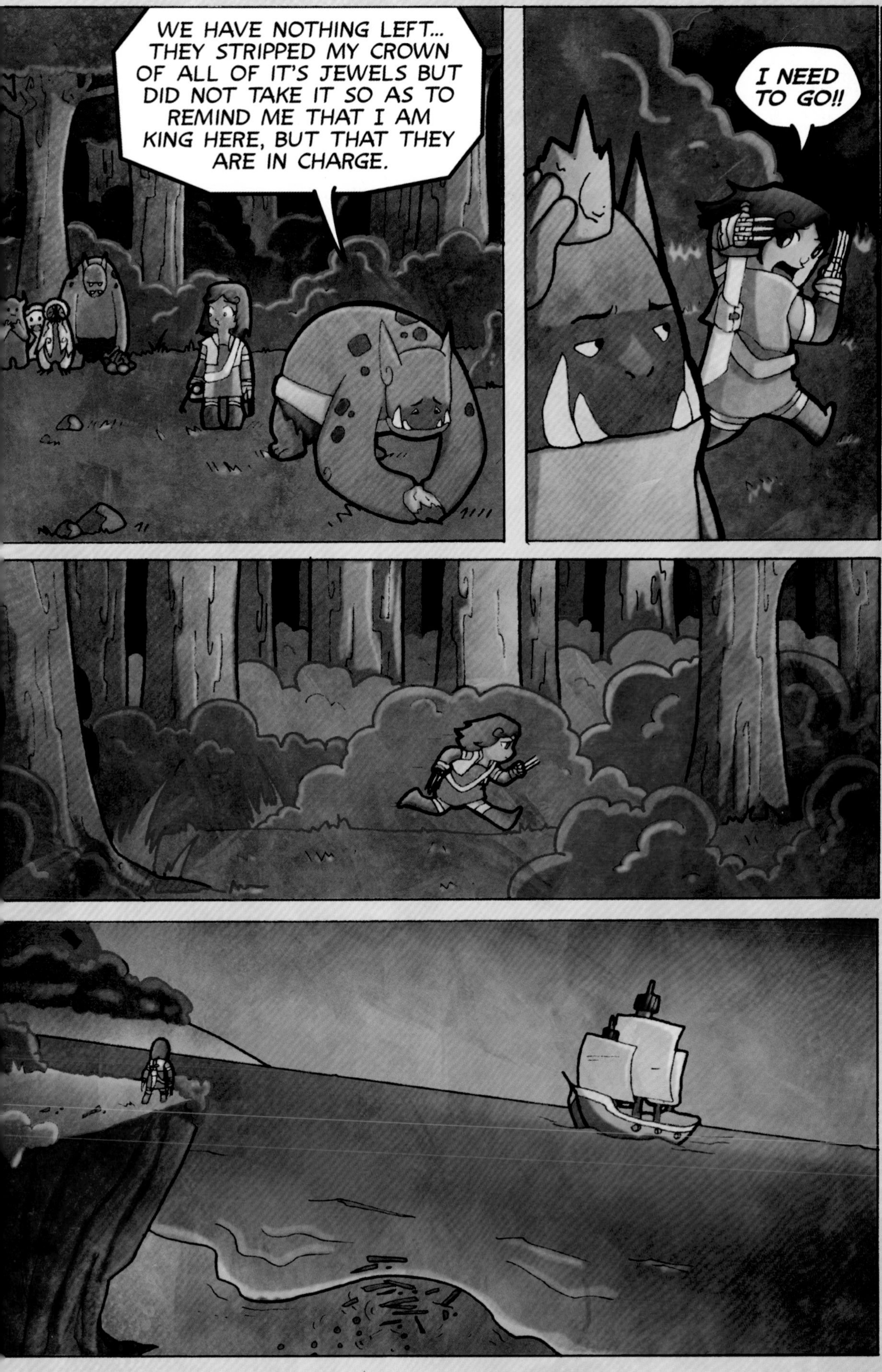
WE HAVE NOTHING LEFT... THEY STRIPPED MY CROWN OF ALL OF IT'S JEWELS BUT DID NOT TAKE IT SO AS TO REMIND ME THAT I AM KING HERE, BUT THAT THEY ARE IN CHARGE.
I NEED TO GO!!

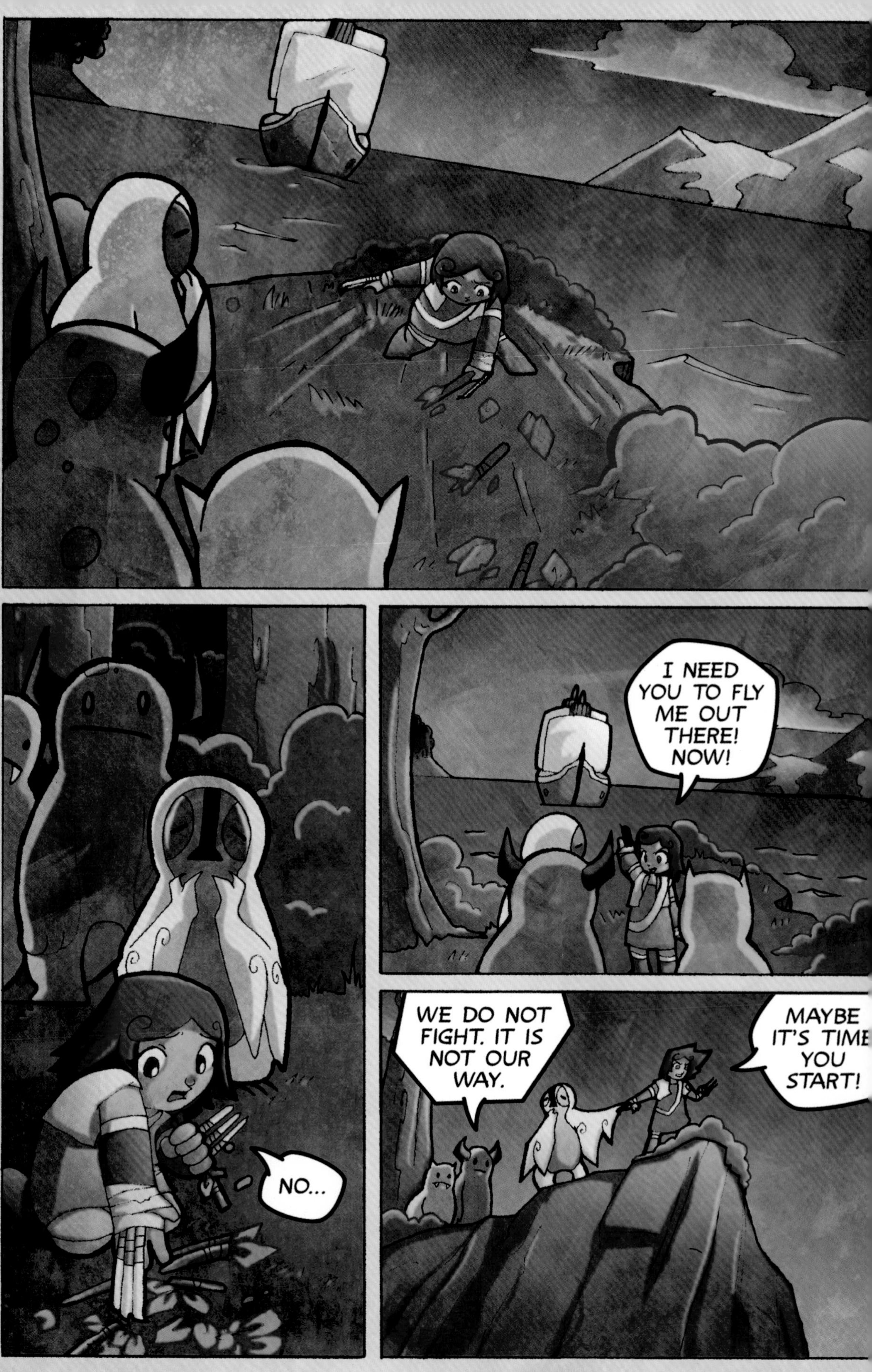
NO...
I NEED YOU TO FLY ME OUT THERE! NOW!
WE DO NOT FIGHT. IT IS NOT OUR WAY.
MAYBE IT'S TIME YOU START!

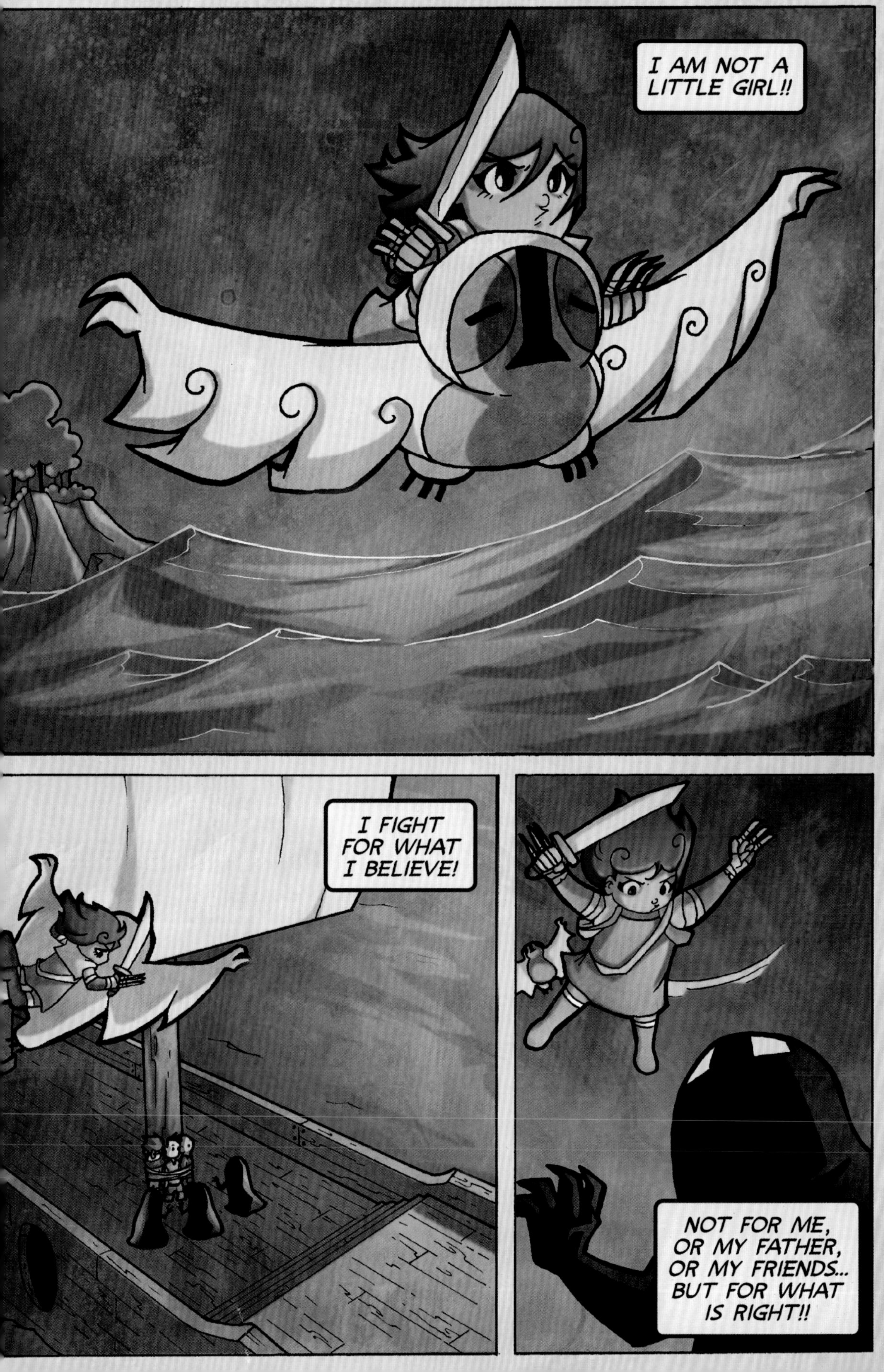
I AM NOT A LITTLE GIRL!!
I FIGHT FOR WHAT I BELIEVE!
NOT FOR ME, OR MY FATHER, OR MY FRIENDS... BUT FOR WHAT IS RIGHT!!

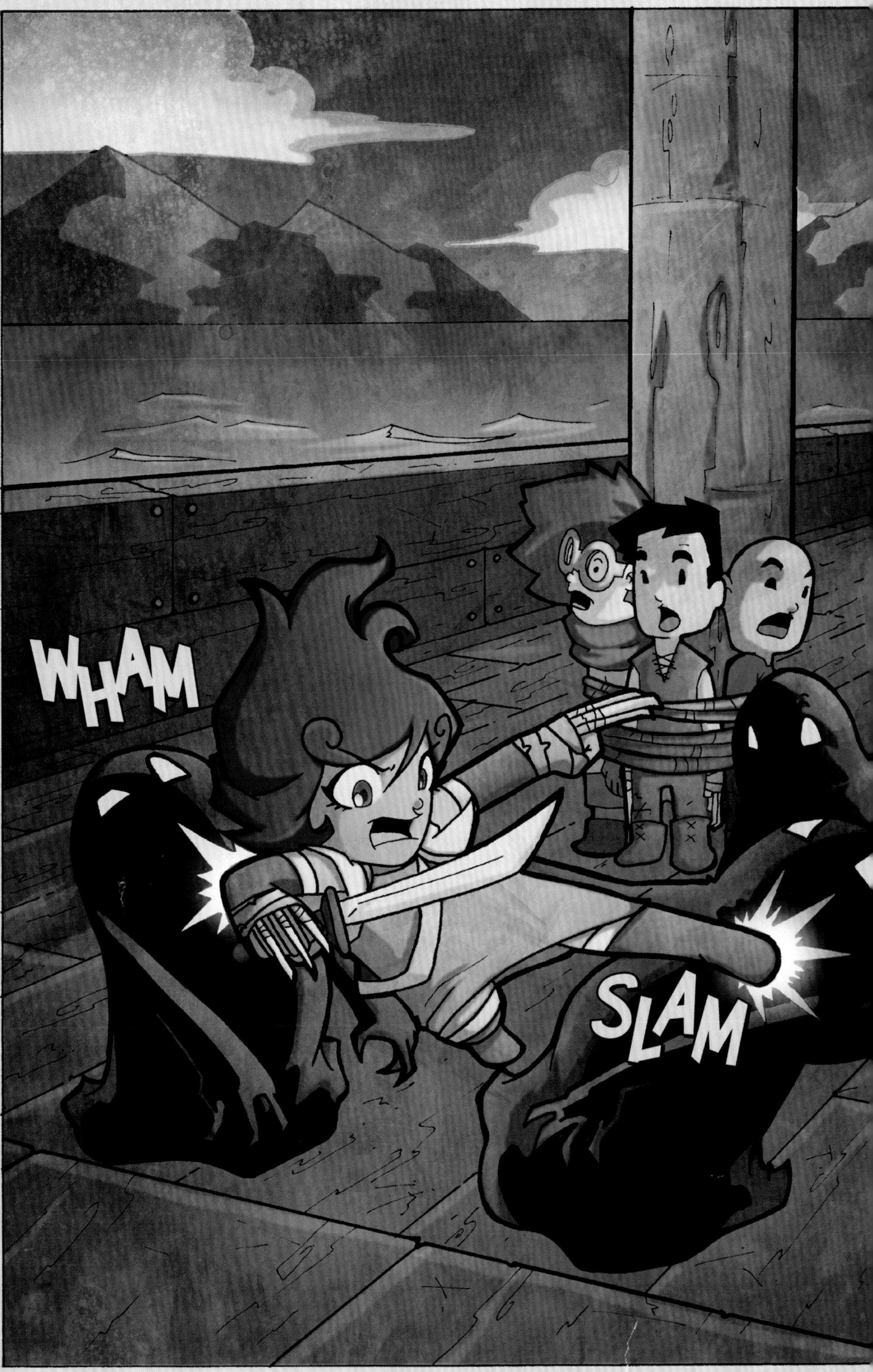
WHAM
SLAM

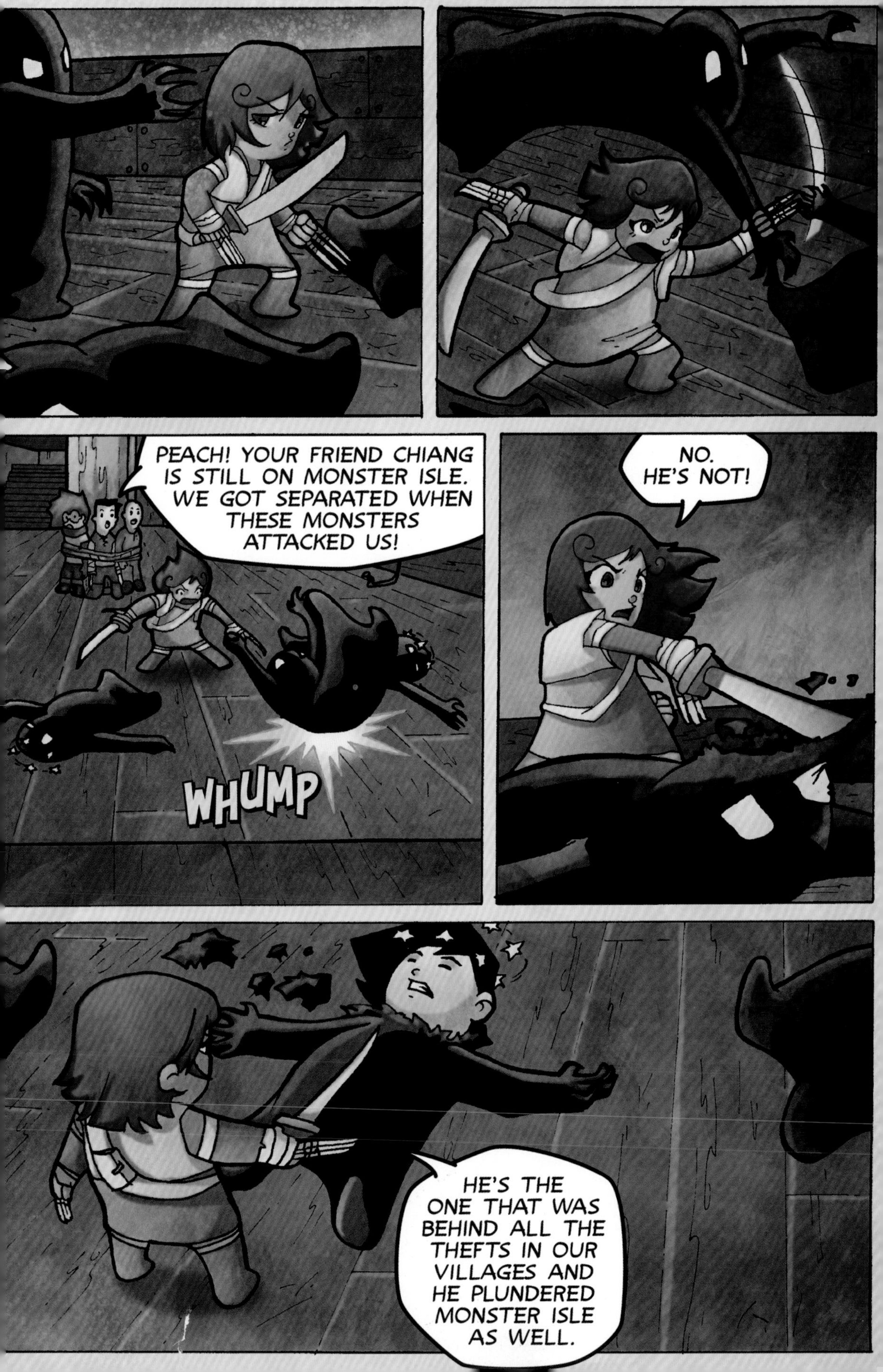
PEACH! YOUR FRIEND CHIANG IS STILL ON MONSTER ISLE. WE GOT SEPARATED WHEN THESE MONSTERS ATTACKED US!
WHUMP
NO. HE'S NOT!
HE'S THE ONE THAT WAS BEHIND ALL THE THEFTS IN OUR VILLAGES AND HE PLUNDERED MONSTER ISLE AS WELL.

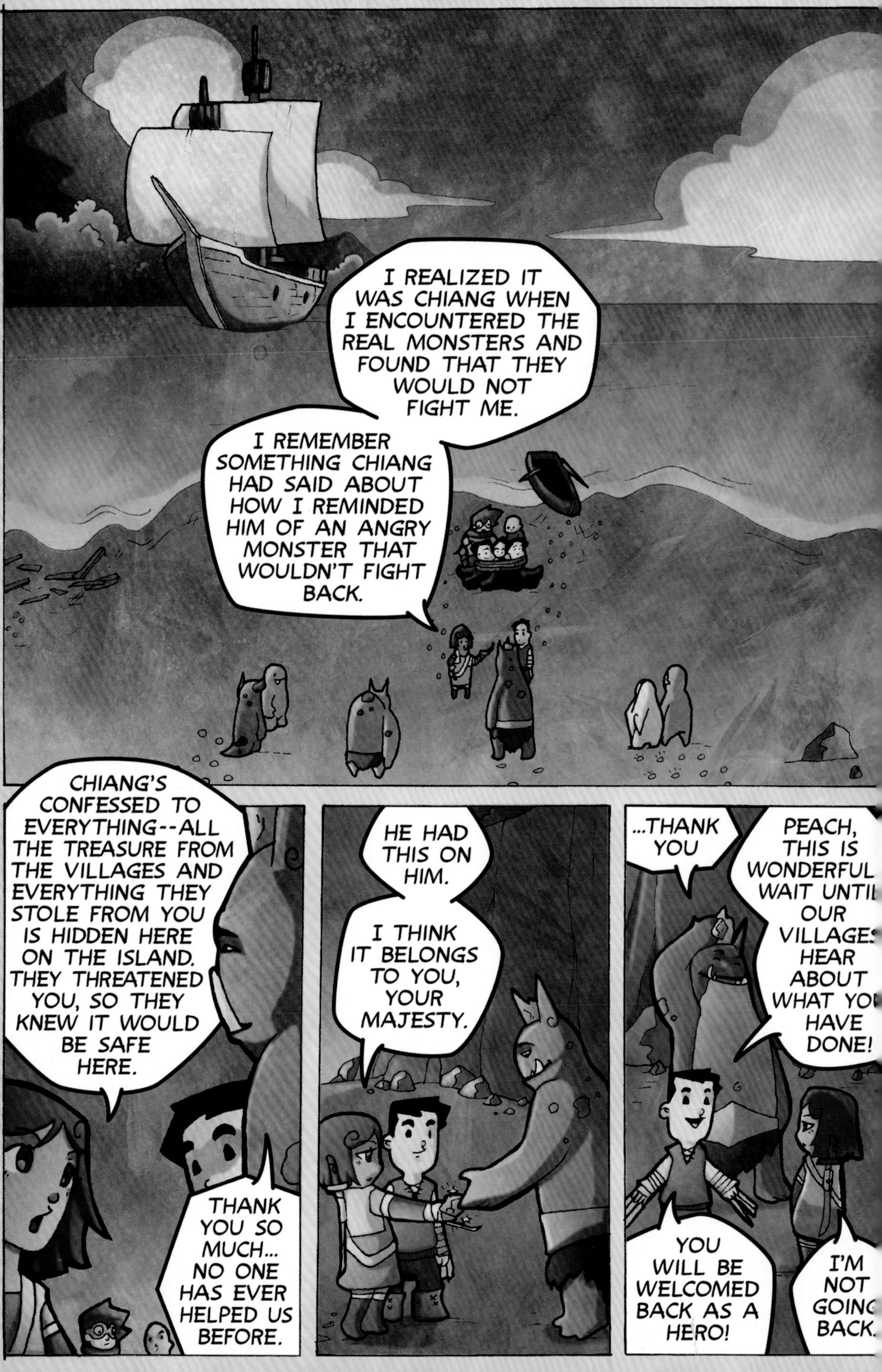
I REALIZED IT WAS CHIANG WHEN I ENCOUNTERED THE REAL MONSTERS AND FOUND THAT THEY WOULD NOT FIGHT ME.
I REMEMBER SOMETHING CHIANG HAD SAID ABOUT HOW I REMINDED HIM OF AN ANGRY MONSTER THAT WOULDN'T FIGHT BACK.
CHIANG'S CONFESSED TO EVERYTHING--ALL THE TREASURE FROM THE VILLAGES AND EVERYTHING THEY STOLE FROM YOU IS HIDDEN HERE ON THE ISLAND. THEY THREATENED YOU, SO THEY KNEW IT WOULD BE SAFE HERE.
THANK YOU SO MUCH... NO ONE HAS EVER HELPED US BEFORE.
HE HAD THIS ON HIM.
I THINK IT BELONGS TO YOU, YOUR MAJESTY.
...THANK YOU
YOU WILL BE WELCOMED BACK AS A HERO!
I'M NOT GOING BACK.

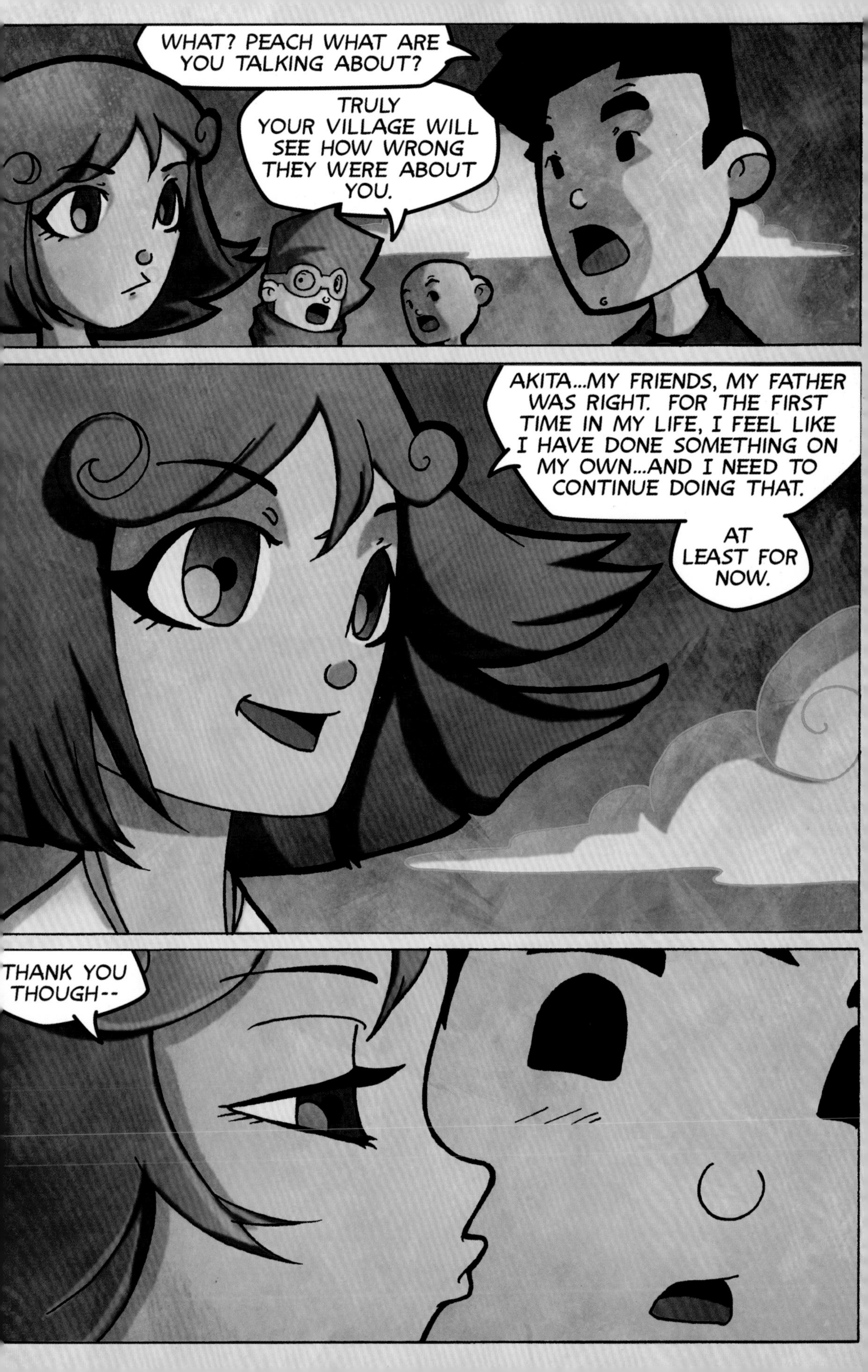
WHAT? PEACH WHAT ARE YOU TALKING ABOUT?
TRULY YOUR VILLAGE WILL SEE HOW WRONG THEY WERE ABOUT YOU.
AKITA...MY FRIENDS, MY FATHER WAS RIGHT. FOR THE FIRST TIME IN MY LIFE, I FEEL LIKE I HAVE DONE SOMETHING ON MY OWN...AND I NEED TO CONTINUE DOING THAT.
AT LEAST FOR NOW.
THANK YOU THOUGH--

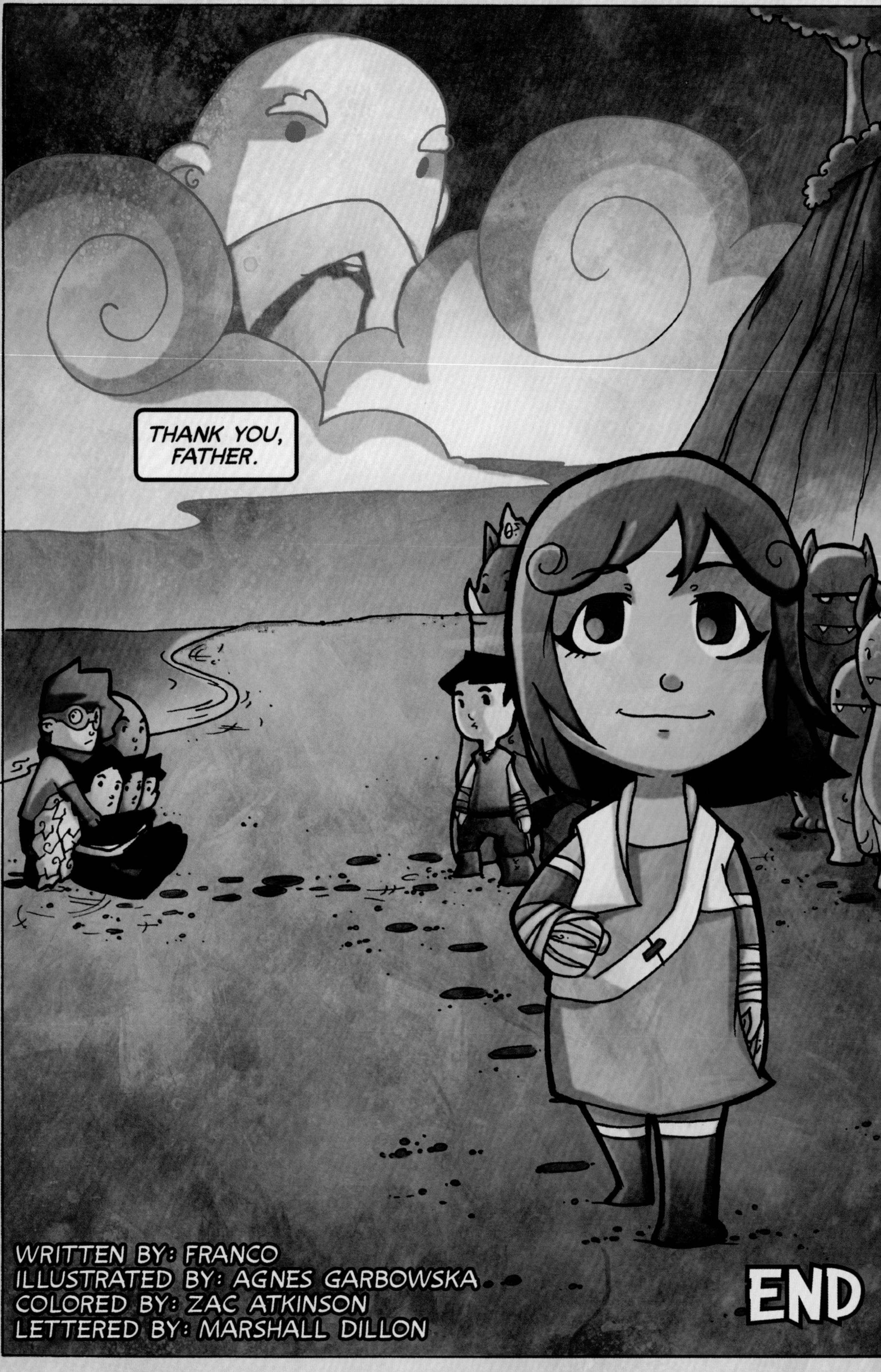
THANK YOU, FATHER.
WRITTEN BY: FRANCO
ILLUSTRATED BY: AGNES GARBOWSKA
COLORED BY: ZAC ATKINSON
LETTERED BY: MARSHALL DILLON
END

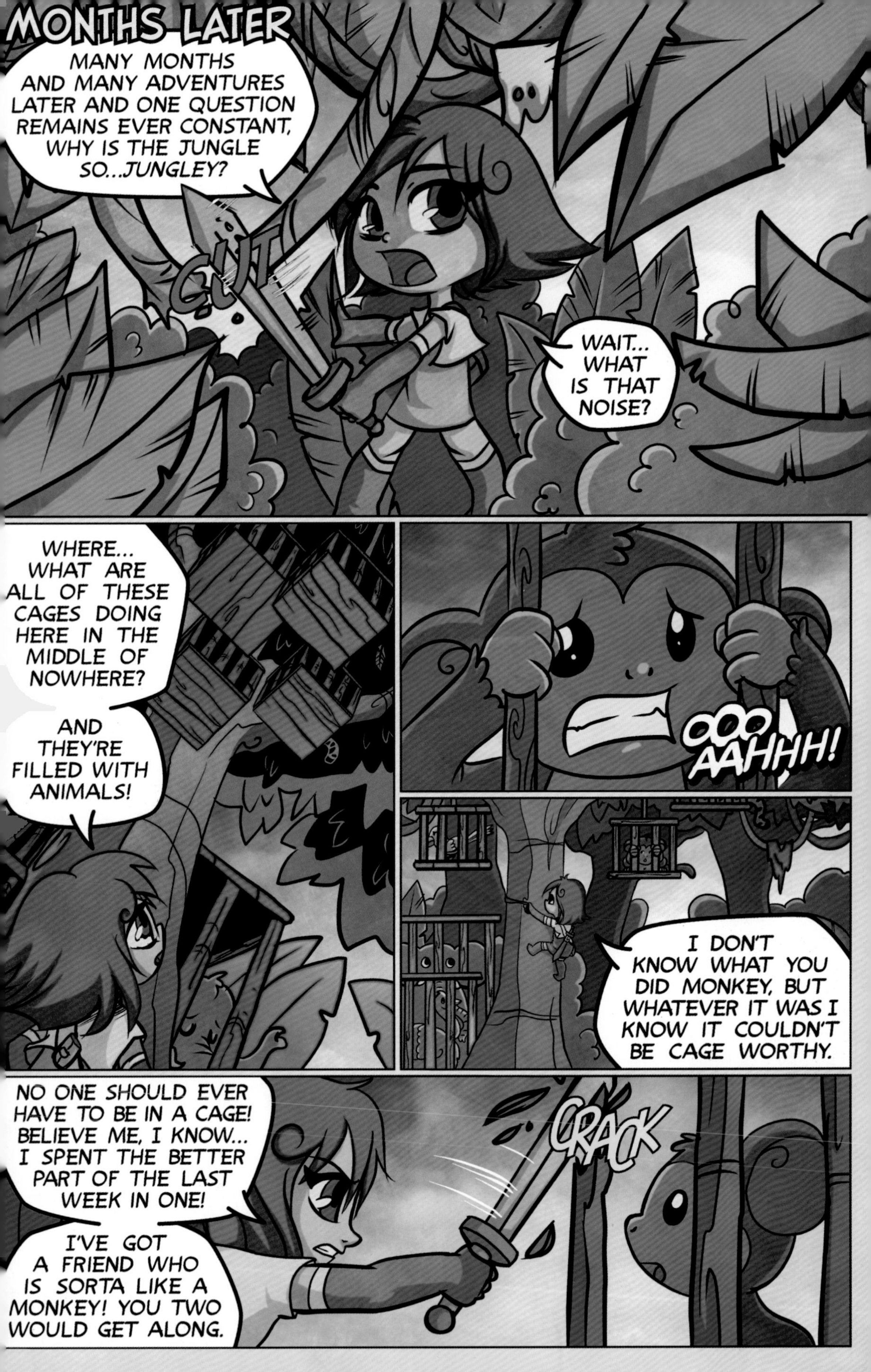
MONTHS LATER
MANY MONTHS AND MANY ADVENTURES LATER AND ONE QUESTION REMAINS EVER CONSTANT, WHY IS THE JUNGLE SO...JUNGLEY?
CUT
WAIT... WHAT IS THAT NOISE?
WHERE... WHAT ARE ALL OF THESE CAGES DOING HERE IN THE MIDDLE OF NOWHERE?
AND THEY'RE FILLED WITH ANIMALS!
OOO AAHHH!
I DON'T KNOW WHAT YOU DID MONKEY, BUT WHATEVER IT WAS I KNOW IT COULDN'T BE CAGE WORTHY.
NO ONE SHOULD EVER HAVE TO BE IN A CAGE! BELIEVE ME, I KNOW... I SPENT THE BETTER PART OF THE LAST WEEK IN ONE!
CRACK
I'VE GOT A FRIEND WHO IS SORTA LIKE A MONKEY! YOU TWO WOULD GET ALONG.

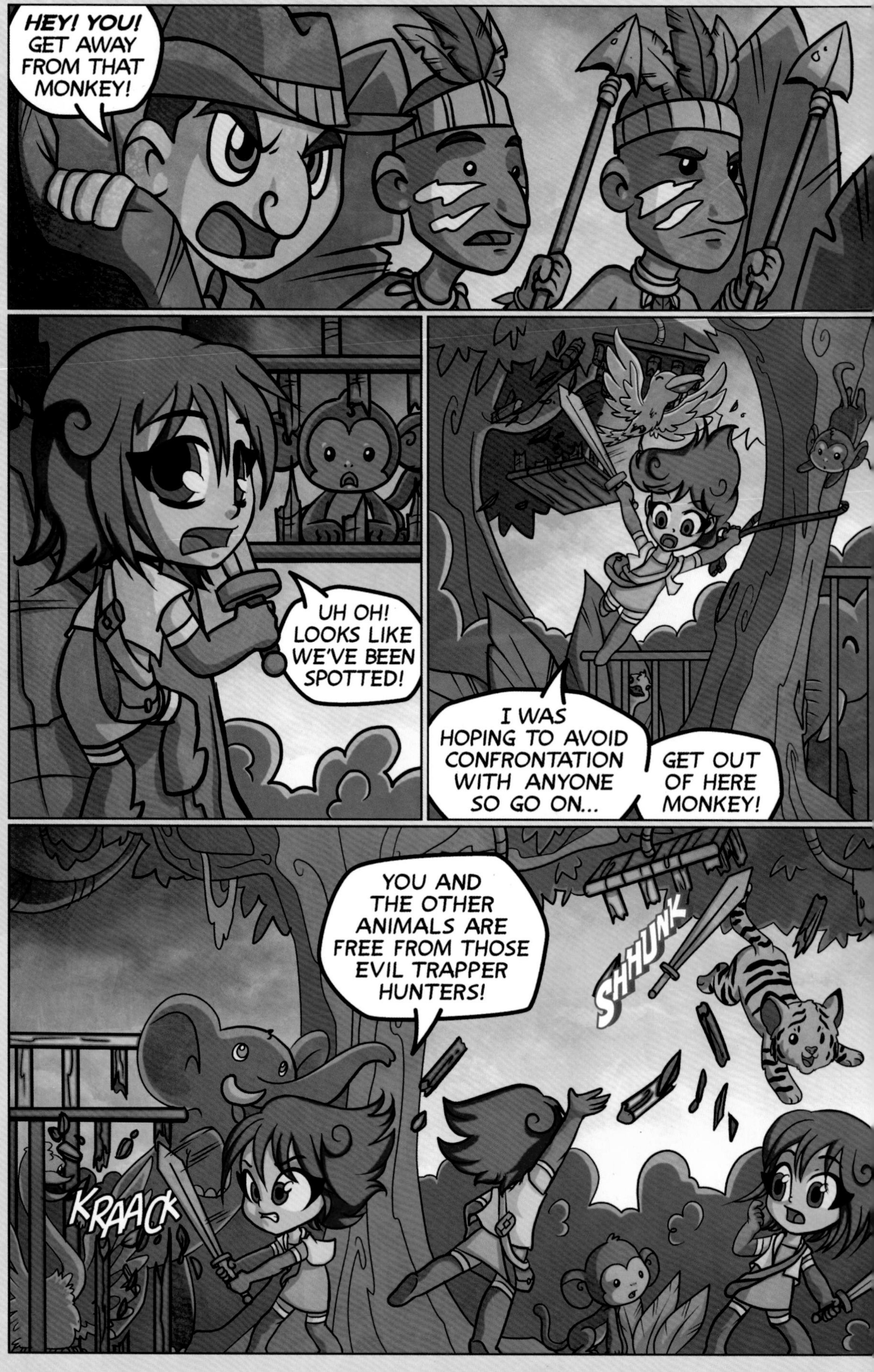
HEY! YOU! GET AWAY FROM THAT MONKEY!
UH OH! LOOKS LIKE WE'VE BEEN SPOTTED!
I WAS HOPING TO AVOID CONFRONTATION WITH ANYONE SO GO ON...
GET OUT OF HERE MONKEY!
YOU AND THE OTHER ANIMALS ARE FREE FROM THOSE EVIL TRAPPER HUNTERS!
SHHUNK
KRAACK

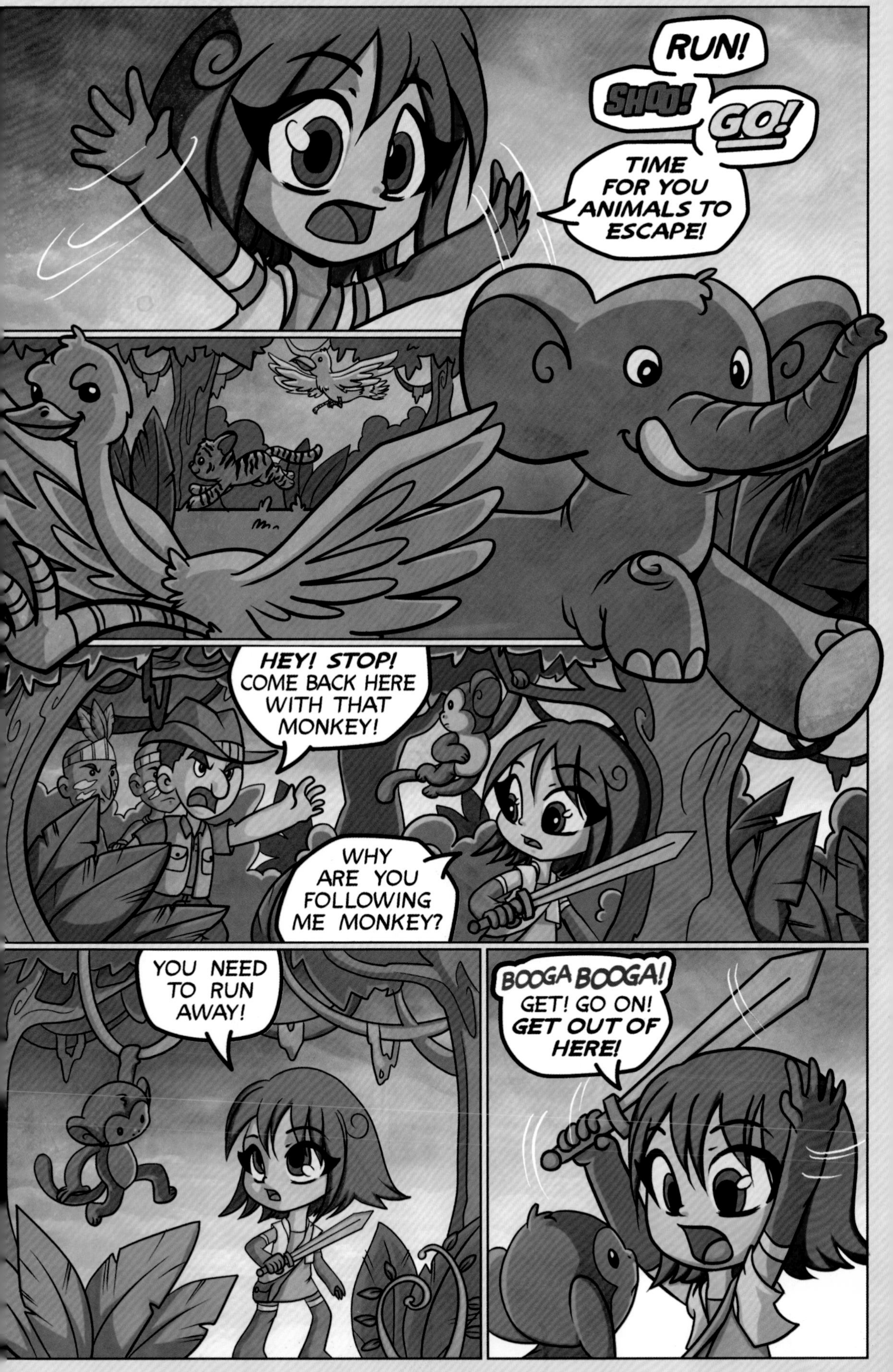
RUN!
SHOO!
GO!
TIME FOR YOU ANIMALS TO ESCAPE!
HEY! STOP! COME BACK HERE WITH THAT MONKEY!
WHY ARE YOU FOLLOWING ME MONKEY?
YOU NEED TO RUN AWAY!
BOOGA BOOGA! GET! GO ON! GET OUT OF HERE!

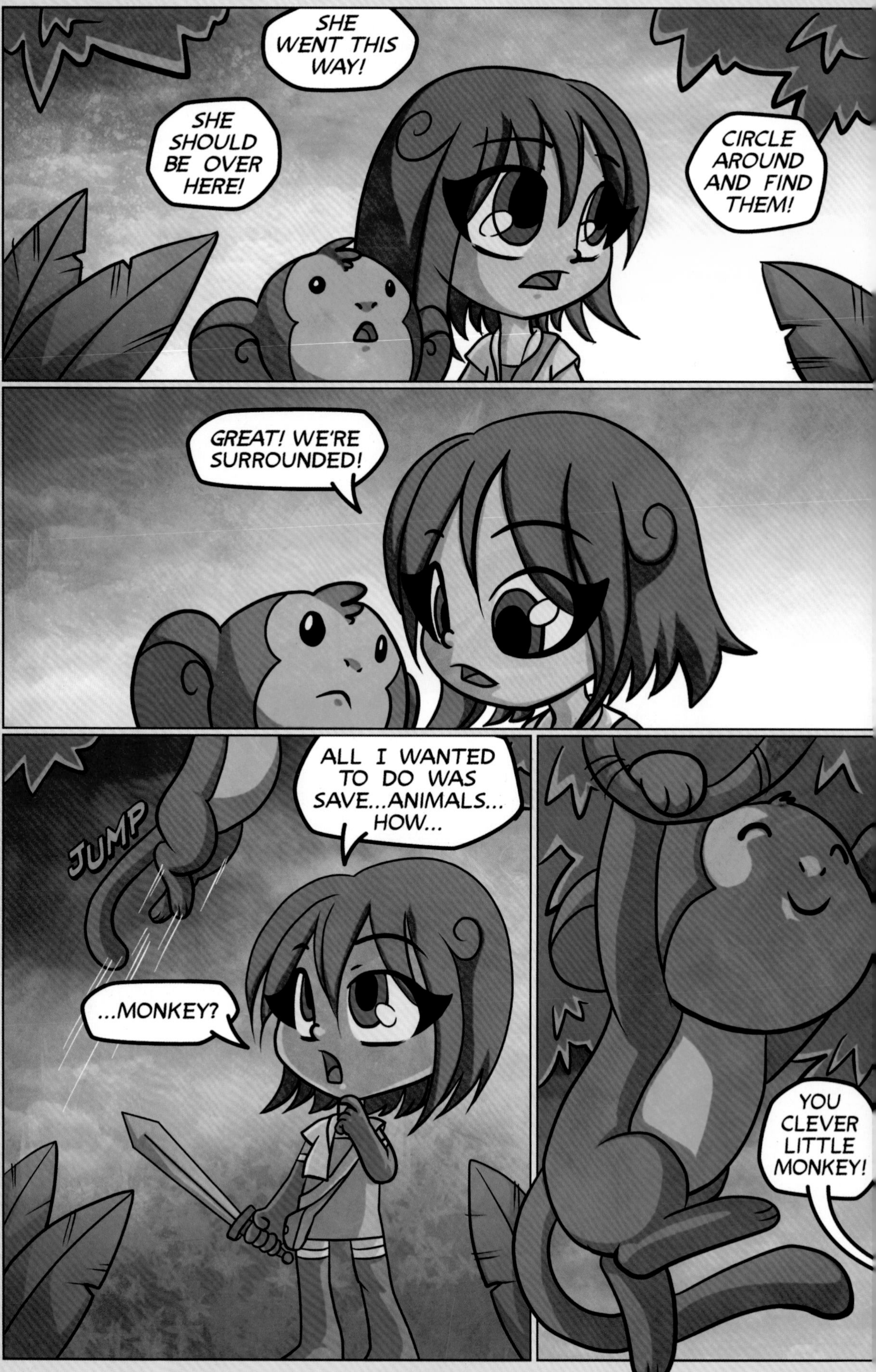
SHE WENT THIS WAY!
SHE SHOULD BE OVER HERE!
CIRCLE AROUND AND FIND THEM!
GREAT! WE'RE SURROUNDED!
ALL I WANTED TO DO WAS SAVE...ANIMALS... HOW...
JUMP
...MONKEY?
YOU CLEVER LITTLE MONKEY!

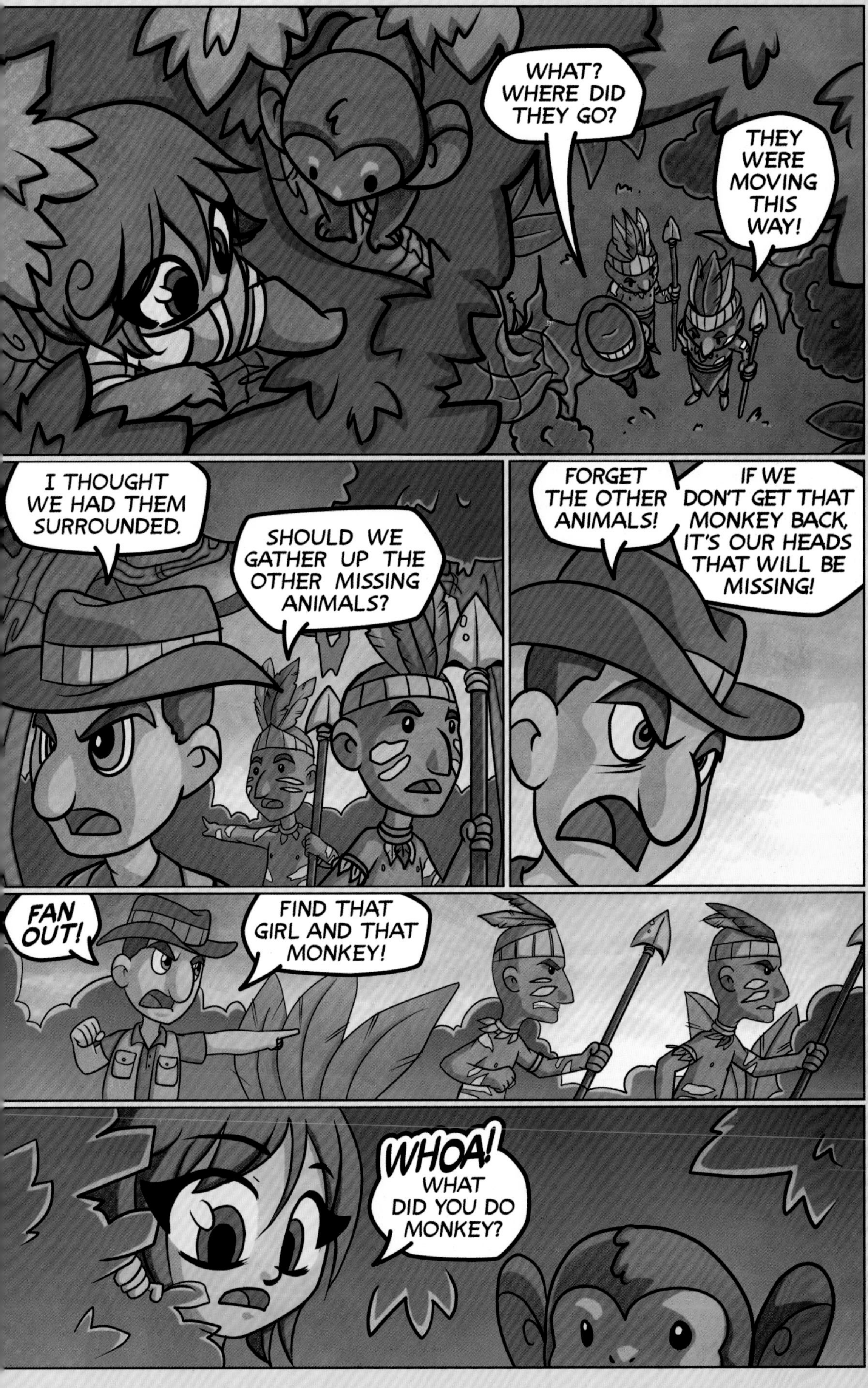
WHAT? WHERE DID THEY GO?
THEY WERE MOVING THIS WAY!
I THOUGHT WE HAD THEM SURROUNDED.
SHOULD WE GATHER UP THE OTHER MISSING ANIMALS?
FORGET THE OTHER ANIMALS!
IF WE DON'T GET THAT MONKEY BACK, IT'S OUR HEADS THAT WILL BE MISSING!
FAN OUT!
FIND THAT GIRL AND THAT MONKEY!
WHOA! WHAT DID YOU DO MONKEY?

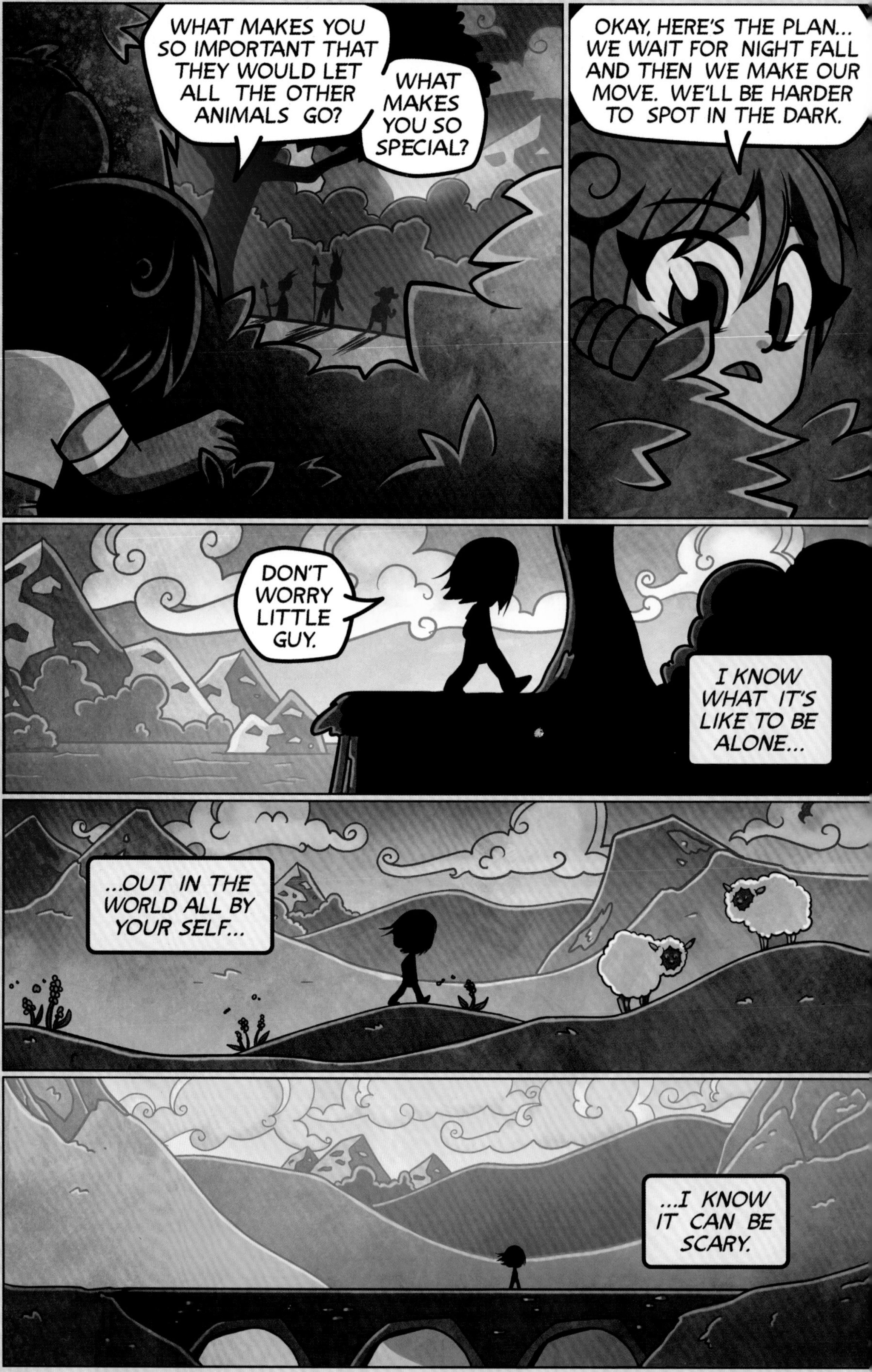
WHAT MAKES YOU SO IMPORTANT THAT THEY WOULD LET ALL THE OTHER ANIMALS GO?
WHAT MAKES YOU SO SPECIAL?
OKAY, HERE'S THE PLAN... WE WAIT FOR NIGHT FALL AND THEN WE MAKE OUR MOVE. WE'LL BE HARDER TO SPOT IN THE DARK.
DON'T WORRY LITTLE GUY.
I KNOW WHAT IT'S LIKE TO BE ALONE...
...OUT IN THE WORLD ALL BY YOUR SELF...
...I KNOW IT CAN BE SCARY.

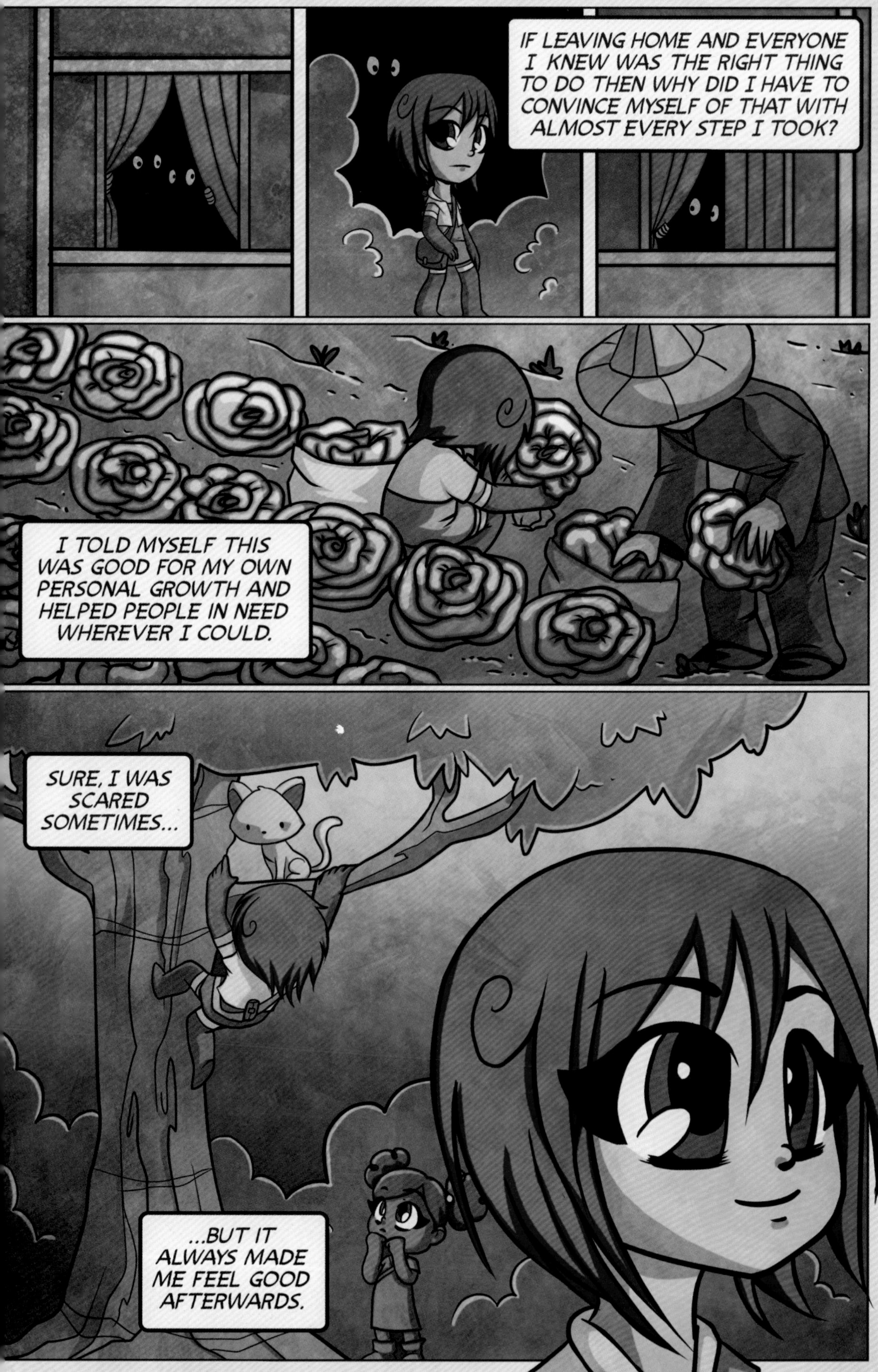
IF LEAVING HOME AND EVERYONE I KNEW WAS THE RIGHT THING TO DO THEN WHY DID I HAVE TO CONVINCE MYSELF OF THAT WITH ALMOST EVERY STEP I TOOK?
I TOLD MYSELF THIS WAS GOOD FOR MY OWN PERSONAL GROWTH AND HELPED PEOPLE IN NEED WHEREVER I COULD.
SURE, I WAS SCARED SOMETIMES...
...BUT IT ALWAYS MADE ME FEEL GOOD AFTERWARDS.

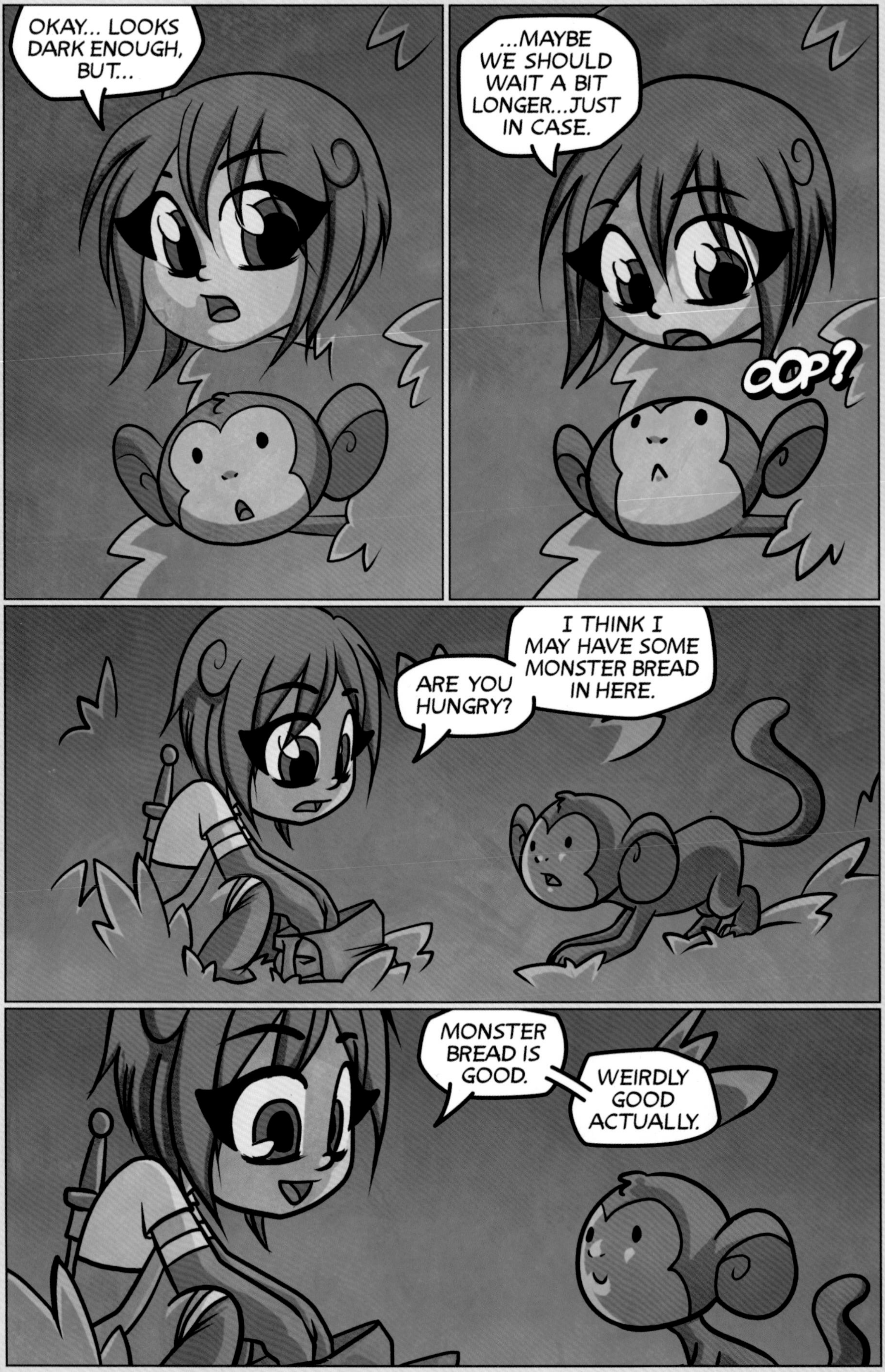
OKAY... LOOKS DARK ENOUGH, BUT...
...MAYBE WE SHOULD WAIT A BIT LONGER...JUST IN CASE.
OOP?
ARE YOU HUNGRY?
I THINK I MAY HAVE SOME MONSTER BREAD IN HERE.
MONSTER BREAD IS GOOD.
WEIRDLY GOOD ACTUALLY.

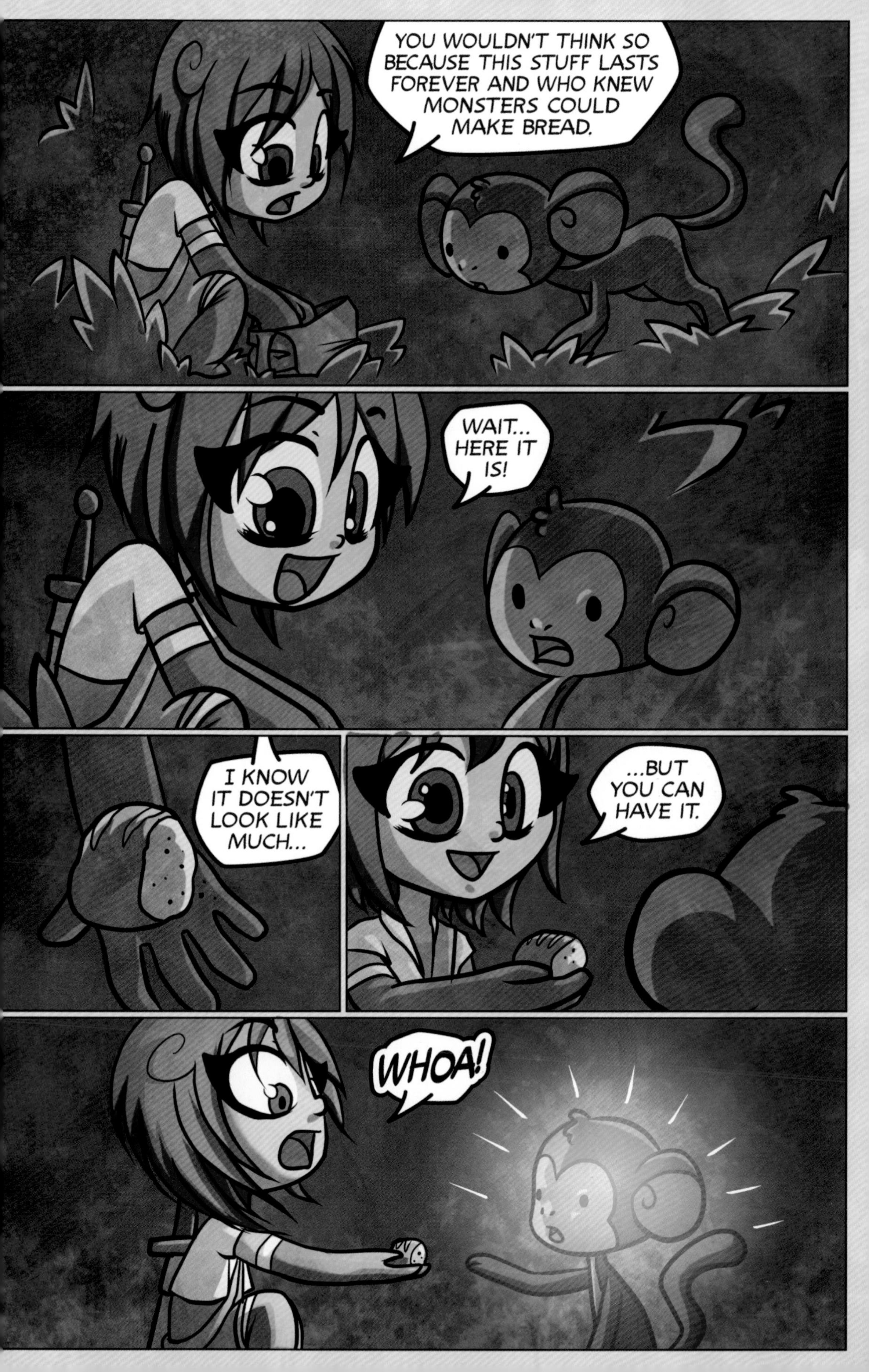
YOU WOULDN'T THINK SO BECAUSE THIS STUFF LASTS FOREVER AND WHO KNEW MONSTERS COULD MAKE BREAD.
WAIT... HERE IT IS!
I KNOW IT DOESN'T LOOK LIKE MUCH...
...BUT YOU CAN HAVE IT.
WHOA!

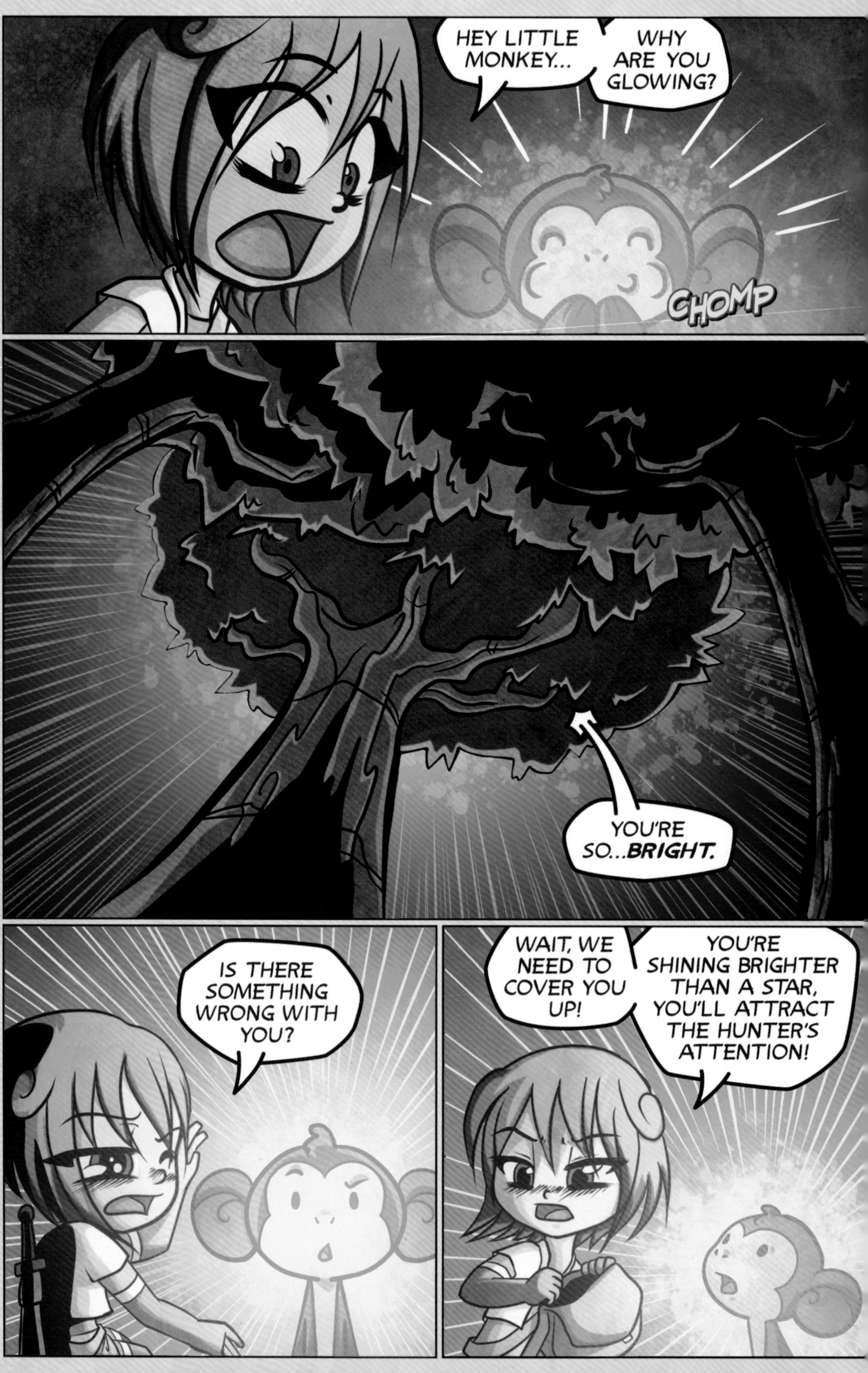
HEY LITTLE MONKEY...
WHY ARE YOU GLOWING?
CHOMP
YOU'RE SO...BRIGHT.
IS THERE SOMETHING WRONG WITH YOU?
WAIT, WE NEED TO COVER YOU UP!
YOU'RE SHINING BRIGHTER THAN A STAR, YOU'LL ATTRACT THE HUNTER'S ATTENTION!

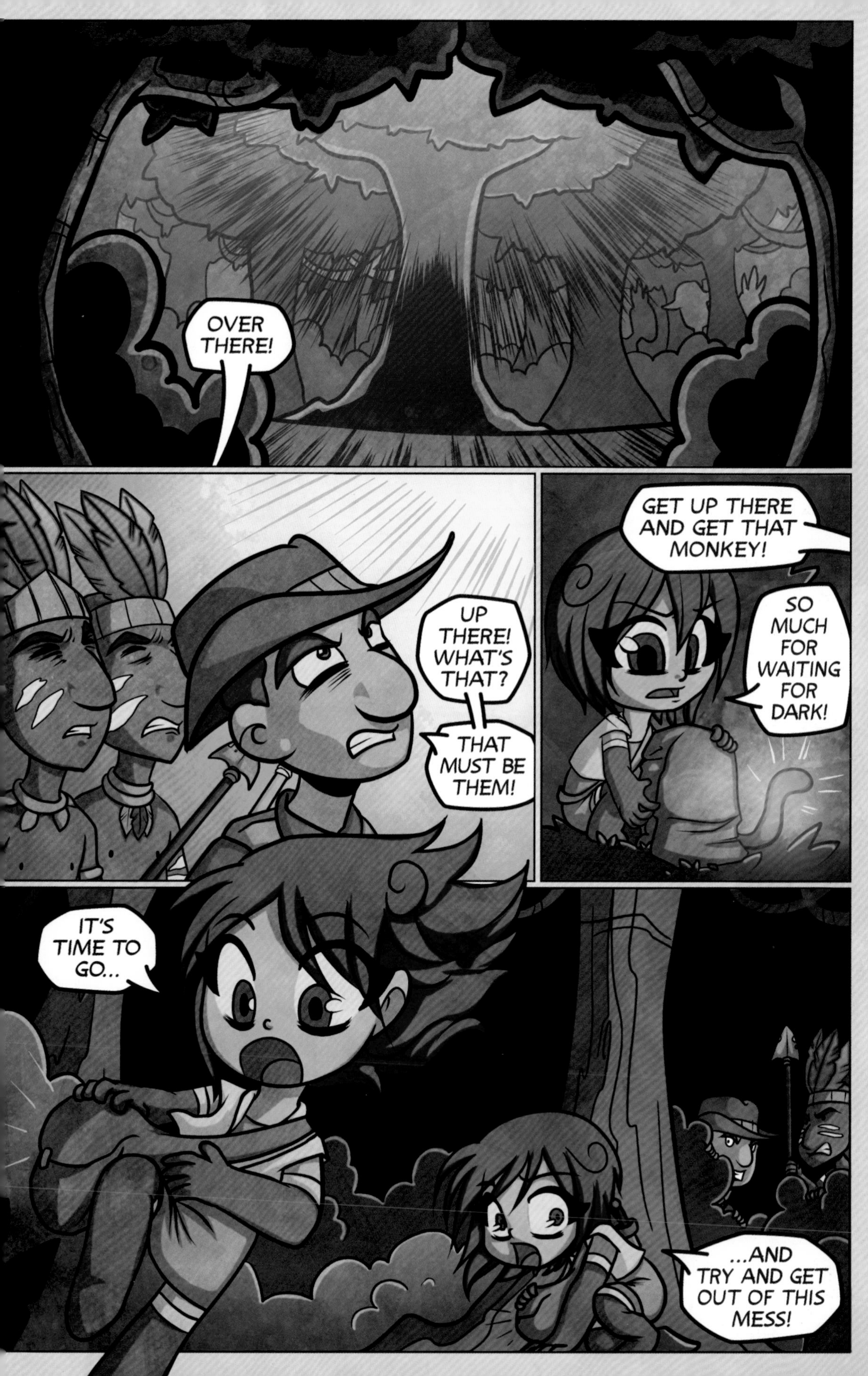
OVER THERE!
UP THERE! WHAT'S THAT?
THAT MUST BE THEM!
GET UP THERE AND GET THAT MONKEY!
SO MUCH FOR WAITING FOR DARK!
IT'S TIME TO GO...
...AND TRY AND GET OUT OF THIS MESS!

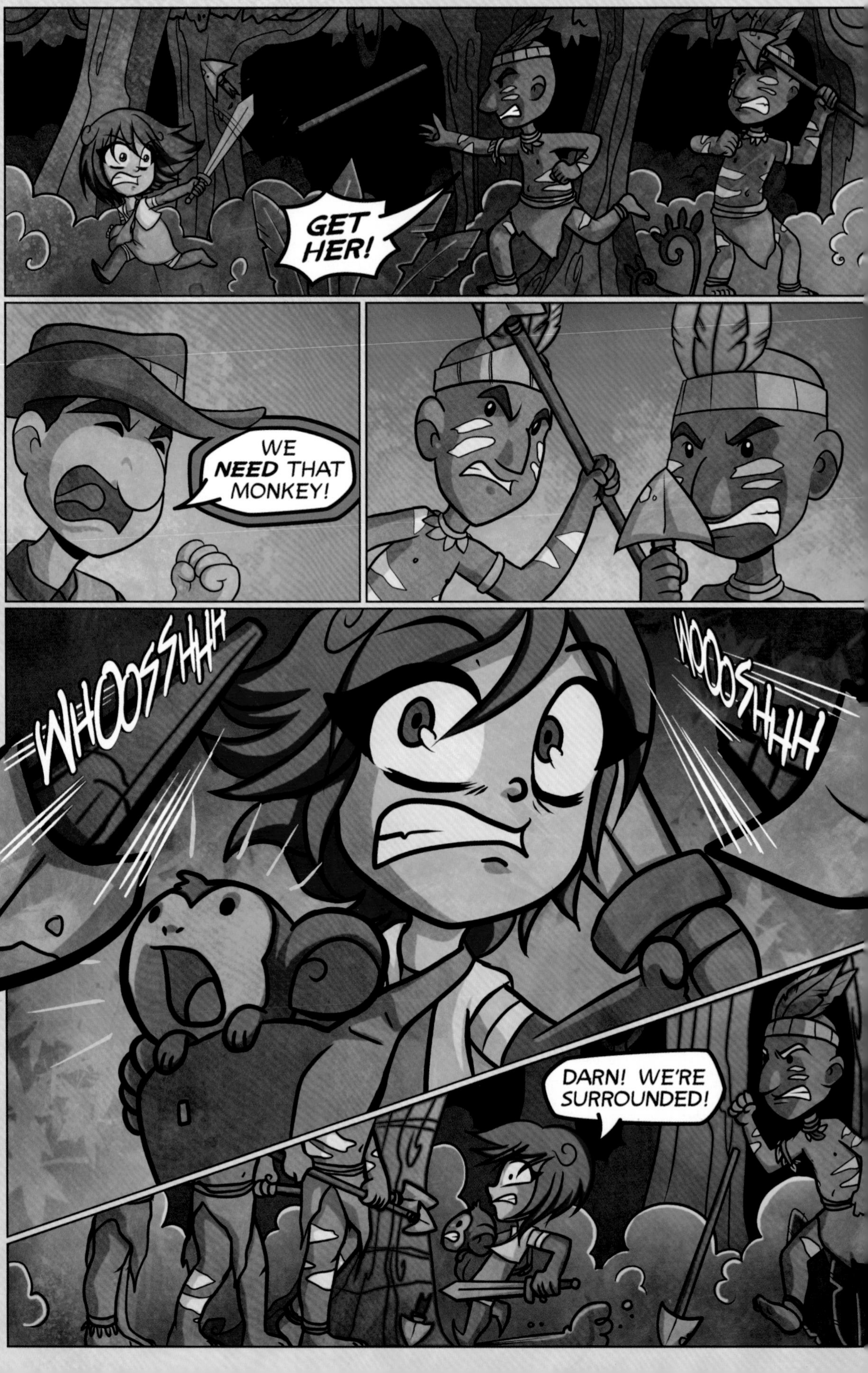
GET HER!
WE NEED THAT MONKEY!
WHOOSSHHH
WOOOSHHH
DARN! WE'RE SURROUNDED!

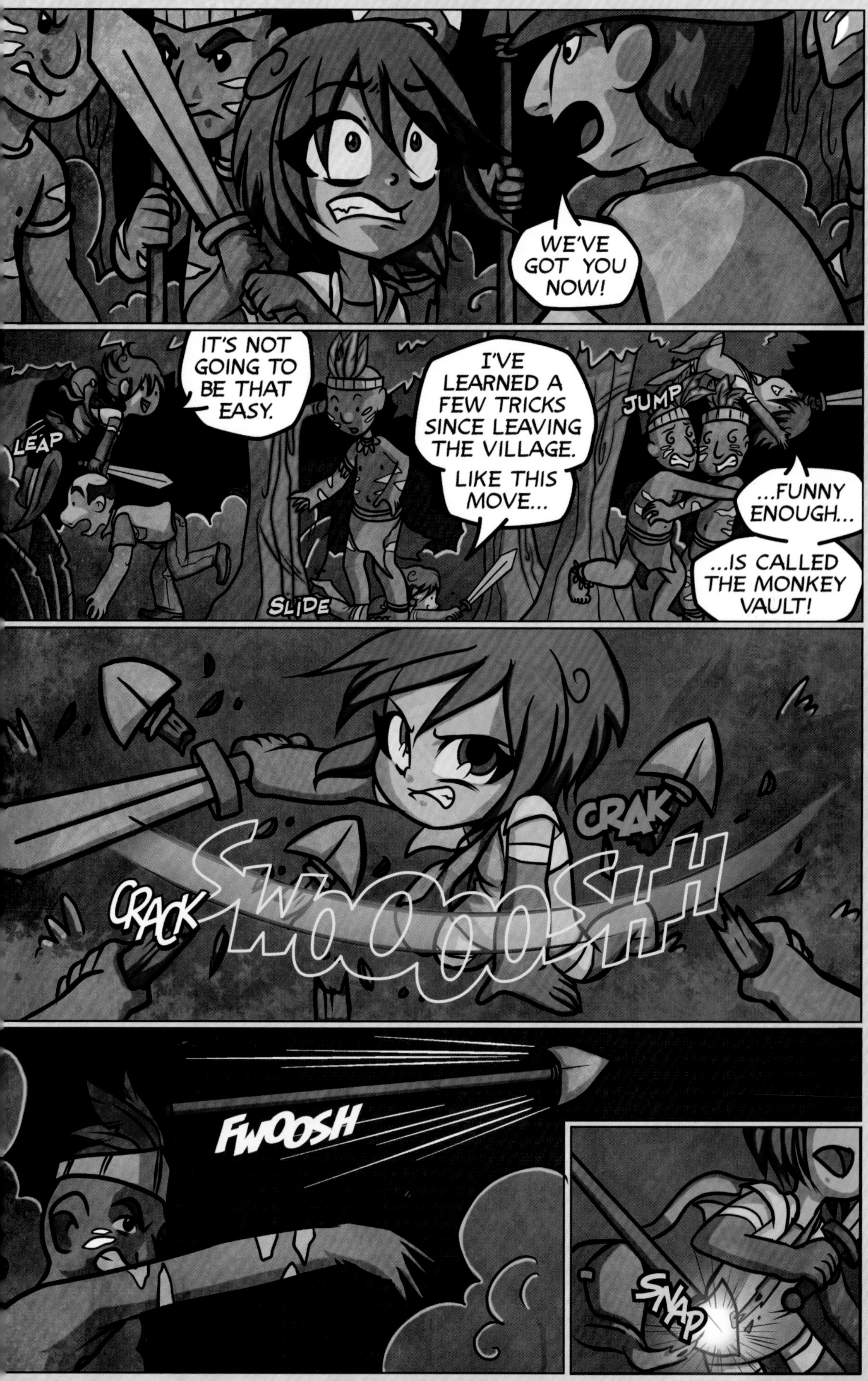
WE'VE GOT YOU NOW!
IT'S NOT GOING TO BE THAT EASY.
LEAP
I'VE LEARNED A FEW TRICKS SINCE LEAVING THE VILLAGE.
LIKE THIS MOVE...
SLIDE
JUMP
...FUNNY ENOUGH...
...IS CALLED THE MONKEY VAULT!
CRAK
CRACK
SWOOOOSHH
FWOOSH
SNAP

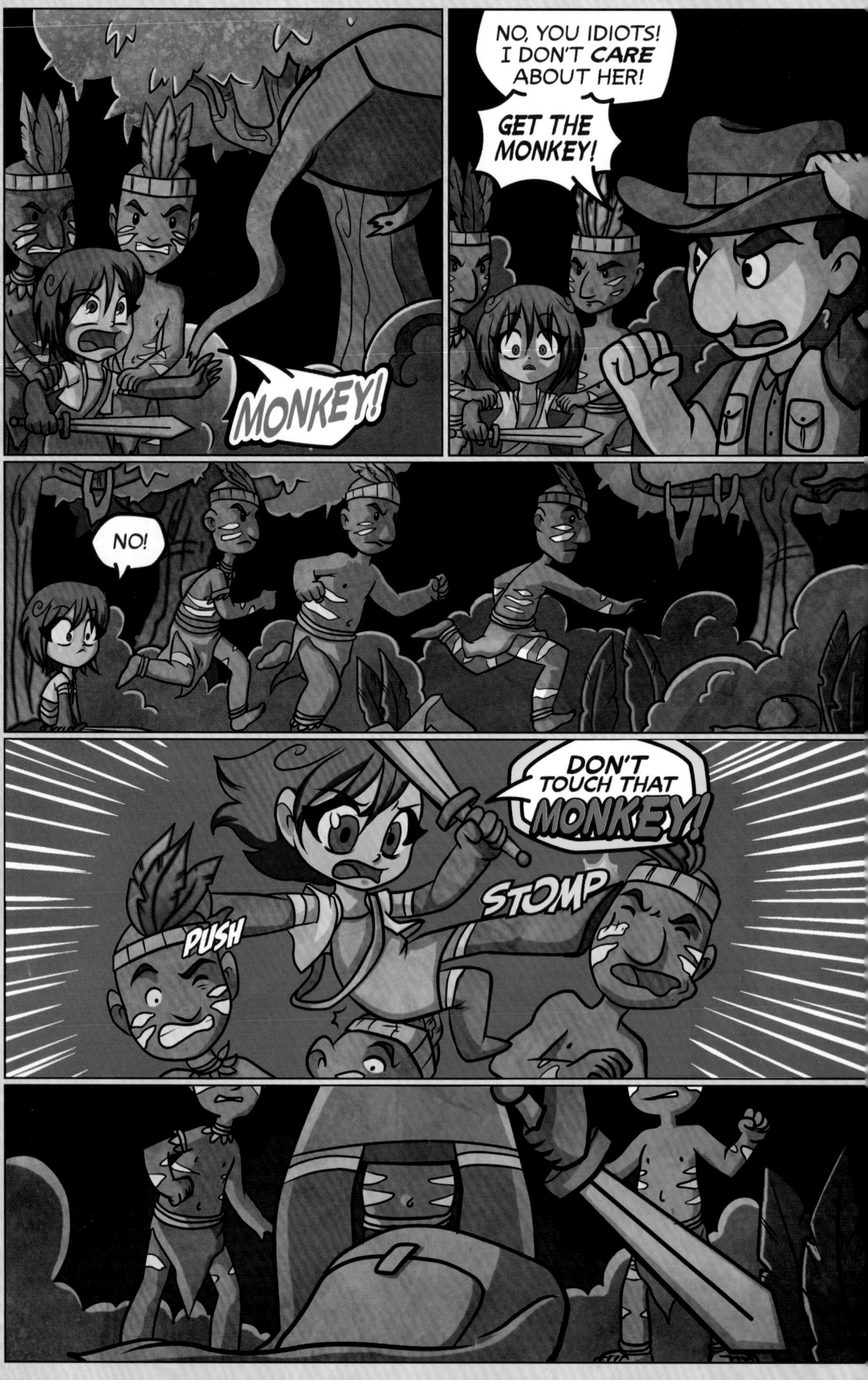
MONKEY!
NO, YOU IDIOTS! I DON'T CARE ABOUT HER!
GET THE MONKEY!
NO!
DON'T TOUCH THAT MONKEY!
STOMP
PUSH

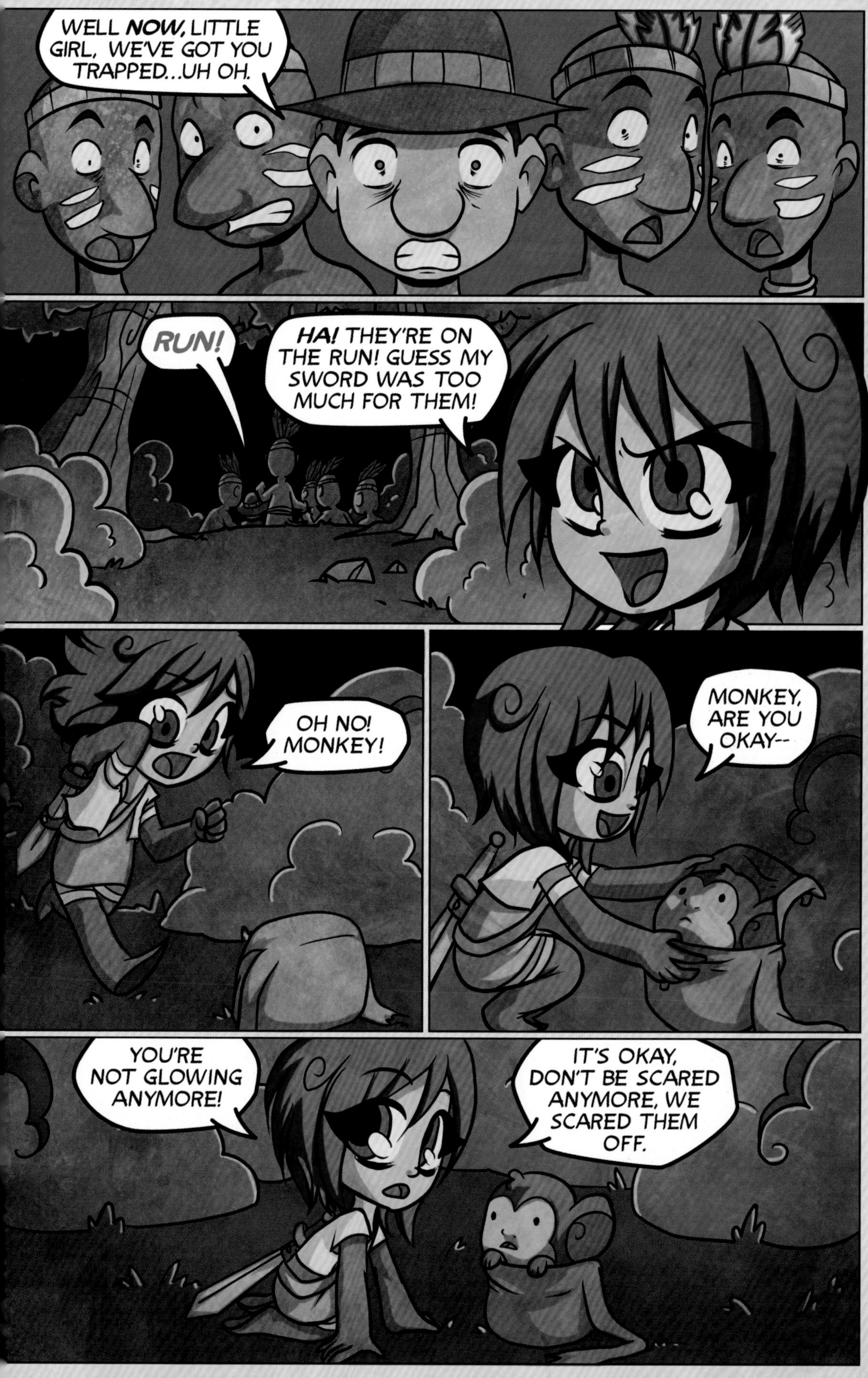

WELL *NOW*, LITTLE GIRL, WE'VE GOT YOU TRAPPED...UH OH.
RUN!
HA! THEY'RE ON THE RUN! GUESS MY SWORD WAS TOO MUCH FOR THEM!
OH NO! MONKEY!
MONKEY, ARE YOU OKAY--
YOU'RE NOT GLOWING ANYMORE!
IT'S OKAY, DON'T BE SCARED ANYMORE, WE SCARED THEM OFF.

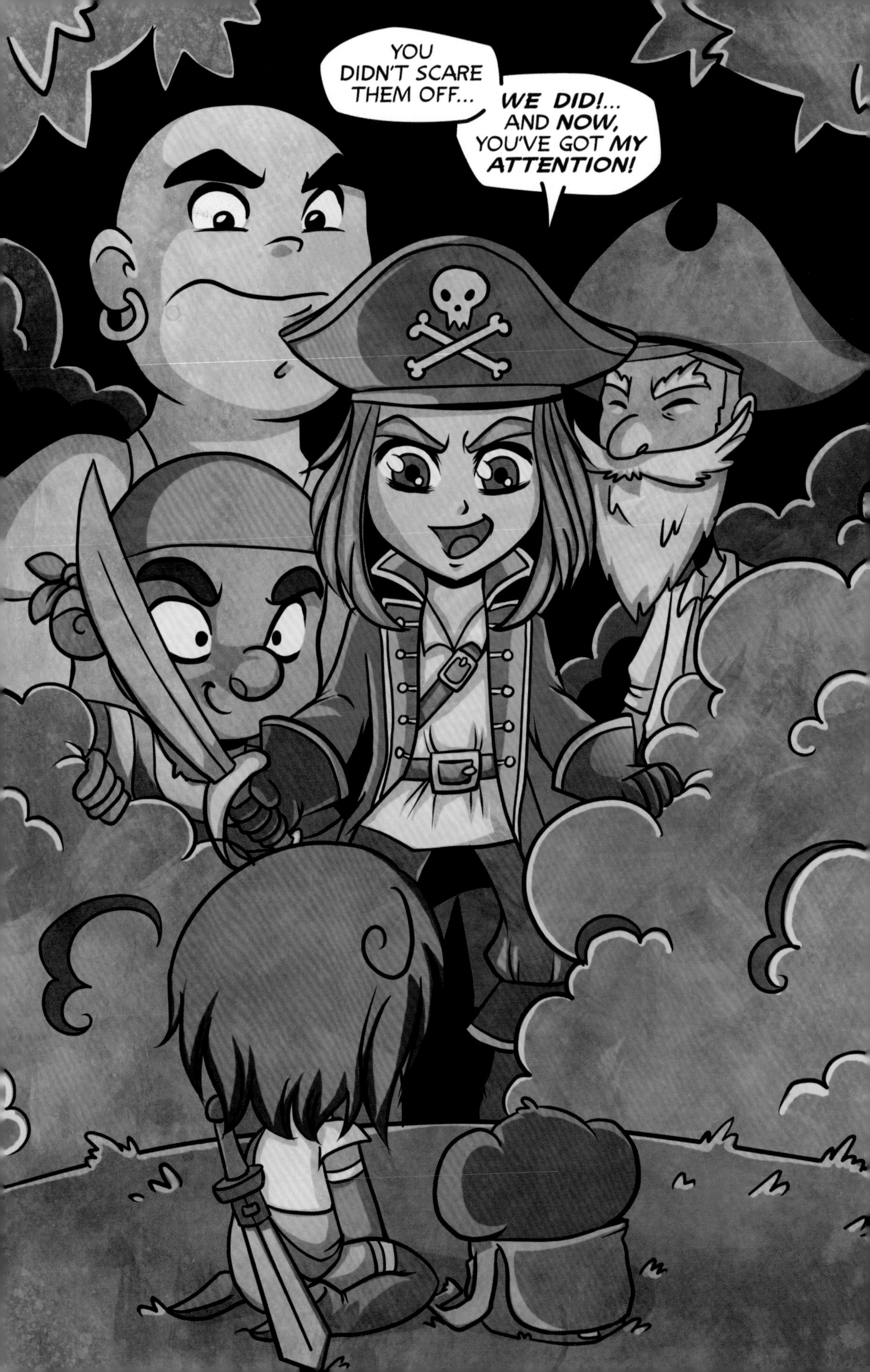
YOU DIDN'T SCARE THEM OFF...
WE DID!... AND *NOW*, YOU'VE GOT *MY ATTENTION!*

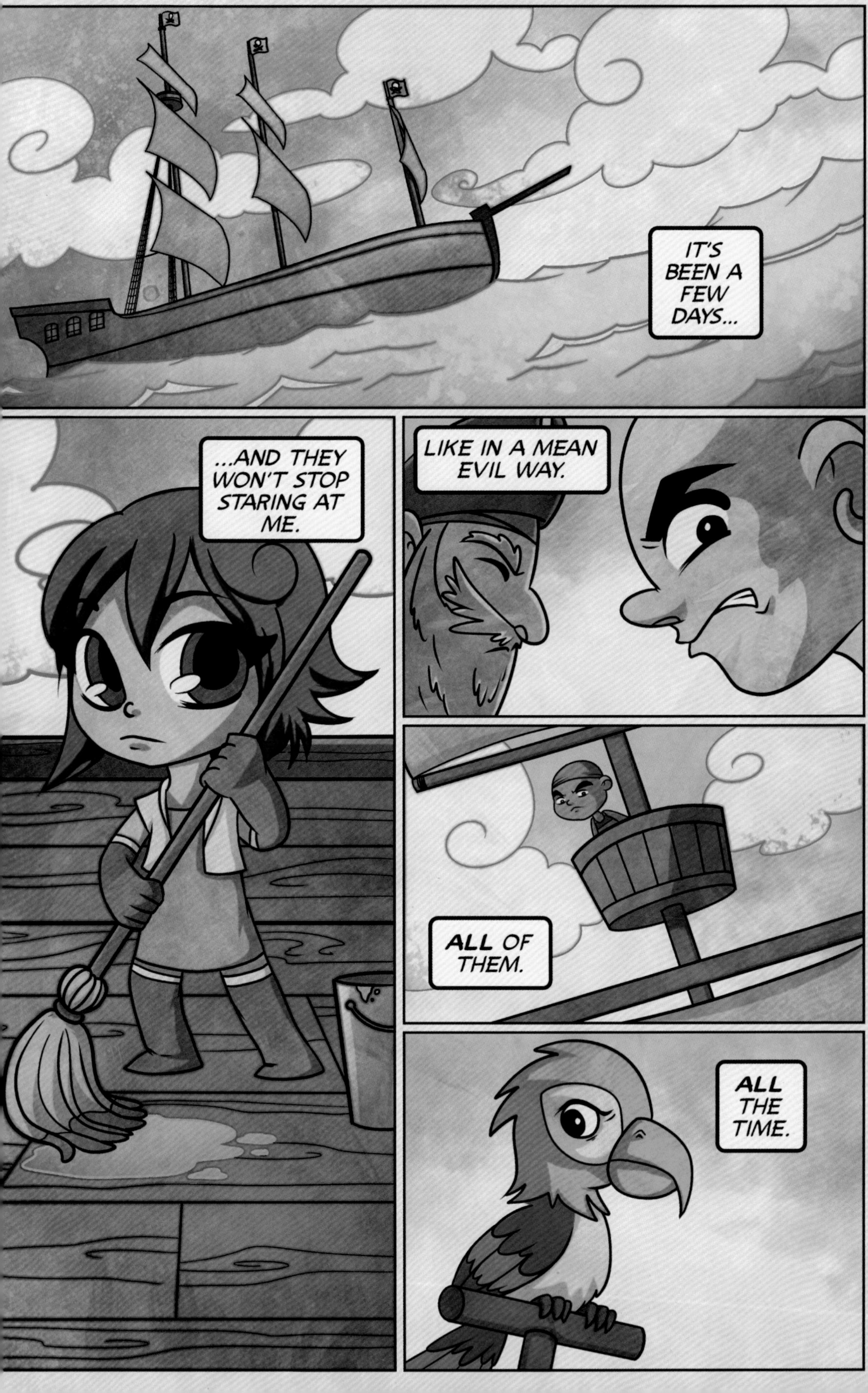
IT'S BEEN A FEW DAYS...
...AND THEY WON'T STOP STARING AT ME.
LIKE IN A MEAN EVIL WAY.
ALL OF THEM.
ALL THE TIME.

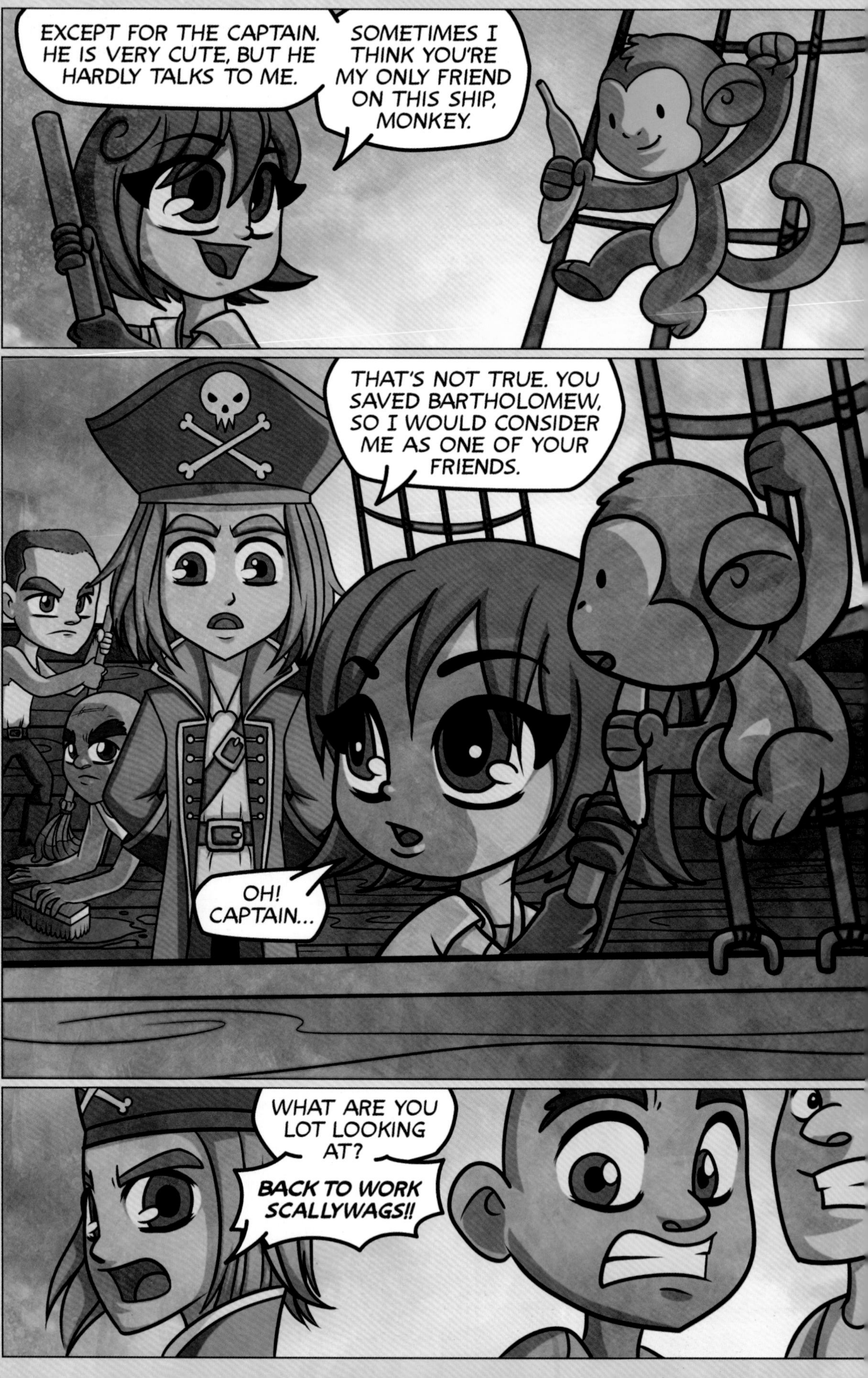
EXCEPT FOR THE CAPTAIN. HE IS VERY CUTE, BUT HE HARDLY TALKS TO ME.
SOMETIMES I THINK YOU'RE MY ONLY FRIEND ON THIS SHIP, MONKEY.
THAT'S NOT TRUE. YOU SAVED BARTHOLOMEW, SO I WOULD CONSIDER ME AS ONE OF YOUR FRIENDS.
OH! CAPTAIN...
WHAT ARE YOU LOT LOOKING AT?
BACK TO WORK SCALLYWAGS!!

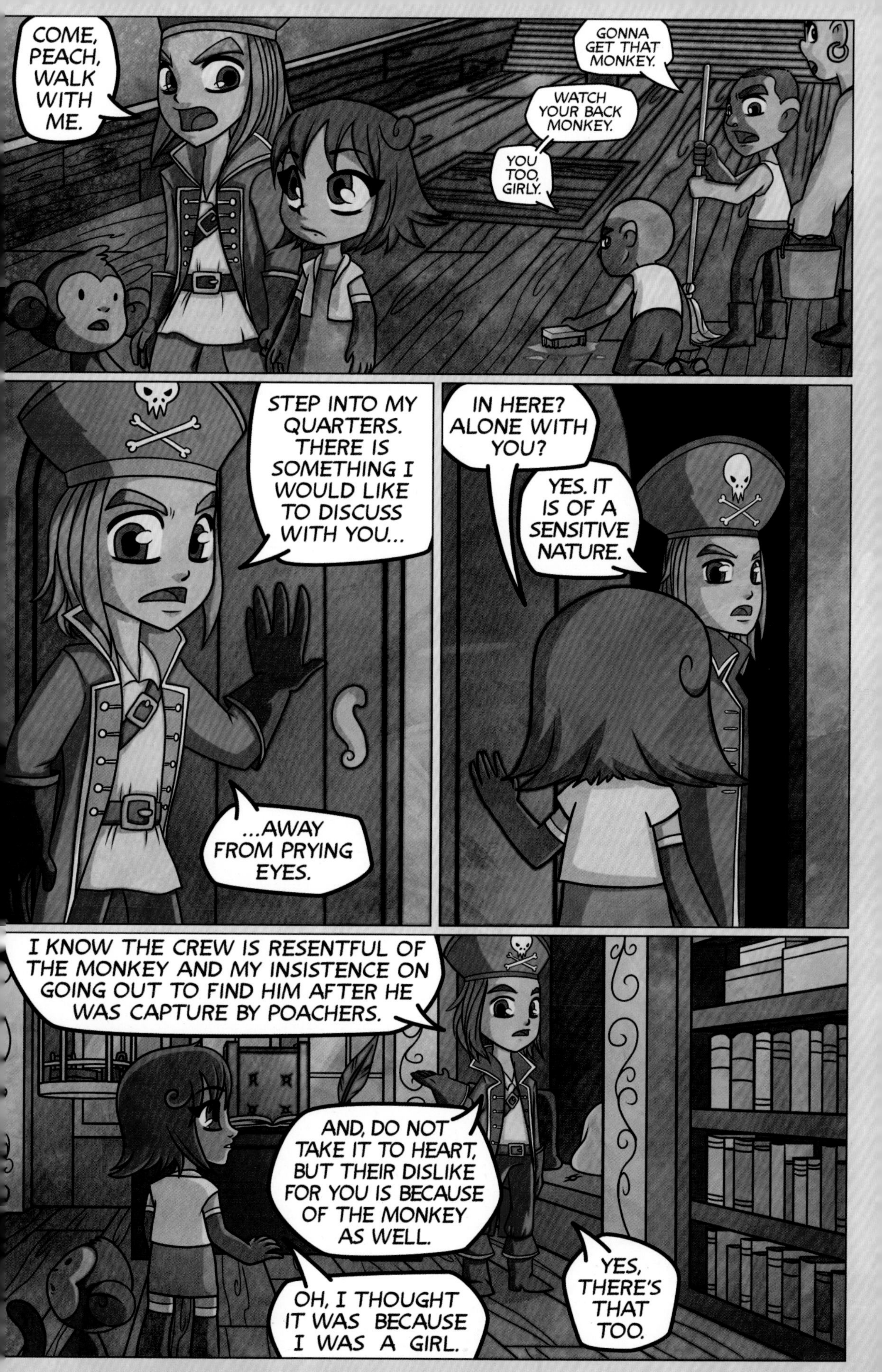
COME, PEACH, WALK WITH ME.
GONNA GET THAT MONKEY.
WATCH YOUR BACK MONKEY.
YOU TOO, GIRLY.
STEP INTO MY QUARTERS. THERE IS SOMETHING I WOULD LIKE TO DISCUSS WITH YOU...
...AWAY FROM PRYING EYES.
IN HERE? ALONE WITH YOU?
YES. IT IS OF A SENSITIVE NATURE.
I KNOW THE CREW IS RESENTFUL OF THE MONKEY AND MY INSISTENCE ON GOING OUT TO FIND HIM AFTER HE WAS CAPTURE BY POACHERS.
AND, DO NOT TAKE IT TO HEART, BUT THEIR DISLIKE FOR YOU IS BECAUSE OF THE MONKEY AS WELL.
OH, I THOUGHT IT WAS BECAUSE I WAS A GIRL.
YES, THERE'S THAT TOO.

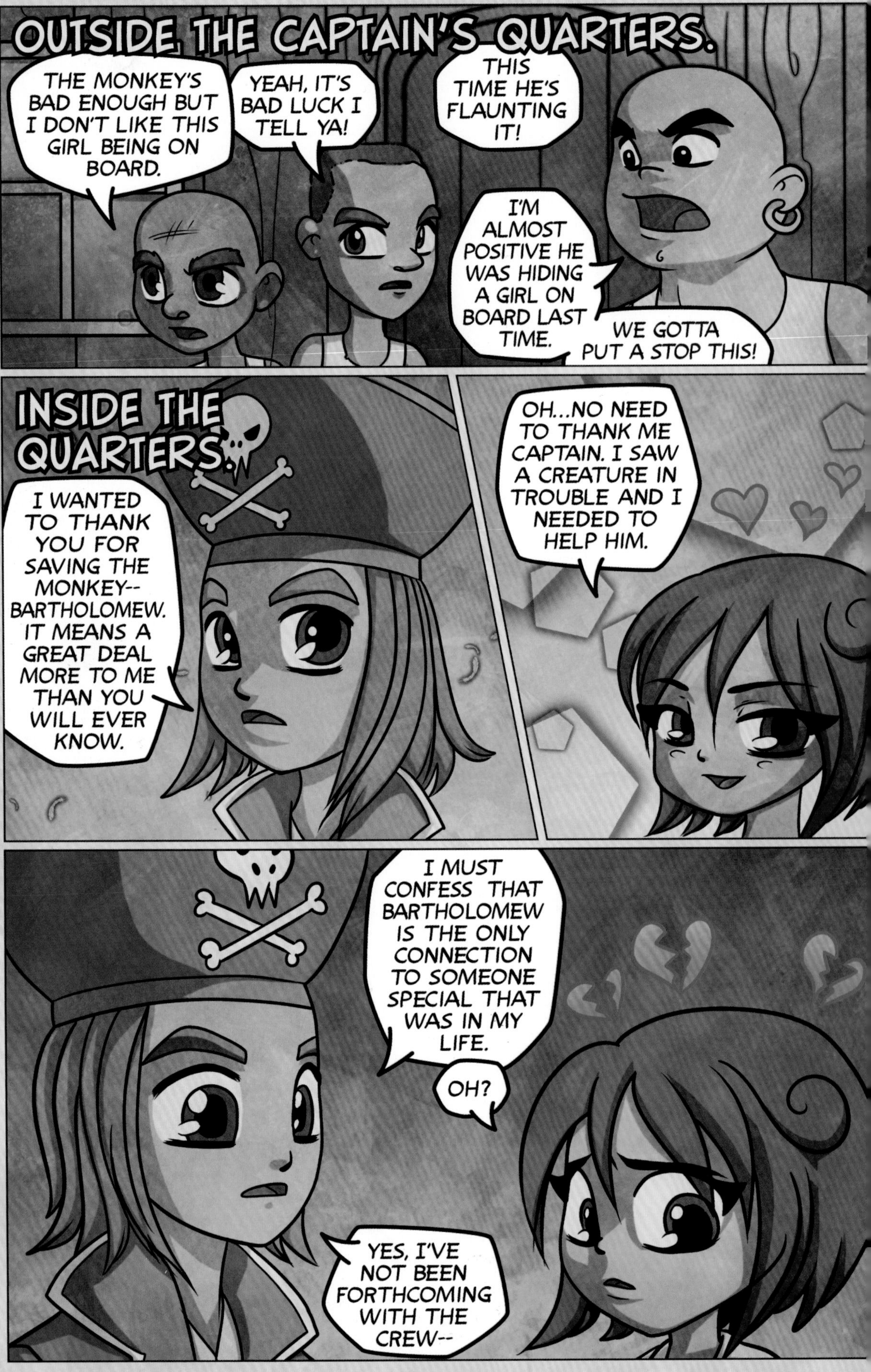
OUTSIDE THE CAPTAIN'S QUARTERS.
THE MONKEY'S BAD ENOUGH BUT I DON'T LIKE THIS GIRL BEING ON BOARD.
YEAH, IT'S BAD LUCK I TELL YA!
THIS TIME HE'S FLAUNTING IT!
I'M ALMOST POSITIVE HE WAS HIDING A GIRL ON BOARD LAST TIME.
WE GOTTA PUT A STOP THIS!
INSIDE THE QUARTERS.
I WANTED TO THANK YOU FOR SAVING THE MONKEY--BARTHOLOMEW. IT MEANS A GREAT DEAL MORE TO ME THAN YOU WILL EVER KNOW.
OH...NO NEED TO THANK ME CAPTAIN. I SAW A CREATURE IN TROUBLE AND I NEEDED TO HELP HIM.
I MUST CONFESS THAT BARTHOLOMEW IS THE ONLY CONNECTION TO SOMEONE SPECIAL THAT WAS IN MY LIFE.
OH?
YES, I'VE NOT BEEN FORTHCOMING WITH THE CREW--

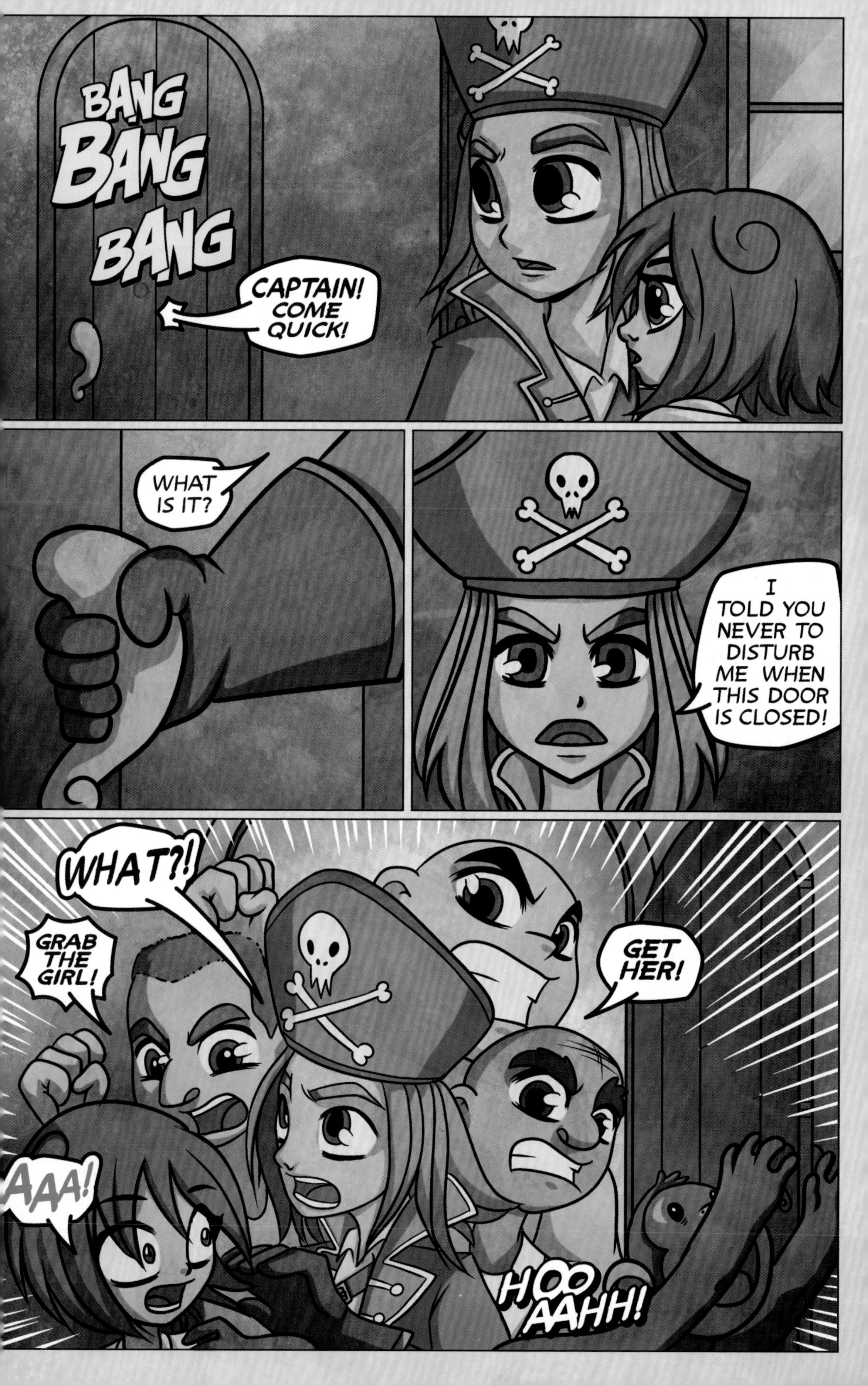
BANG
BANG
BANG
CAPTAIN! COME QUICK!
WHAT IS IT?
I TOLD YOU NEVER TO DISTURB ME WHEN THIS DOOR IS CLOSED!
WHAT?!
GRAB THE GIRL!
GET HER!
AAA!
HOO AAHH!

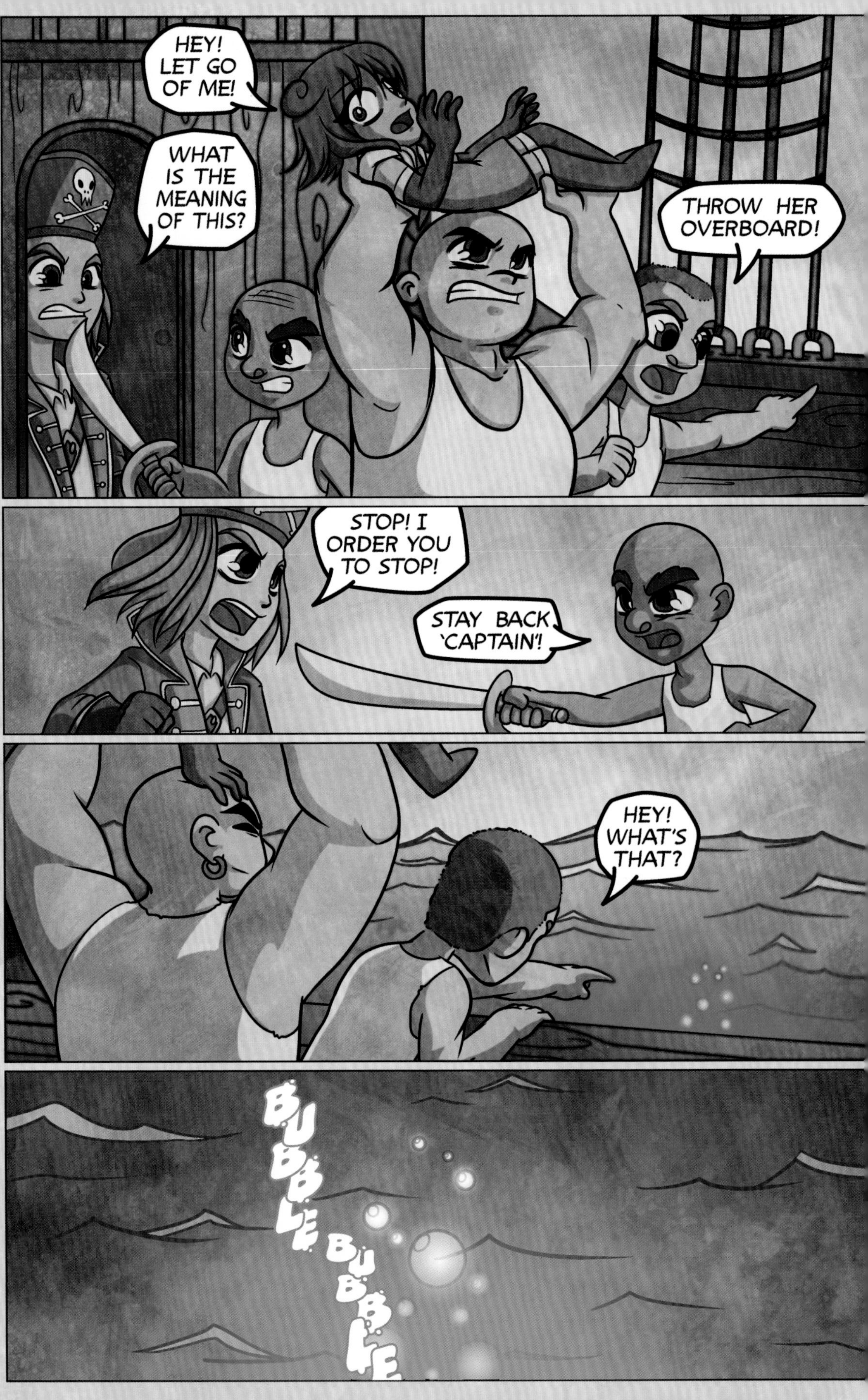
HEY! LET GO OF ME!
WHAT IS THE MEANING OF THIS?
THROW HER OVERBOARD!
STOP! I ORDER YOU TO STOP!
STAY BACK 'CAPTAIN'!
HEY! WHAT'S THAT?
BUBBLE
BUBBLE

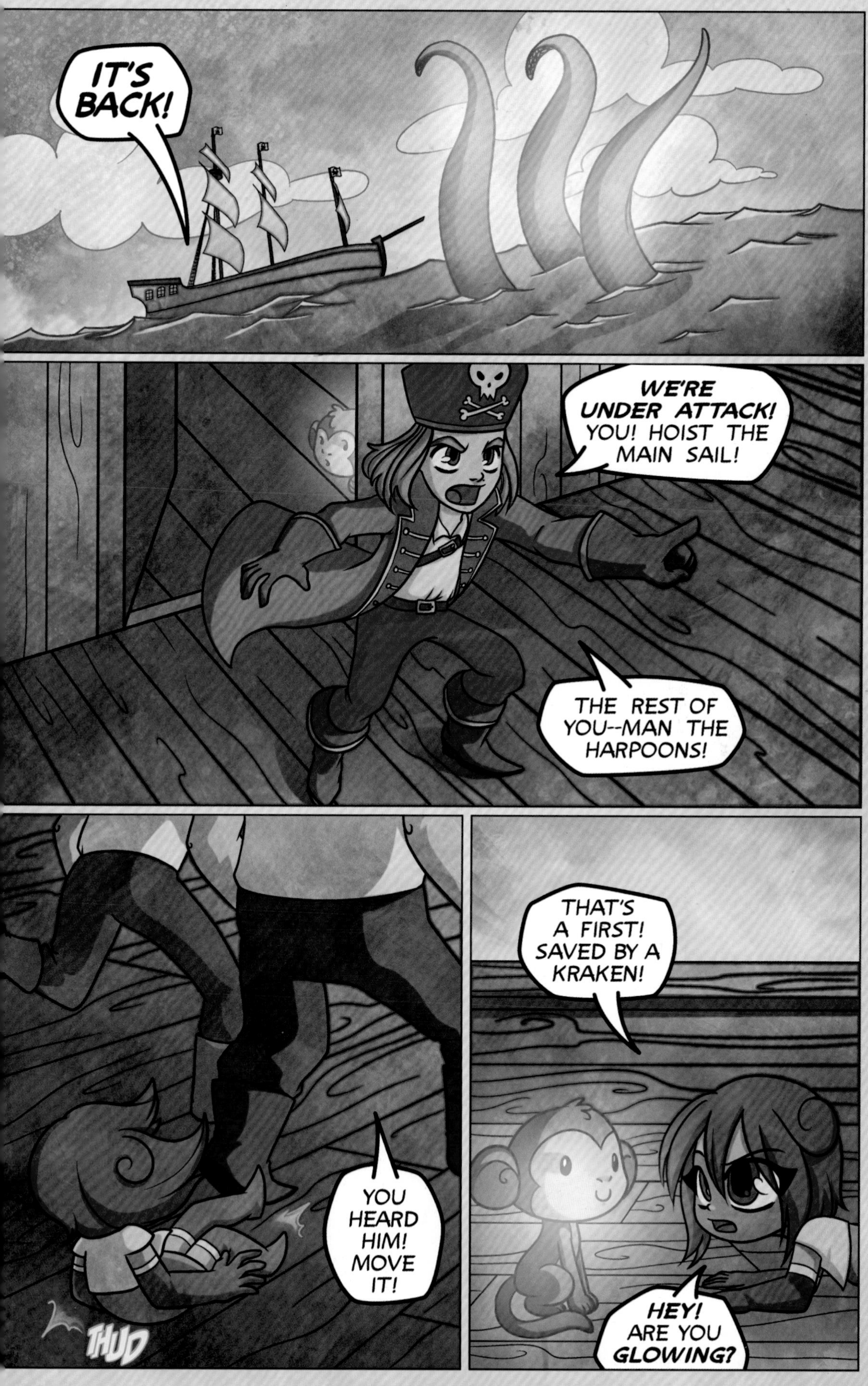
IT'S BACK!
WE'RE UNDER ATTACK! YOU! HOIST THE MAIN SAIL!
THE REST OF YOU--MAN THE HARPOONS!
YOU HEARD HIM! MOVE IT!
THUD
THAT'S A FIRST! SAVED BY A KRAKEN!
HEY! ARE YOU GLOWING?

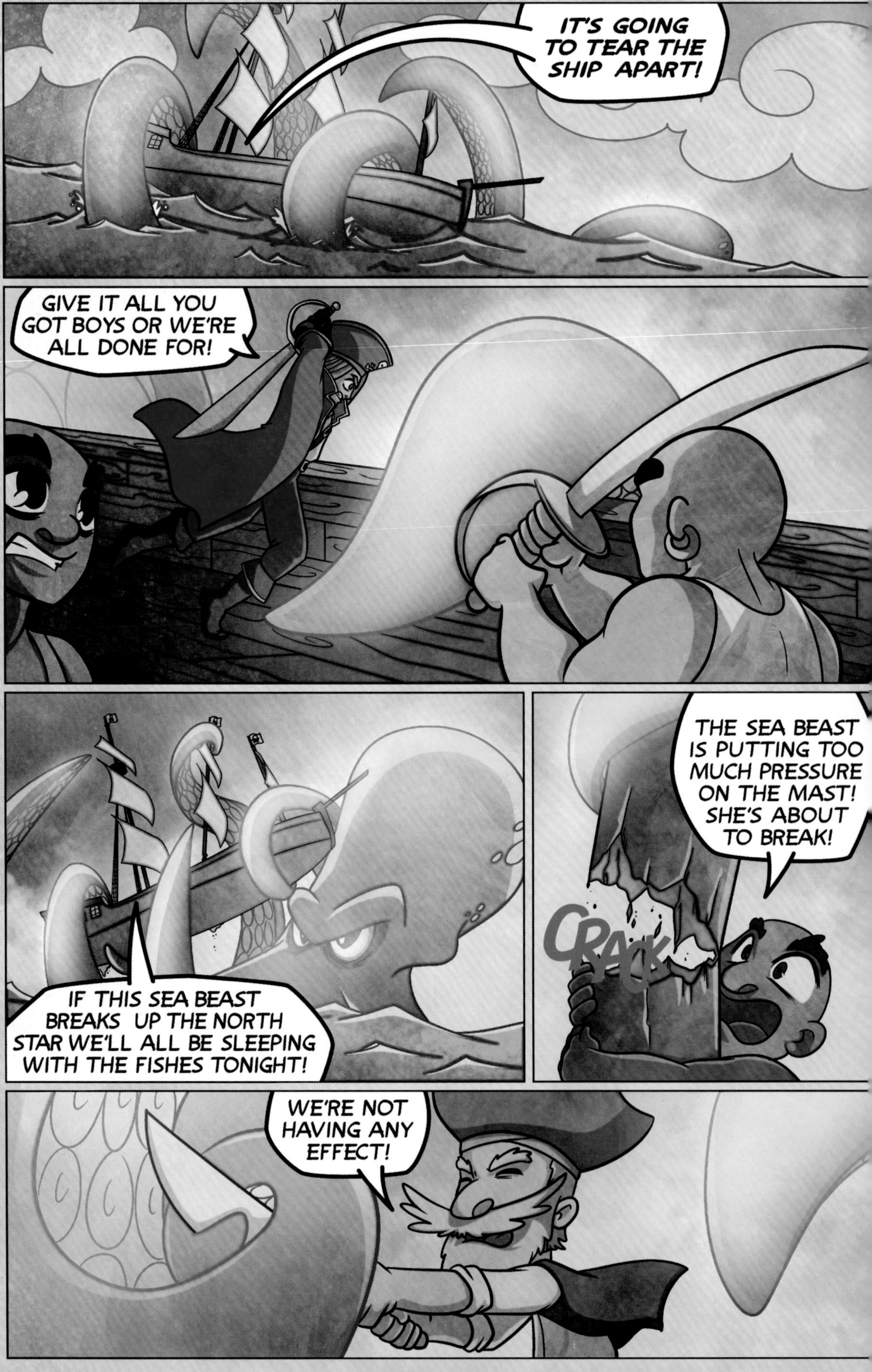
IT'S GOING TO TEAR THE SHIP APART!
GIVE IT ALL YOU GOT BOYS OR WE'RE ALL DONE FOR!
IF THIS SEA BEAST BREAKS UP THE NORTH STAR WE'LL ALL BE SLEEPING WITH THE FISHES TONIGHT!
THE SEA BEAST IS PUTTING TOO MUCH PRESSURE ON THE MAST! SHE'S ABOUT TO BREAK!
CRACK
WE'RE NOT HAVING ANY EFFECT!

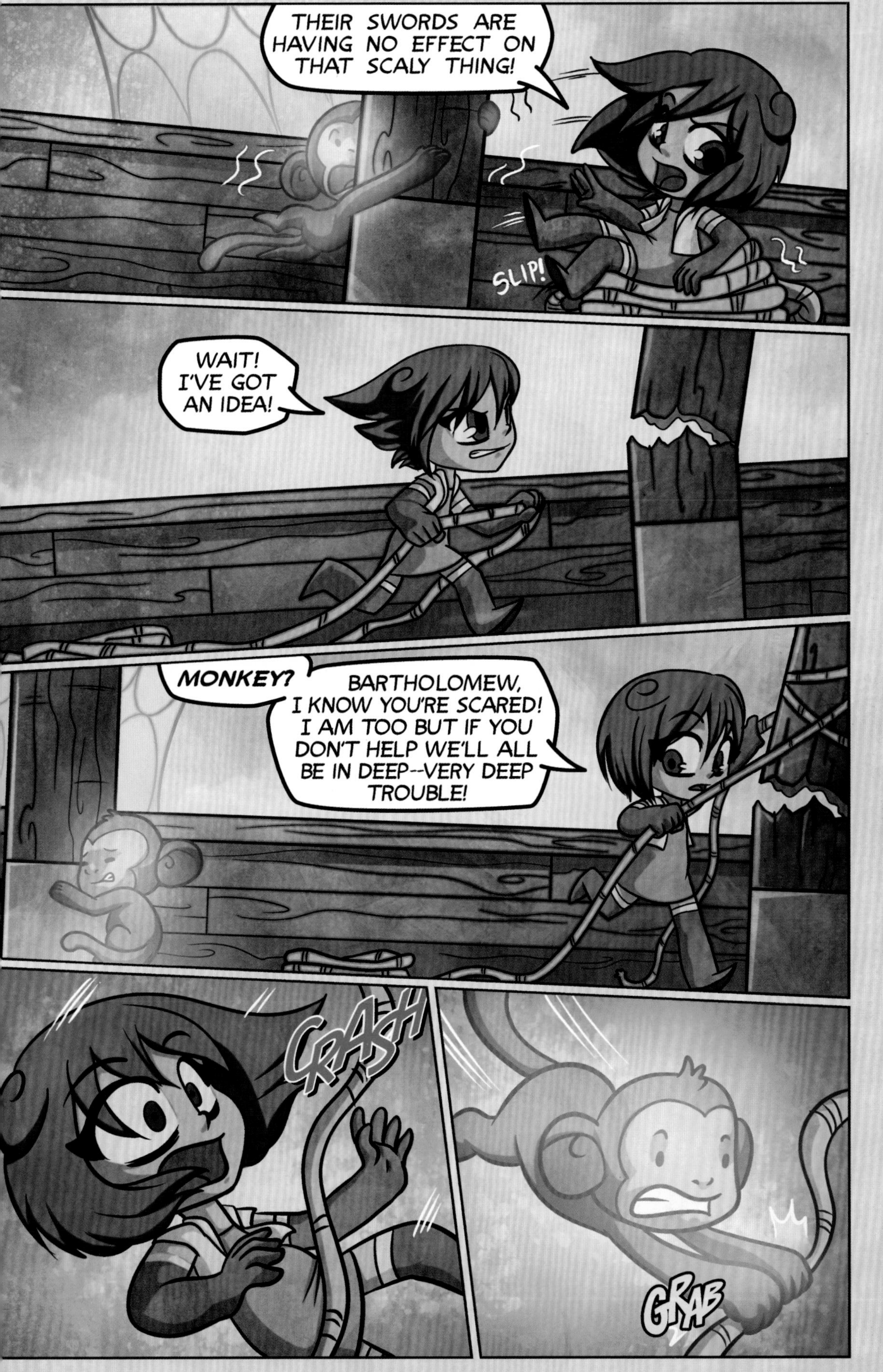
THEIR SWORDS ARE HAVING NO EFFECT ON THAT SCALY THING!
SLIP!
WAIT! I'VE GOT AN IDEA!
MONKEY?
BARTHOLOMEW, I KNOW YOU'RE SCARED! I AM TOO BUT IF YOU DON'T HELP WE'LL ALL BE IN DEEP--VERY DEEP TROUBLE!
CRASH
GRAB

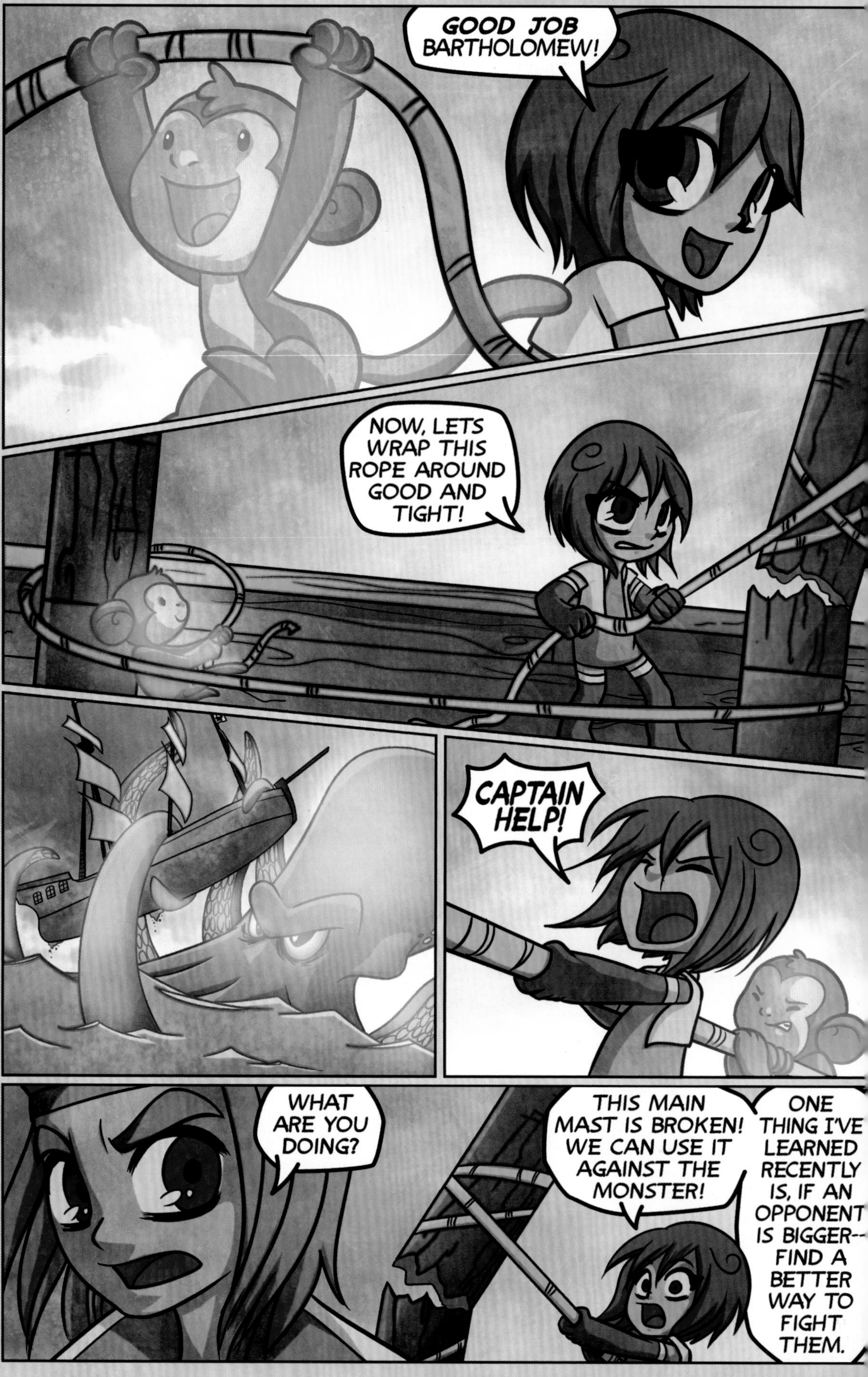
GOOD JOB BARTHOLOMEW!
NOW, LETS WRAP THIS ROPE AROUND GOOD AND TIGHT!
CAPTAIN HELP!
WHAT ARE YOU DOING?
THIS MAIN MAST IS BROKEN! WE CAN USE IT AGAINST THE MONSTER!
ONE THING I'VE LEARNED RECENTLY IS, IF AN OPPONENT IS BIGGER-- FIND A BETTER WAY TO FIGHT THEM.

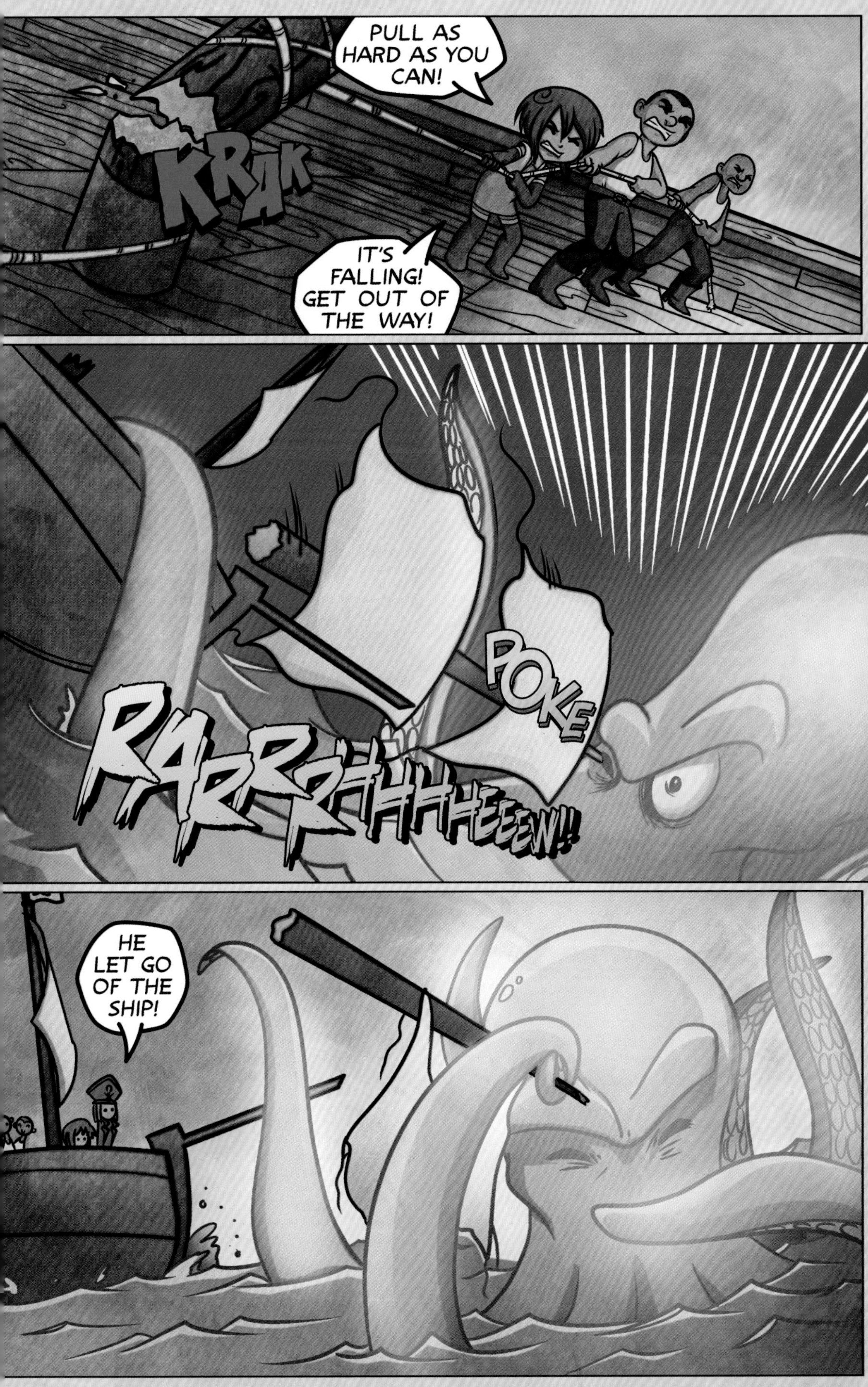
PULL AS HARD AS YOU CAN!
KRAK
IT'S FALLING! GET OUT OF THE WAY!
POKE
RARRRHHHHEEEEN!!
HE LET GO OF THE SHIP!

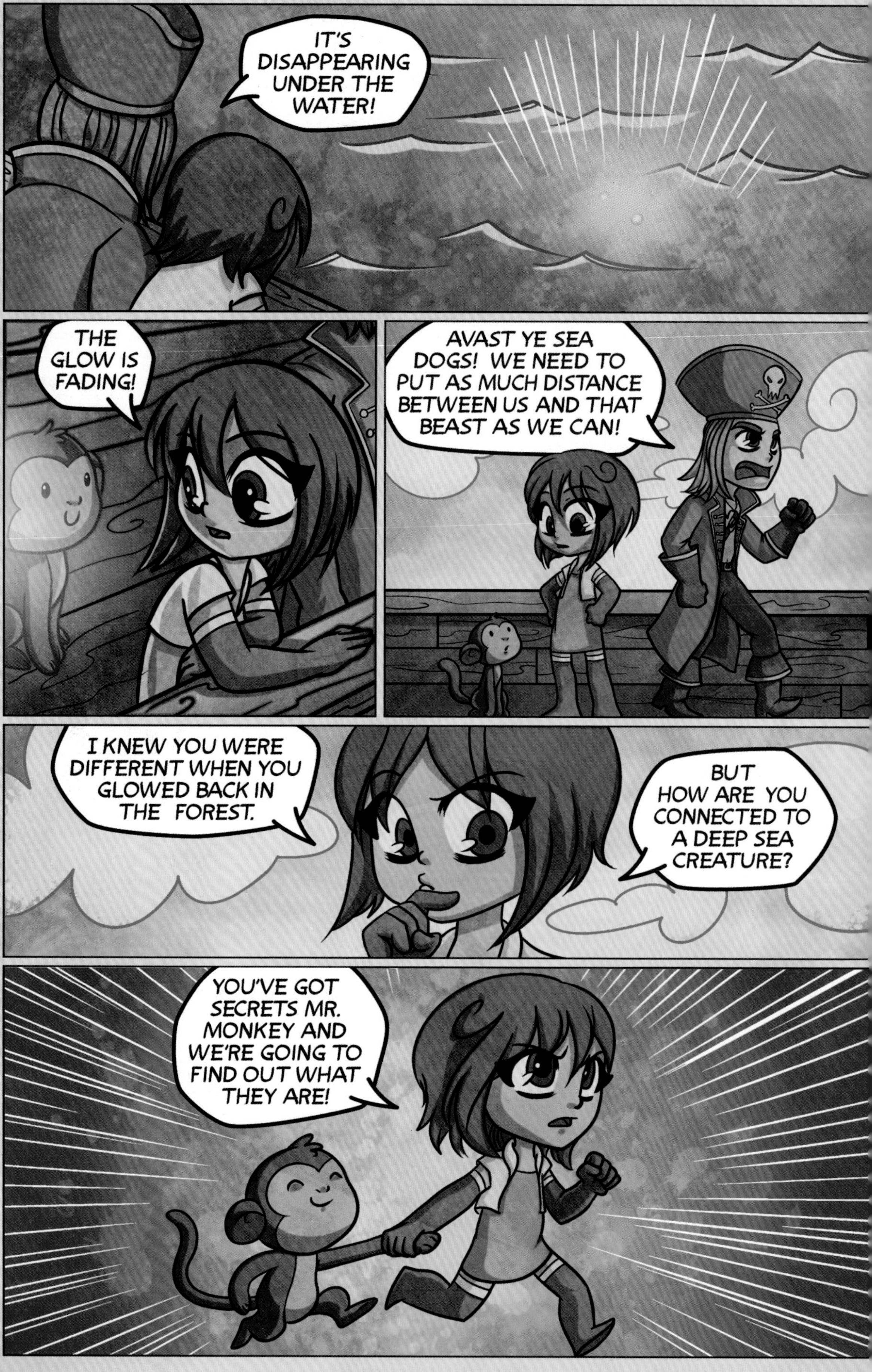
IT'S DISAPPEARING UNDER THE WATER!
THE GLOW IS FADING!
AVAST YE SEA DOGS! WE NEED TO PUT AS MUCH DISTANCE BETWEEN US AND THAT BEAST AS WE CAN!
I KNEW YOU WERE DIFFERENT WHEN YOU GLOWED BACK IN THE FOREST.
BUT HOW ARE YOU CONNECTED TO A DEEP SEA CREATURE?
YOU'VE GOT SECRETS MR. MONKEY AND WE'RE GOING TO FIND OUT WHAT THEY ARE!

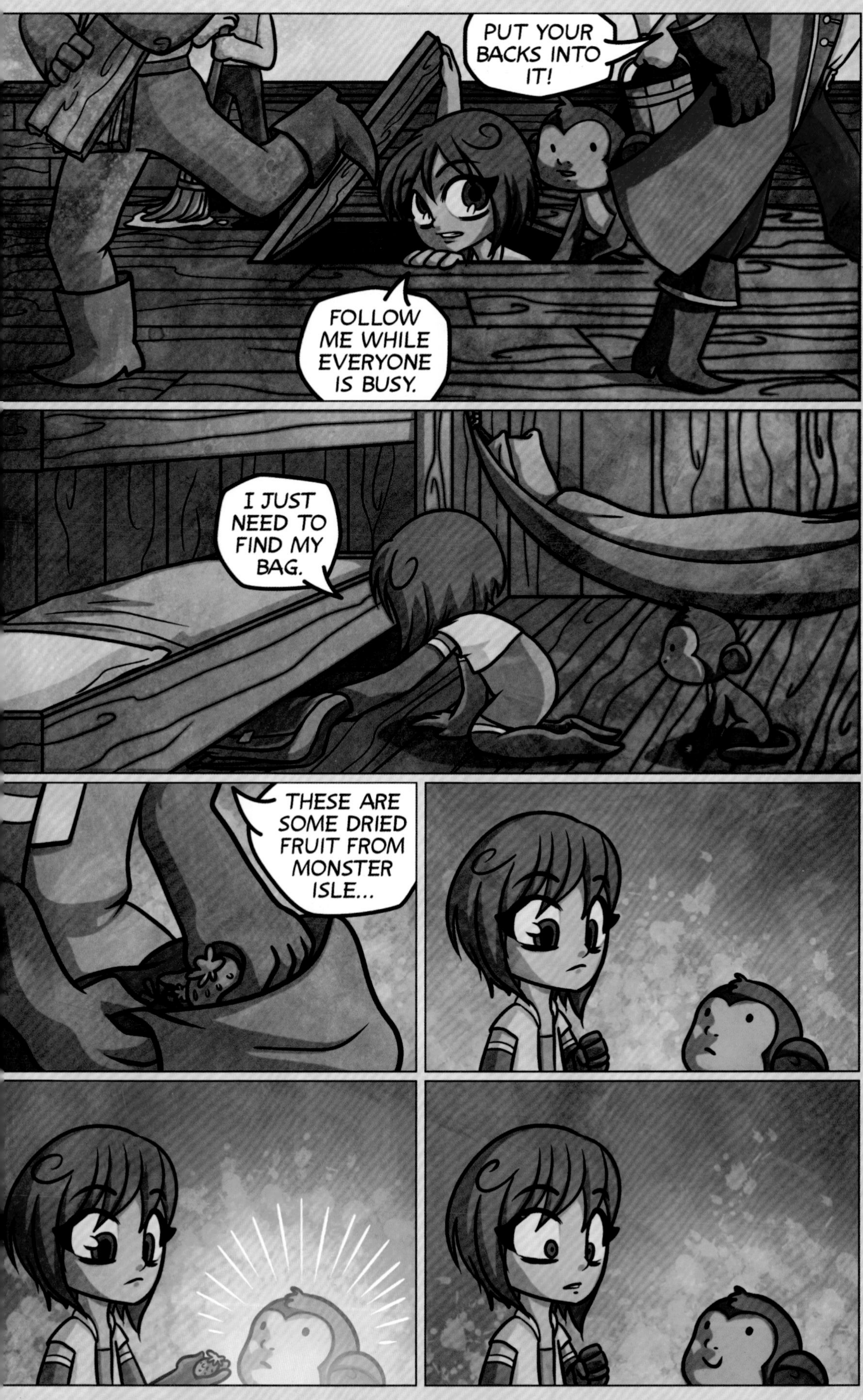
PUT YOUR BACKS INTO IT!
FOLLOW ME WHILE EVERYONE IS BUSY.
I JUST NEED TO FIND MY BAG.
THESE ARE SOME DRIED FRUIT FROM MONSTER ISLE...

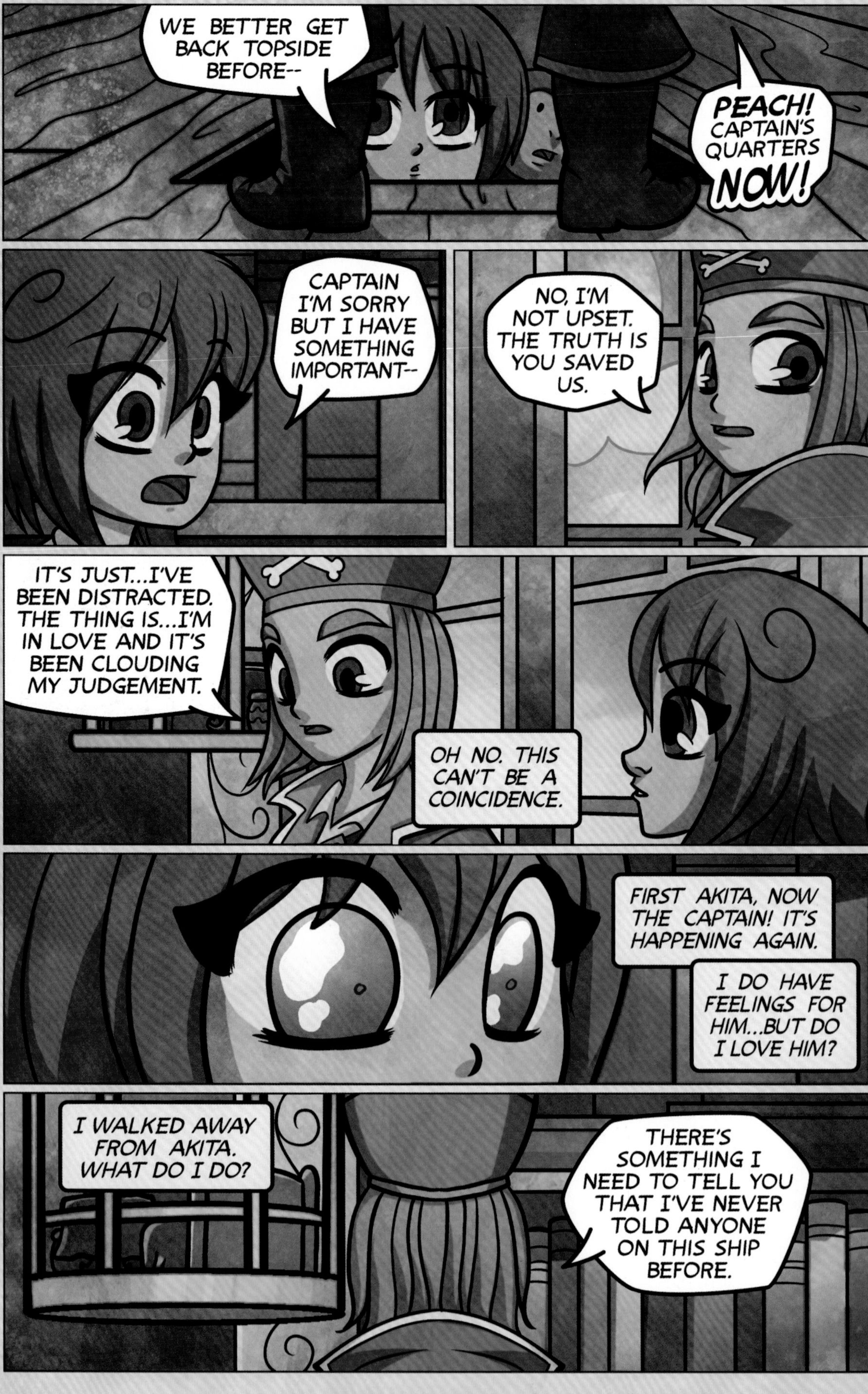
WE BETTER GET BACK TOPSIDE BEFORE--
PEACH! CAPTAIN'S QUARTERS NOW!
CAPTAIN I'M SORRY BUT I HAVE SOMETHING IMPORTANT--
NO, I'M NOT UPSET. THE TRUTH IS YOU SAVED US.
IT'S JUST...I'VE BEEN DISTRACTED. THE THING IS...I'M IN LOVE AND IT'S BEEN CLOUDING MY JUDGEMENT.
OH NO. THIS CAN'T BE A COINCIDENCE.
FIRST AKITA, NOW THE CAPTAIN! IT'S HAPPENING AGAIN.
I DO HAVE FEELINGS FOR HIM...BUT DO I LOVE HIM?
I WALKED AWAY FROM AKITA. WHAT DO I DO?
THERE'S SOMETHING I NEED TO TELL YOU THAT I'VE NEVER TOLD ANYONE ON THIS SHIP BEFORE.

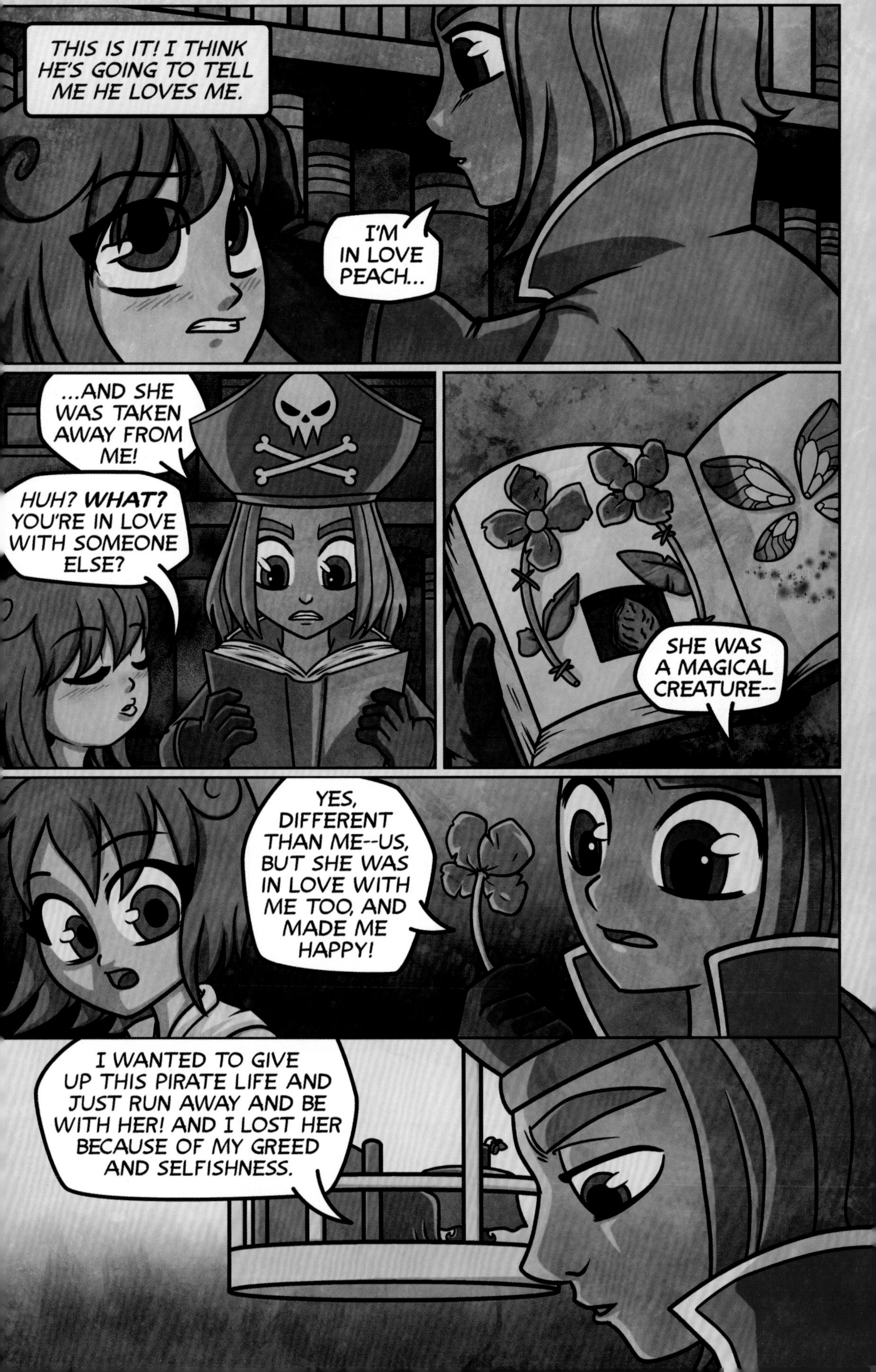
THIS IS IT! I THINK HE'S GOING TO TELL ME HE LOVES ME.
I'M IN LOVE PEACH...
...AND SHE WAS TAKEN AWAY FROM ME!
HUH? **WHAT?** YOU'RE IN LOVE WITH SOMEONE ELSE?
SHE WAS A MAGICAL CREATURE--
YES, DIFFERENT THAN ME--US, BUT SHE WAS IN LOVE WITH ME TOO, AND MADE ME HAPPY!
I WANTED TO GIVE UP THIS PIRATE LIFE AND JUST RUN AWAY AND BE WITH HER! AND I LOST HER BECAUSE OF MY GREED AND SELFISHNESS.

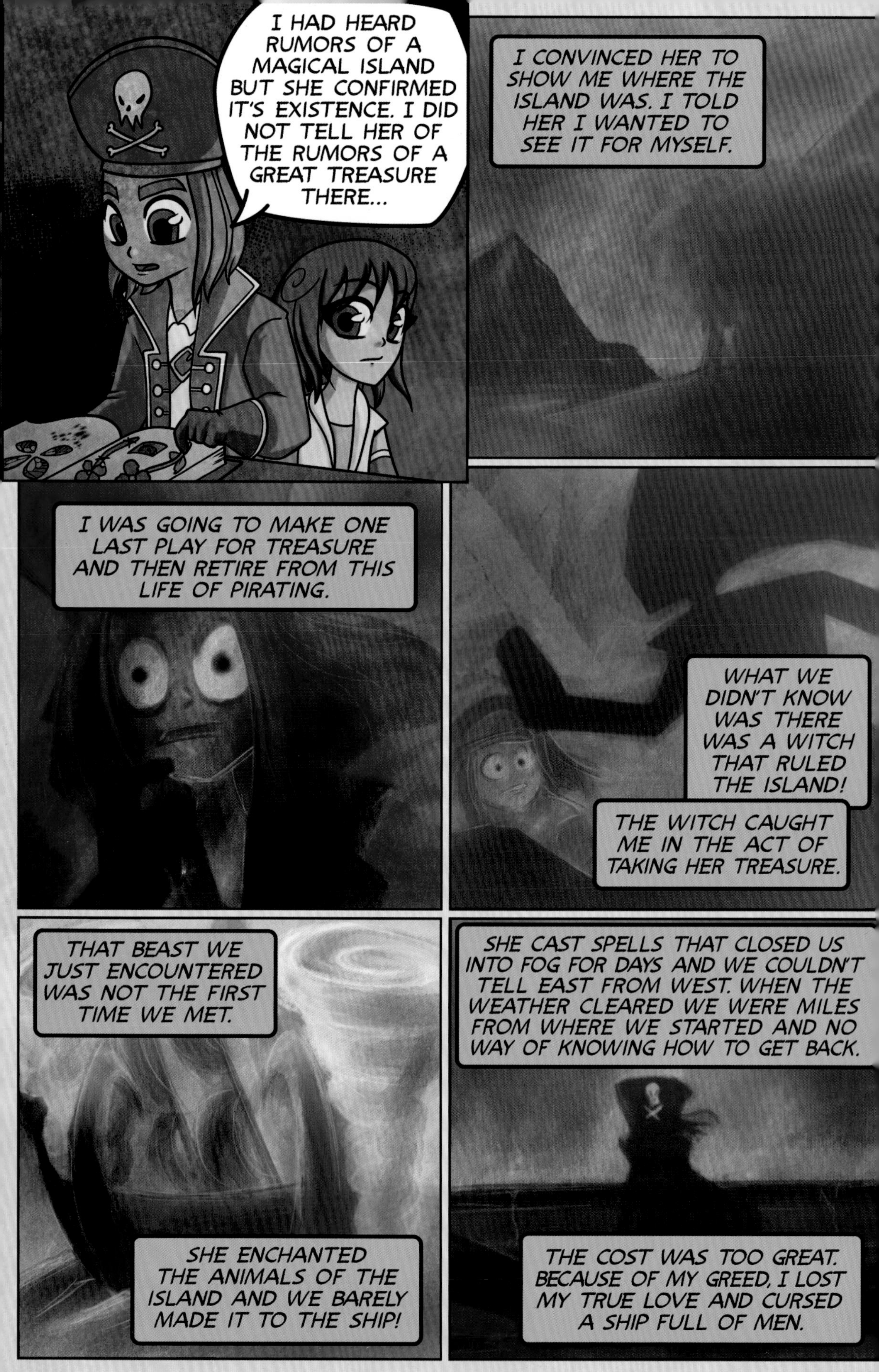
I HAD HEARD RUMORS OF A MAGICAL ISLAND BUT SHE CONFIRMED IT'S EXISTENCE. I DID NOT TELL HER OF THE RUMORS OF A GREAT TREASURE THERE...
I CONVINCED HER TO SHOW ME WHERE THE ISLAND WAS. I TOLD HER I WANTED TO SEE IT FOR MYSELF.
I WAS GOING TO MAKE ONE LAST PLAY FOR TREASURE AND THEN RETIRE FROM THIS LIFE OF PIRATING.
WHAT WE DIDN'T KNOW WAS THERE WAS A WITCH THAT RULED THE ISLAND!
THE WITCH CAUGHT ME IN THE ACT OF TAKING HER TREASURE.
THAT BEAST WE JUST ENCOUNTERED WAS NOT THE FIRST TIME WE MET.
SHE ENCHANTED THE ANIMALS OF THE ISLAND AND WE BARELY MADE IT TO THE SHIP!
SHE CAST SPELLS THAT CLOSED US INTO FOG FOR DAYS AND WE COULDN'T TELL EAST FROM WEST. WHEN THE WEATHER CLEARED WE WERE MILES FROM WHERE WE STARTED AND NO WAY OF KNOWING HOW TO GET BACK.
THE COST WAS TOO GREAT. BECAUSE OF MY GREED, I LOST MY TRUE LOVE AND CURSED A SHIP FULL OF MEN.

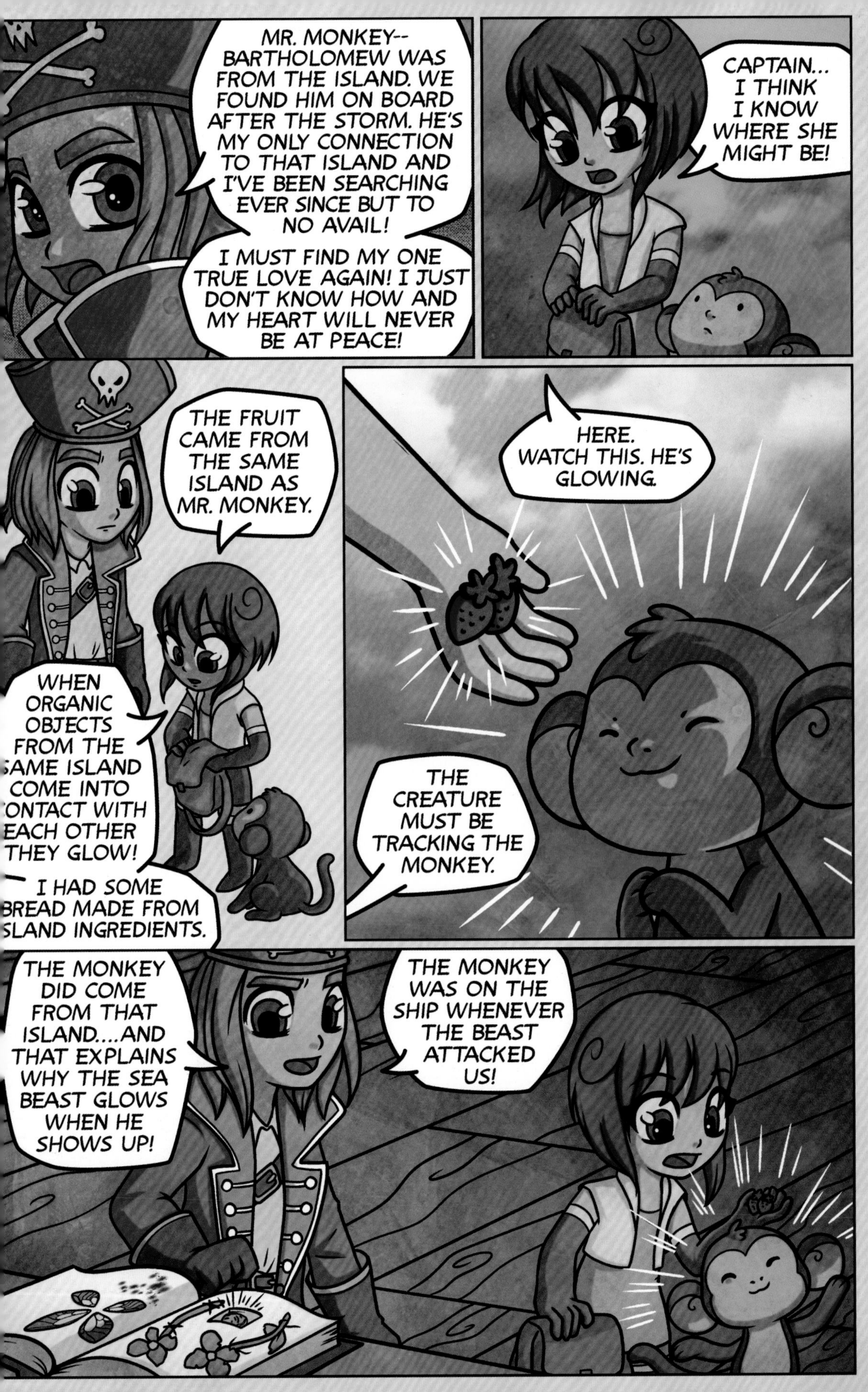
MR. MONKEY-- BARTHOLOMEW WAS FROM THE ISLAND. WE FOUND HIM ON BOARD AFTER THE STORM. HE'S MY ONLY CONNECTION TO THAT ISLAND AND I'VE BEEN SEARCHING EVER SINCE BUT TO NO AVAIL!
I MUST FIND MY ONE TRUE LOVE AGAIN! I JUST DON'T KNOW HOW AND MY HEART WILL NEVER BE AT PEACE!
CAPTAIN... I THINK I KNOW WHERE SHE MIGHT BE!
THE FRUIT CAME FROM THE SAME ISLAND AS MR. MONKEY.
WHEN ORGANIC OBJECTS FROM THE SAME ISLAND COME INTO CONTACT WITH EACH OTHER THEY GLOW!
I HAD SOME BREAD MADE FROM ISLAND INGREDIENTS.
HERE. WATCH THIS. HE'S GLOWING.
THE CREATURE MUST BE TRACKING THE MONKEY.
THE MONKEY DID COME FROM THAT ISLAND....AND THAT EXPLAINS WHY THE SEA BEAST GLOWS WHEN HE SHOWS UP!
THE MONKEY WAS ON THE SHIP WHENEVER THE BEAST ATTACKED US!

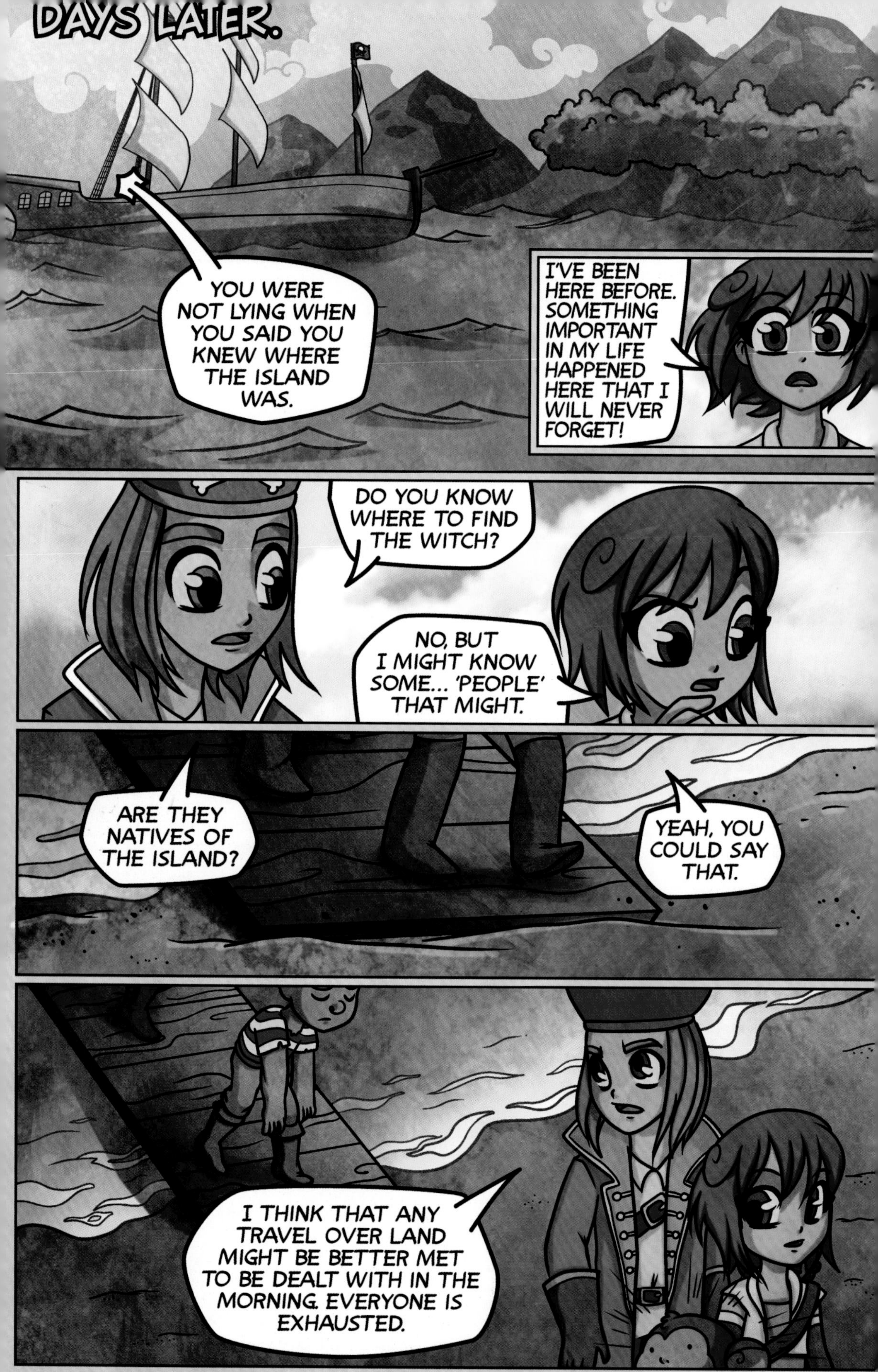
DAYS LATER.
YOU WERE NOT LYING WHEN YOU SAID YOU KNEW WHERE THE ISLAND WAS.
I'VE BEEN HERE BEFORE. SOMETHING IMPORTANT IN MY LIFE HAPPENED HERE THAT I WILL NEVER FORGET!
DO YOU KNOW WHERE TO FIND THE WITCH?
NO, BUT I MIGHT KNOW SOME... 'PEOPLE' THAT MIGHT.
ARE THEY NATIVES OF THE ISLAND?
YEAH, YOU COULD SAY THAT.
I THINK THAT ANY TRAVEL OVER LAND MIGHT BE BETTER MET TO BE DEALT WITH IN THE MORNING. EVERYONE IS EXHAUSTED.

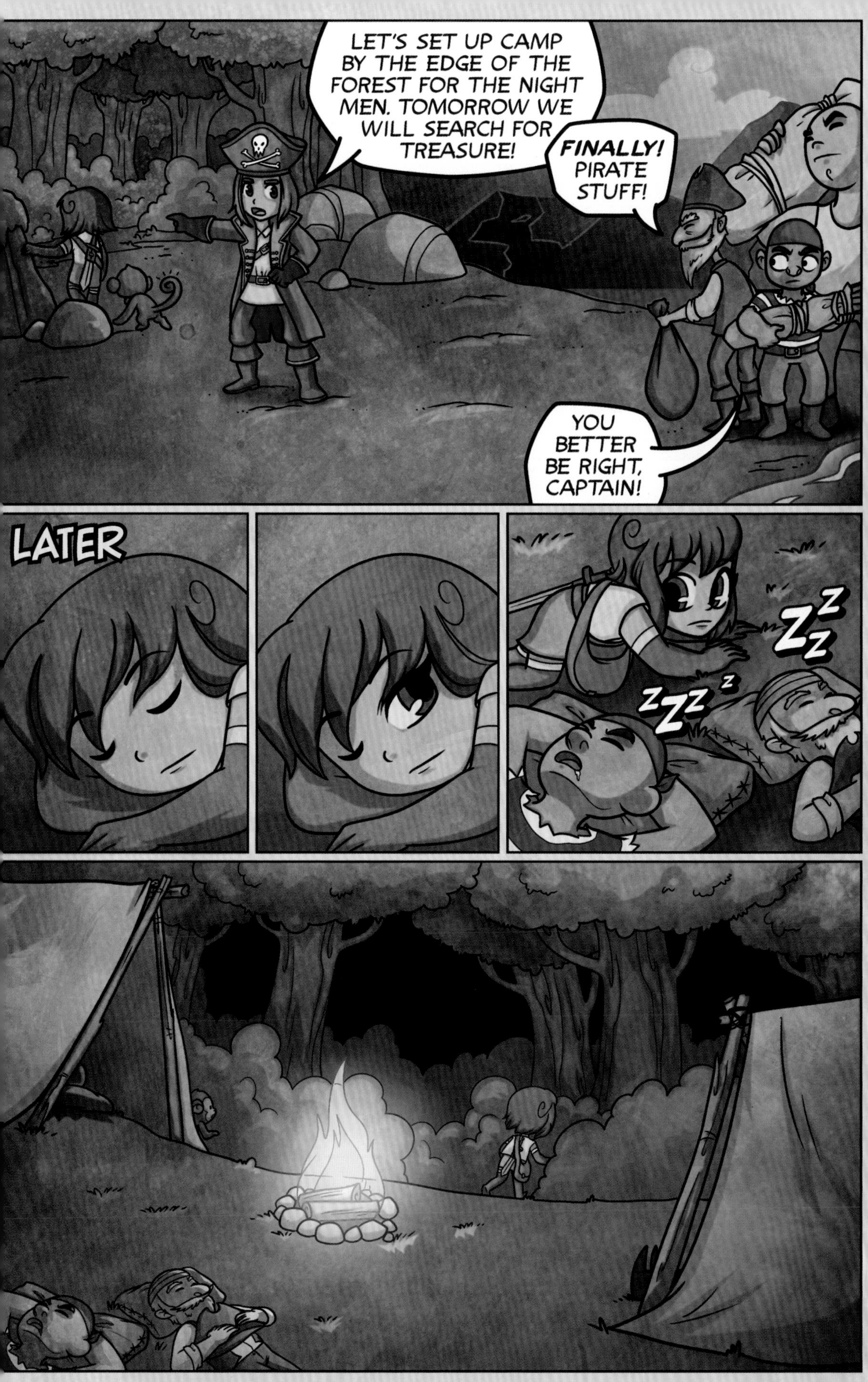
LET'S SET UP CAMP BY THE EDGE OF THE FOREST FOR THE NIGHT MEN. TOMORROW WE WILL SEARCH FOR TREASURE!
FINALLY! PIRATE STUFF!
YOU BETTER BE RIGHT, CAPTAIN!
LATER
ZZZ
ZZZZ

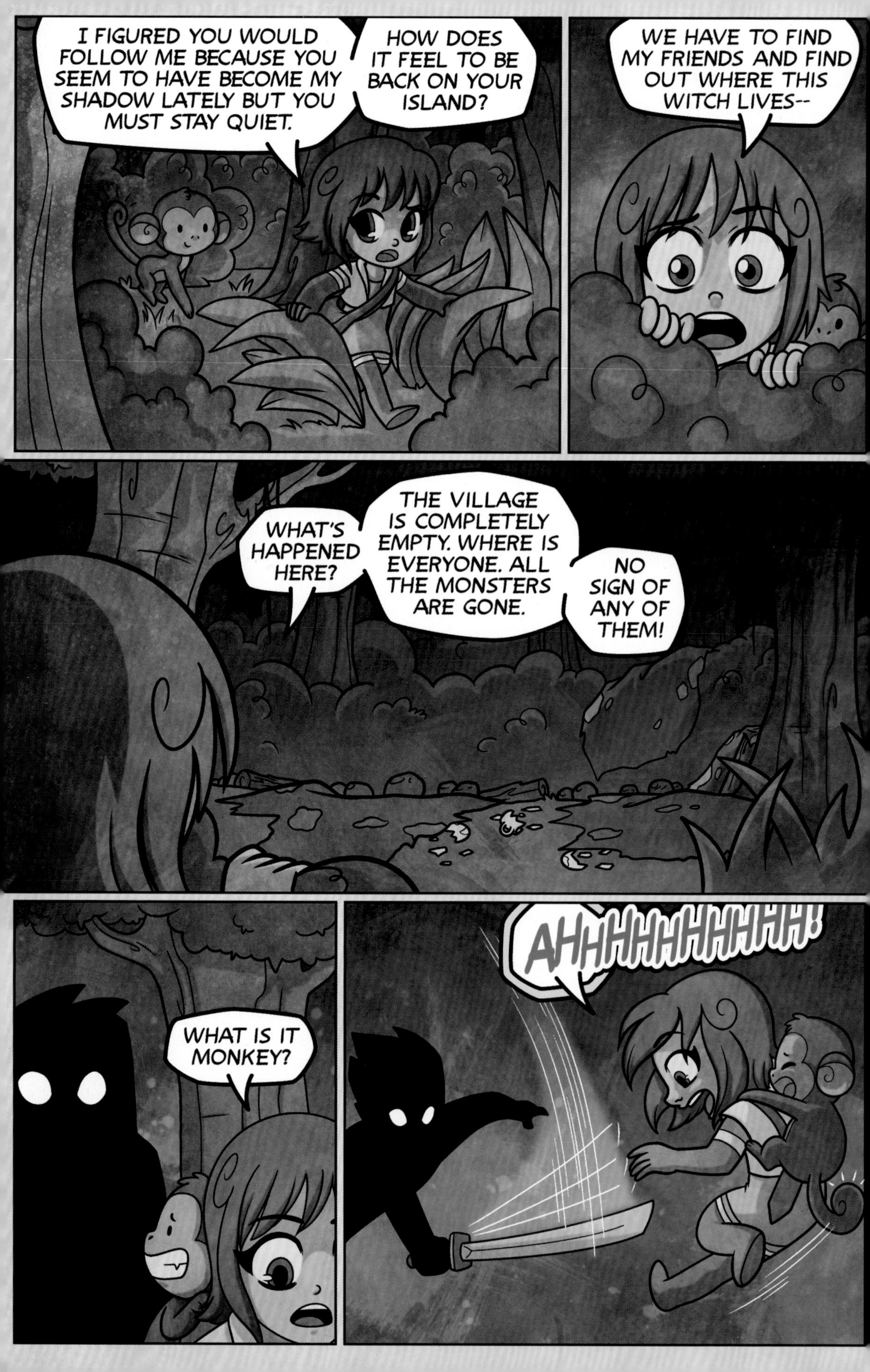
I FIGURED YOU WOULD FOLLOW ME BECAUSE YOU SEEM TO HAVE BECOME MY SHADOW LATELY BUT YOU MUST STAY QUIET.
HOW DOES IT FEEL TO BE BACK ON YOUR ISLAND?
WE HAVE TO FIND MY FRIENDS AND FIND OUT WHERE THIS WITCH LIVES--
WHAT'S HAPPENED HERE?
THE VILLAGE IS COMPLETELY EMPTY. WHERE IS EVERYONE. ALL THE MONSTERS ARE GONE.
NO SIGN OF ANY OF THEM!
WHAT IS IT MONKEY?
AHHHHHHHHHH!

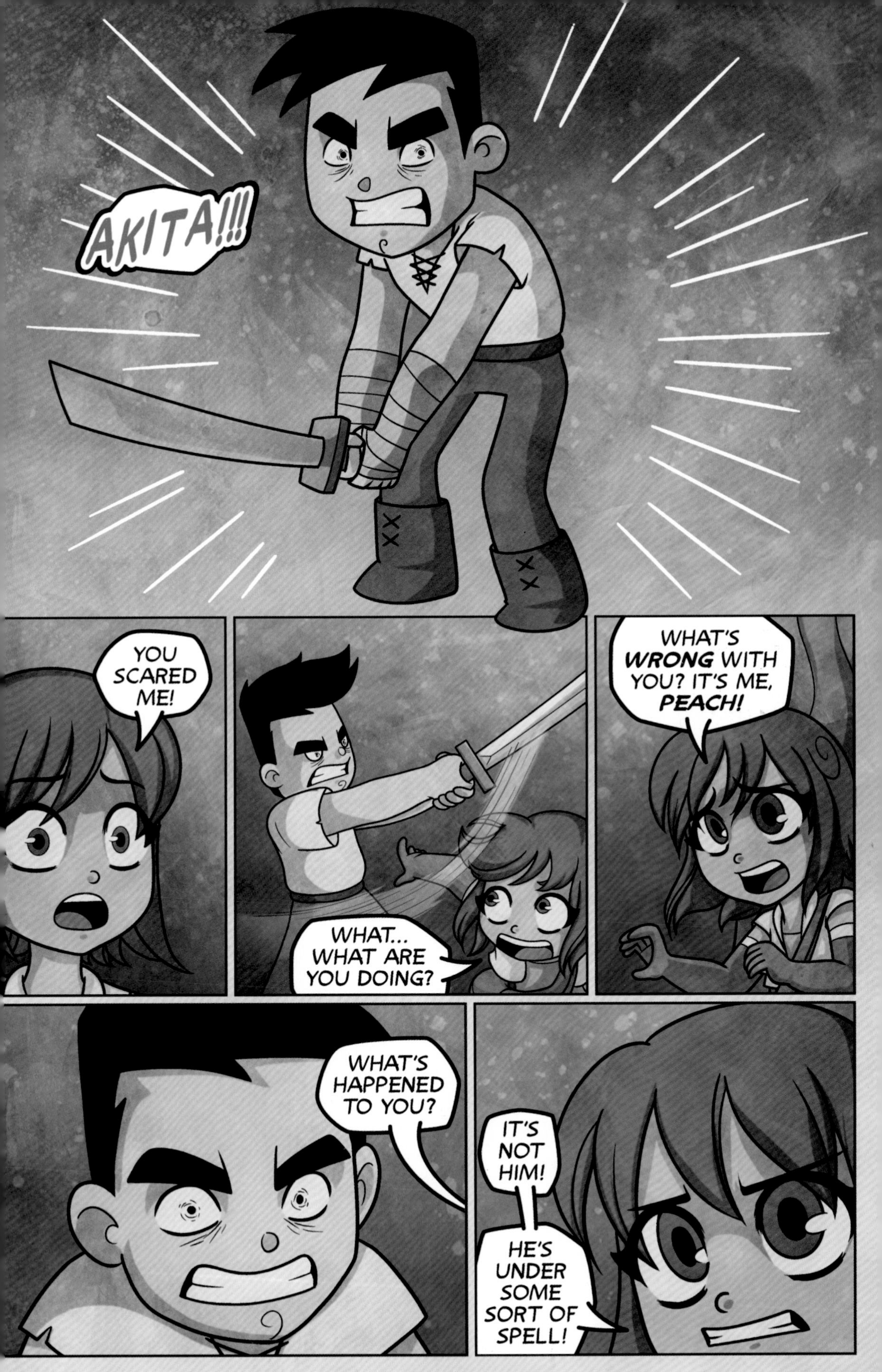
AKITA!!!
YOU SCARED ME!
WHAT... WHAT ARE YOU DOING?
WHAT'S **WRONG** WITH YOU? IT'S ME, **PEACH!**
WHAT'S HAPPENED TO YOU?
IT'S NOT HIM!
HE'S UNDER SOME SORT OF SPELL!

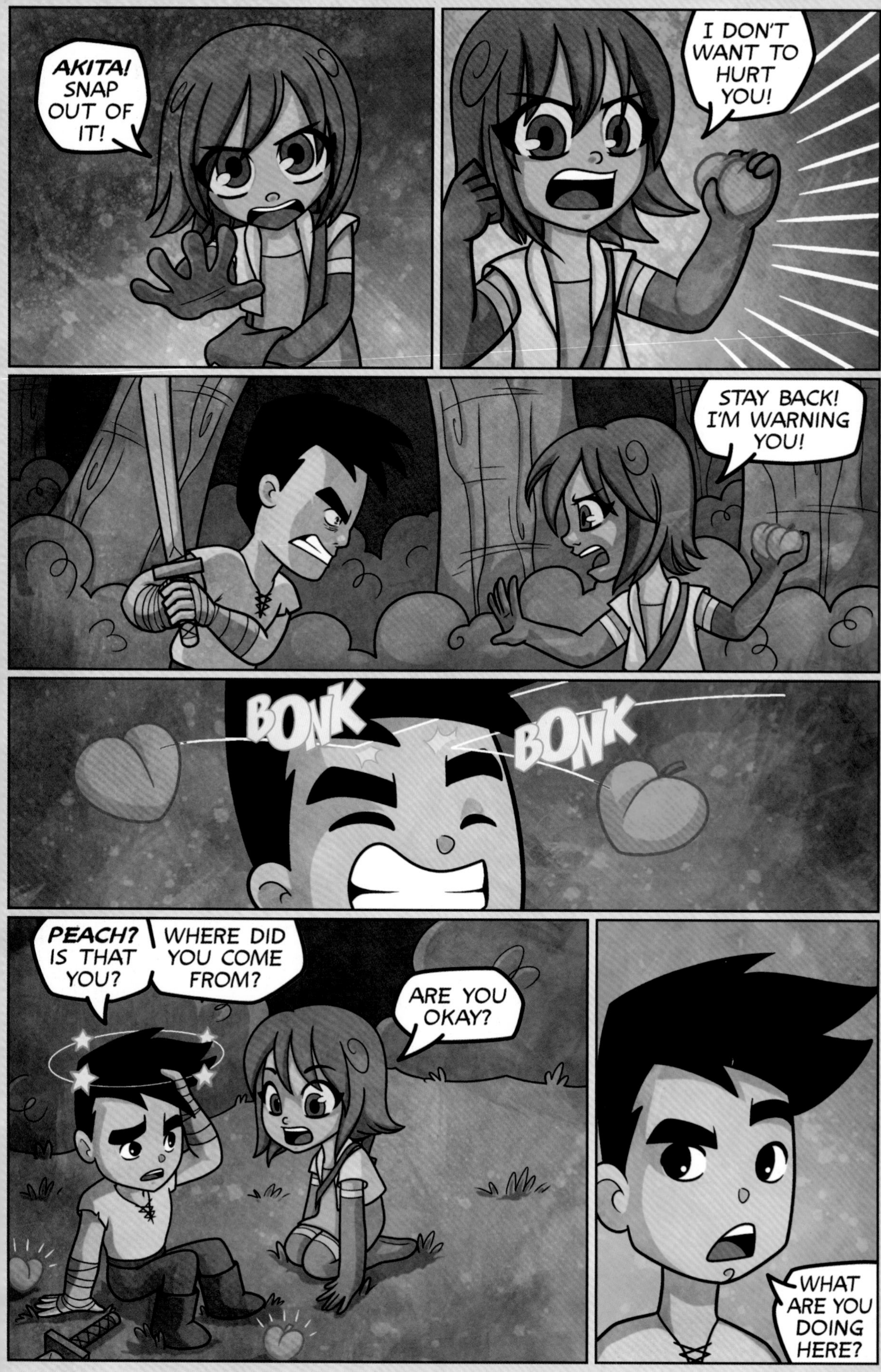
AKITA! SNAP OUT OF IT!
I DON'T WANT TO HURT YOU!
STAY BACK! I'M WARNING YOU!
BONK
BONK
PEACH? IS THAT YOU?
WHERE DID YOU COME FROM?
ARE YOU OKAY?
WHAT ARE YOU DOING HERE?

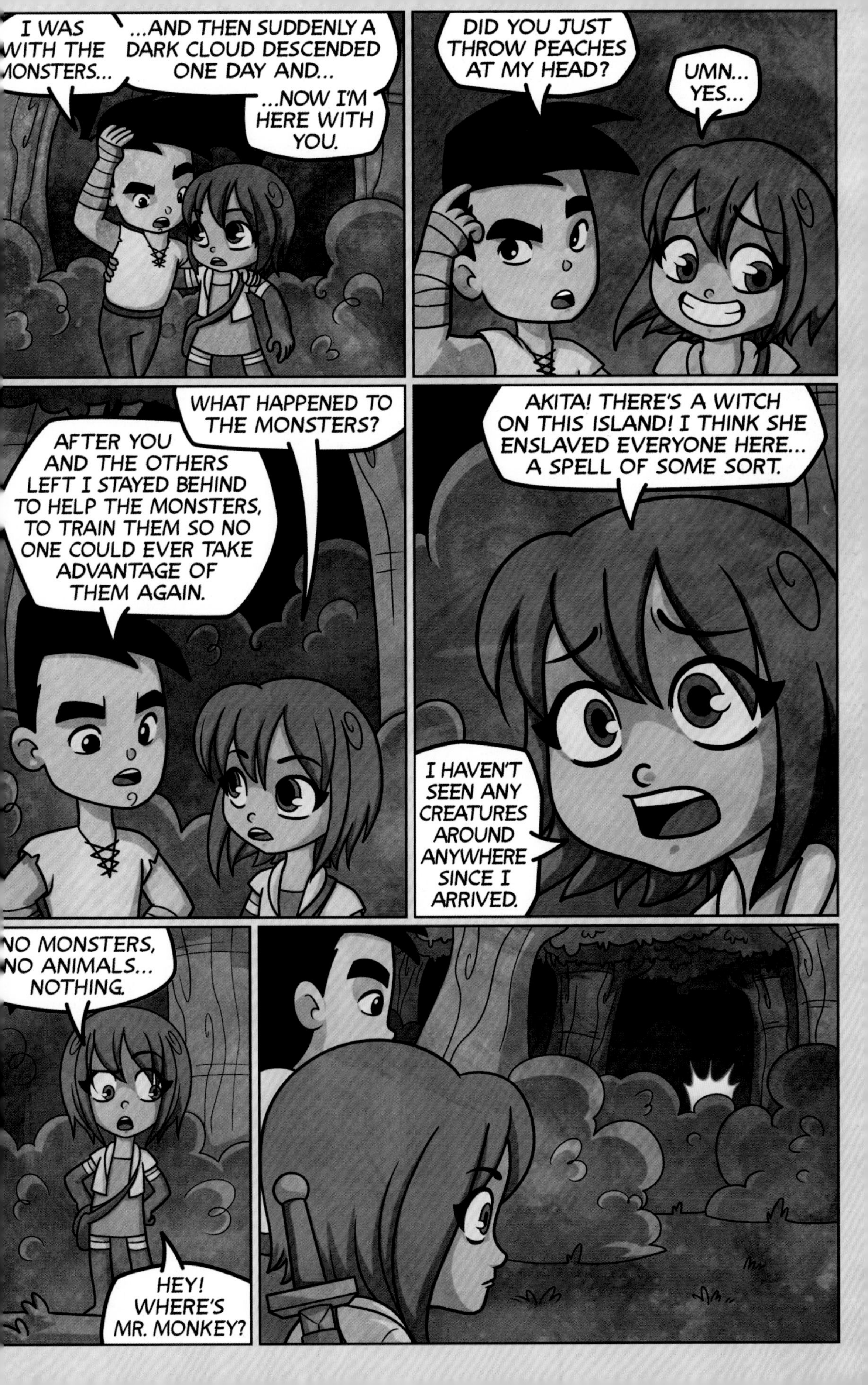
I WAS WITH THE MONSTERS...
...AND THEN SUDDENLY A DARK CLOUD DESCENDED ONE DAY AND...
...NOW I'M HERE WITH YOU.
DID YOU JUST THROW PEACHES AT MY HEAD?
UMN... YES...
WHAT HAPPENED TO THE MONSTERS?
AFTER YOU AND THE OTHERS LEFT I STAYED BEHIND TO HELP THE MONSTERS, TO TRAIN THEM SO NO ONE COULD EVER TAKE ADVANTAGE OF THEM AGAIN.
AKITA! THERE'S A WITCH ON THIS ISLAND! I THINK SHE ENSLAVED EVERYONE HERE... A SPELL OF SOME SORT.
I HAVEN'T SEEN ANY CREATURES AROUND ANYWHERE SINCE I ARRIVED.
NO MONSTERS, NO ANIMALS... NOTHING.
HEY! WHERE'S MR. MONKEY?

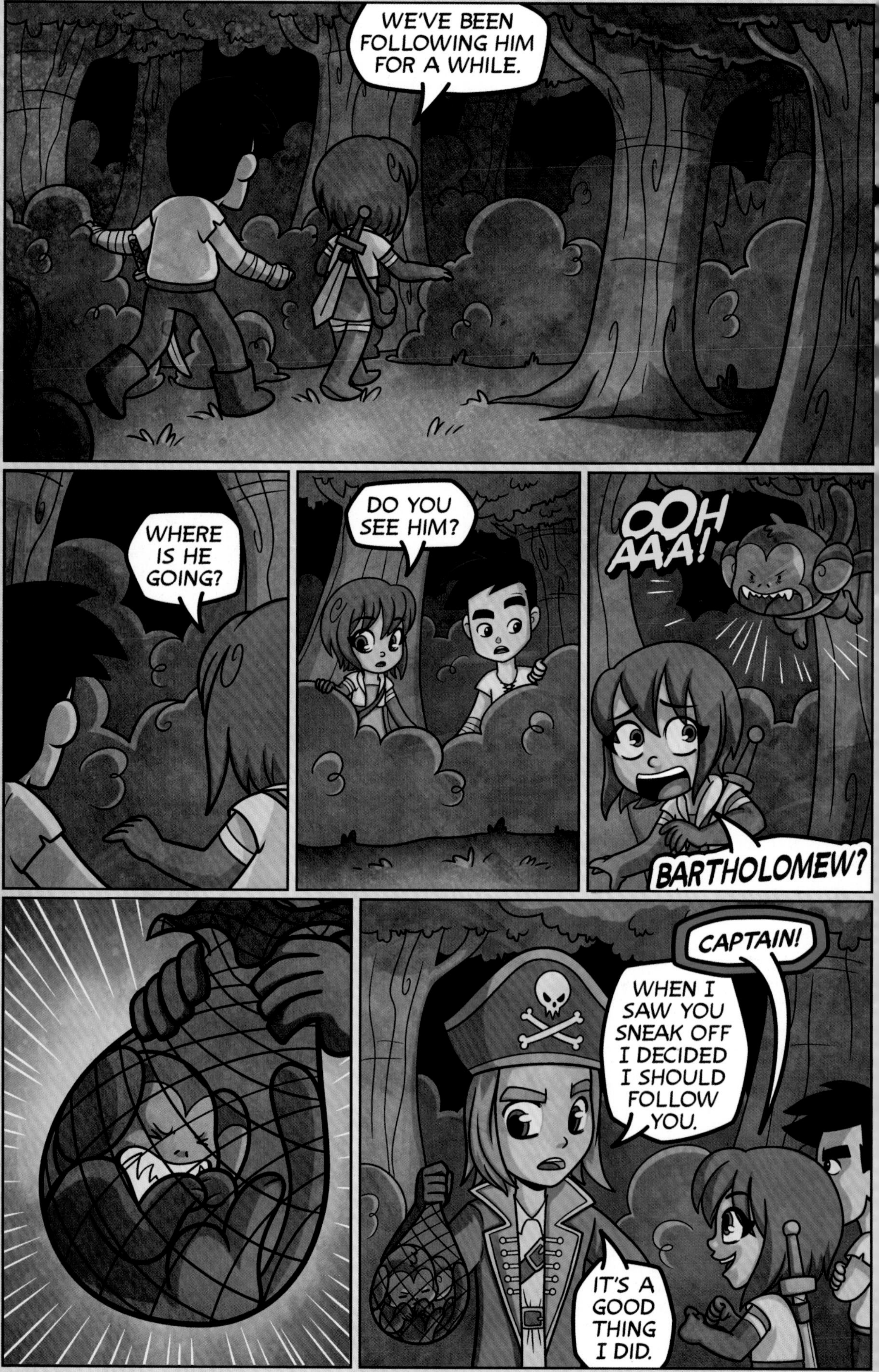
WE'VE BEEN FOLLOWING HIM FOR A WHILE.
WHERE IS HE GOING?
DO YOU SEE HIM?
OOH AAA!
BARTHOLOMEW?
CAPTAIN!
WHEN I SAW YOU SNEAK OFF I DECIDED I SHOULD FOLLOW YOU.
IT'S A GOOD THING I DID.

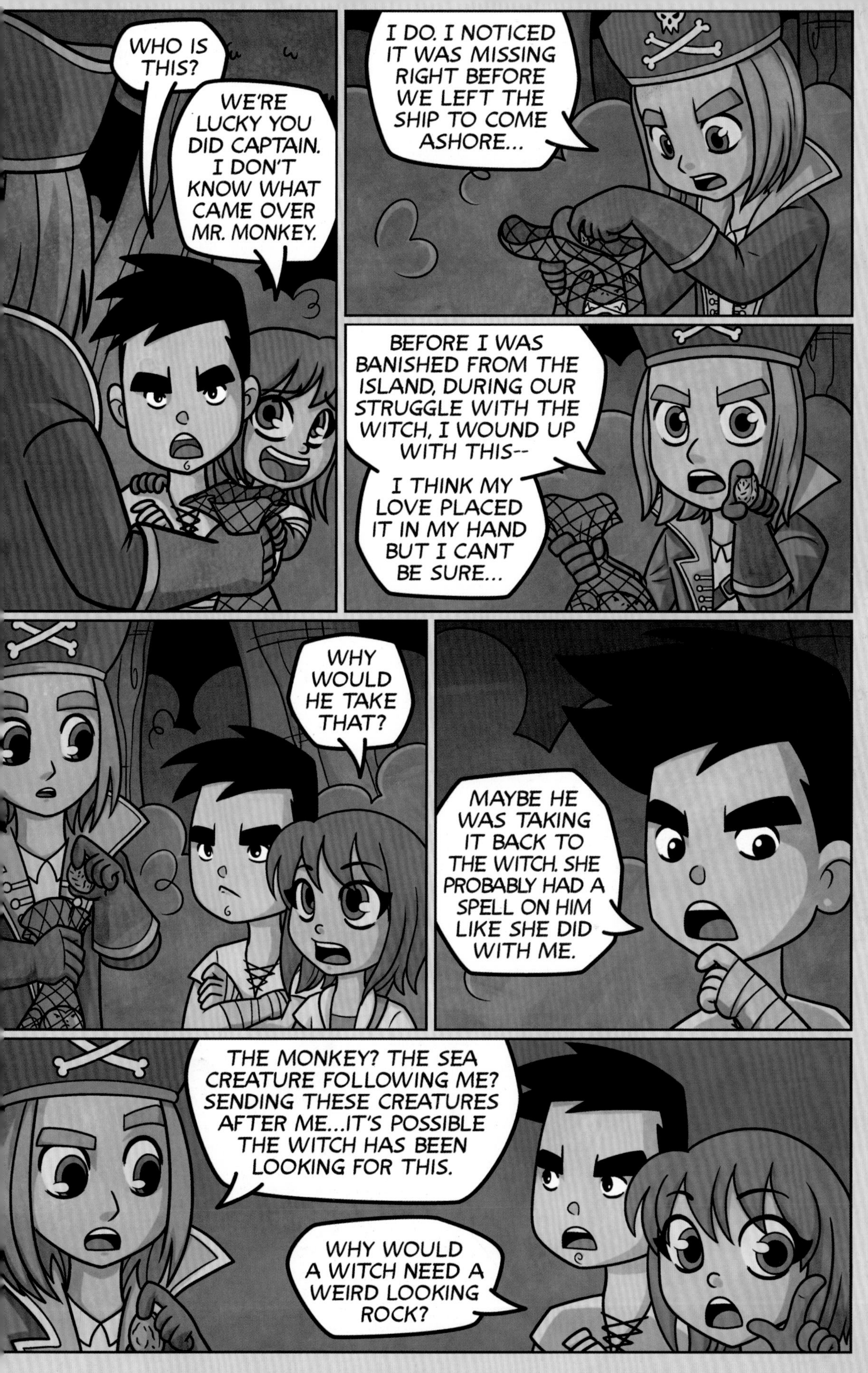
WHO IS THIS?
WE'RE LUCKY YOU DID CAPTAIN. I DON'T KNOW WHAT CAME OVER MR. MONKEY.
I DO. I NOTICED IT WAS MISSING RIGHT BEFORE WE LEFT THE SHIP TO COME ASHORE...
BEFORE I WAS BANISHED FROM THE ISLAND, DURING OUR STRUGGLE WITH THE WITCH, I WOUND UP WITH THIS--
I THINK MY LOVE PLACED IT IN MY HAND BUT I CANT BE SURE...
WHY WOULD HE TAKE THAT?
MAYBE HE WAS TAKING IT BACK TO THE WITCH. SHE PROBABLY HAD A SPELL ON HIM LIKE SHE DID WITH ME.
THE MONKEY? THE SEA CREATURE FOLLOWING ME? SENDING THESE CREATURES AFTER ME...IT'S POSSIBLE THE WITCH HAS BEEN LOOKING FOR THIS.
WHY WOULD A WITCH NEED A WEIRD LOOKING ROCK?

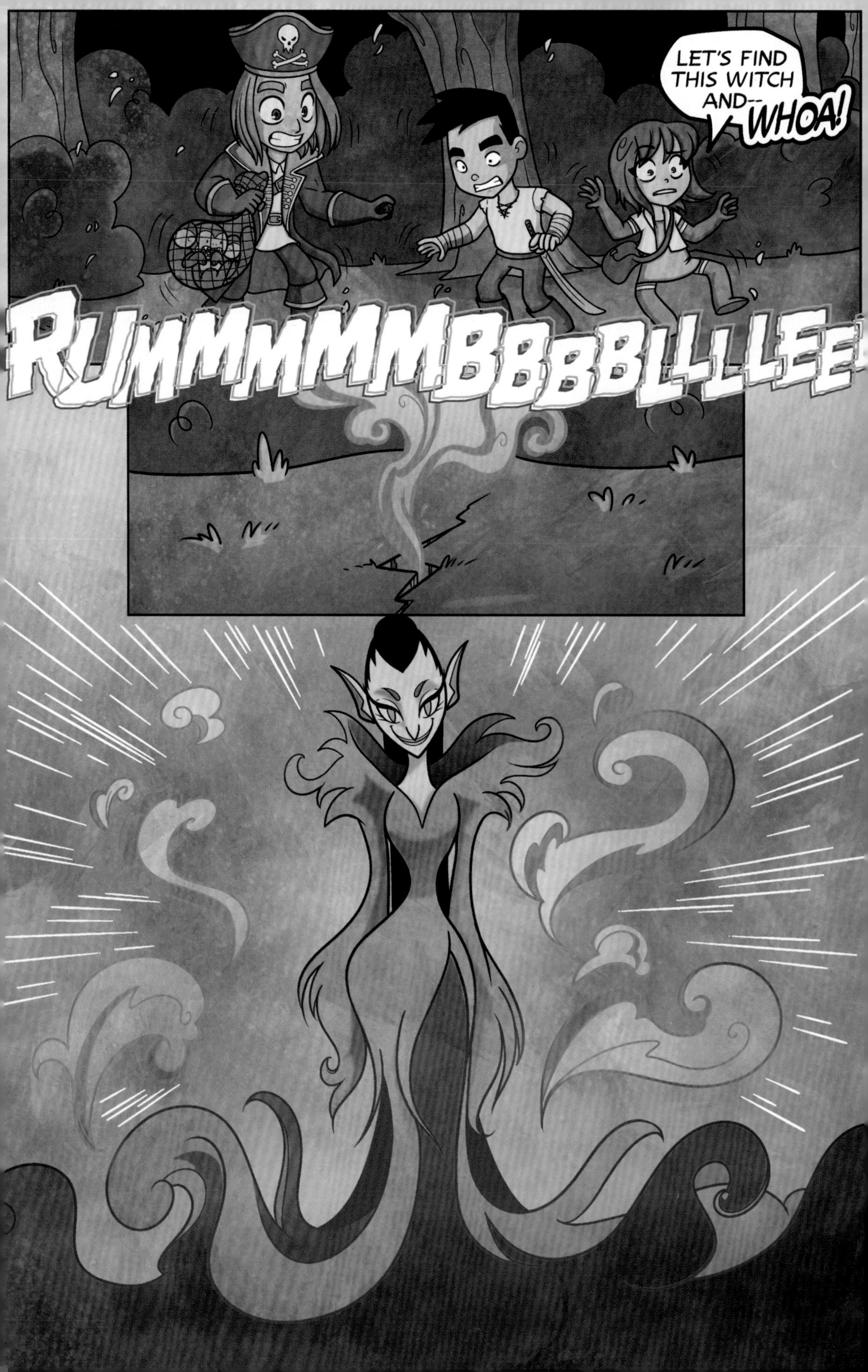
LET'S FIND THIS WITCH AND-- WHOA!
RUMMMMMMBBBBBLLLLEE!

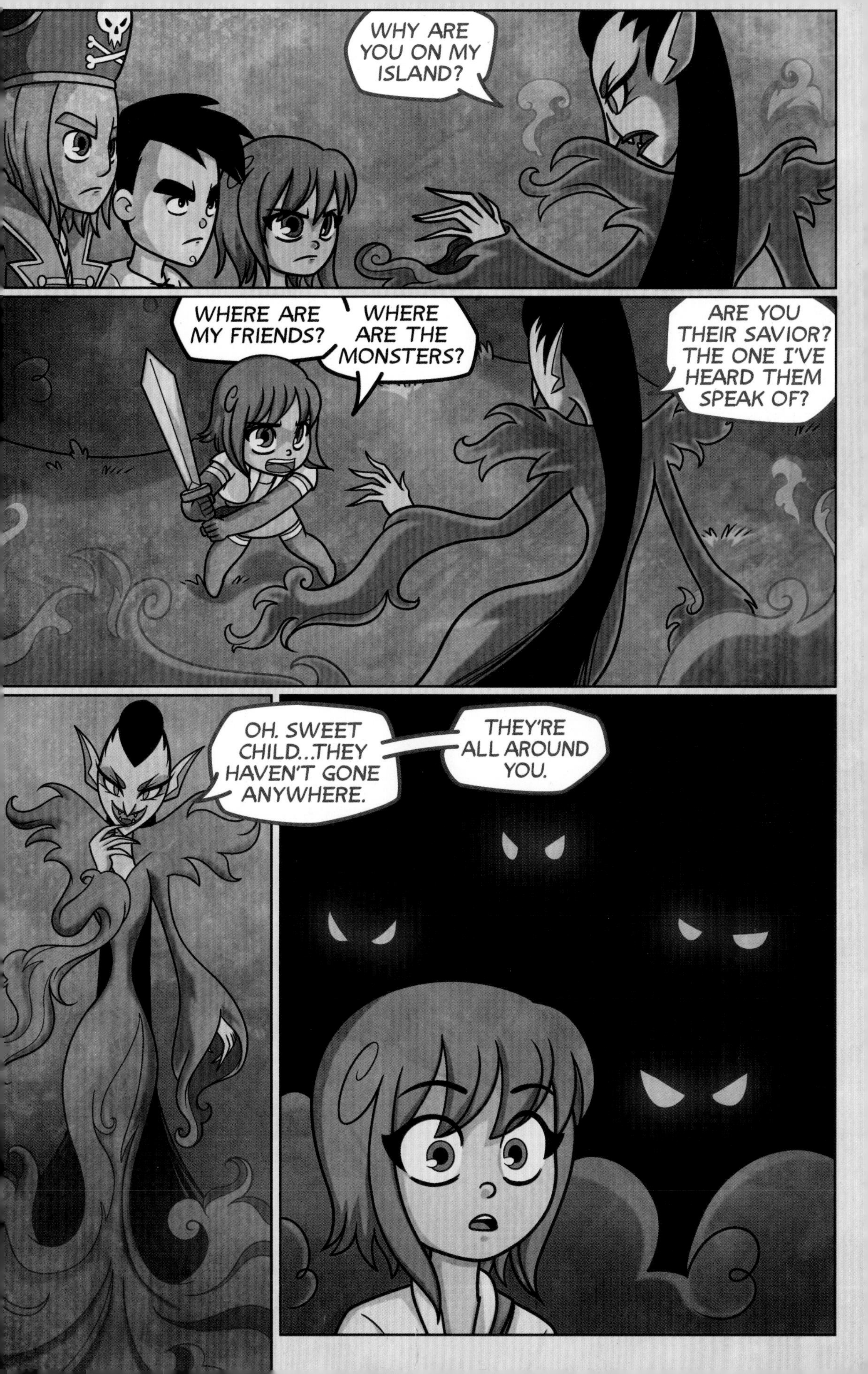
WHY ARE YOU ON MY ISLAND?
WHERE ARE MY FRIENDS?
WHERE ARE THE MONSTERS?
ARE YOU THEIR SAVIOR? THE ONE I'VE HEARD THEM SPEAK OF?
OH. SWEET CHILD...THEY HAVEN'T GONE ANYWHERE.
THEY'RE ALL AROUND YOU.

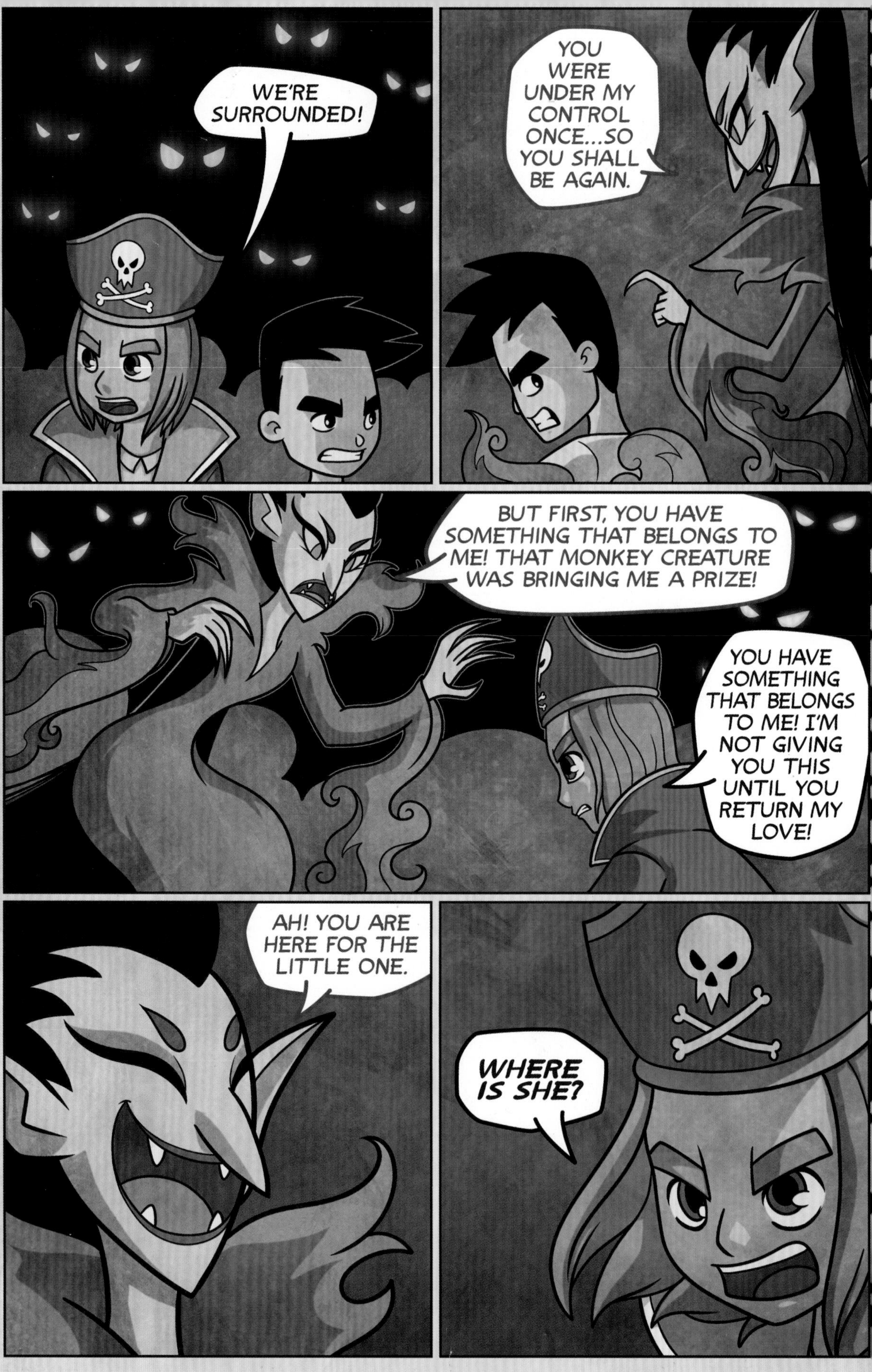
WE'RE SURROUNDED!
YOU WERE UNDER MY CONTROL ONCE...SO YOU SHALL BE AGAIN.
BUT FIRST, YOU HAVE SOMETHING THAT BELONGS TO ME! THAT MONKEY CREATURE WAS BRINGING ME A PRIZE!
YOU HAVE SOMETHING THAT BELONGS TO ME! I'M NOT GIVING YOU THIS UNTIL YOU RETURN MY LOVE!
AH! YOU ARE HERE FOR THE LITTLE ONE.
WHERE IS SHE?

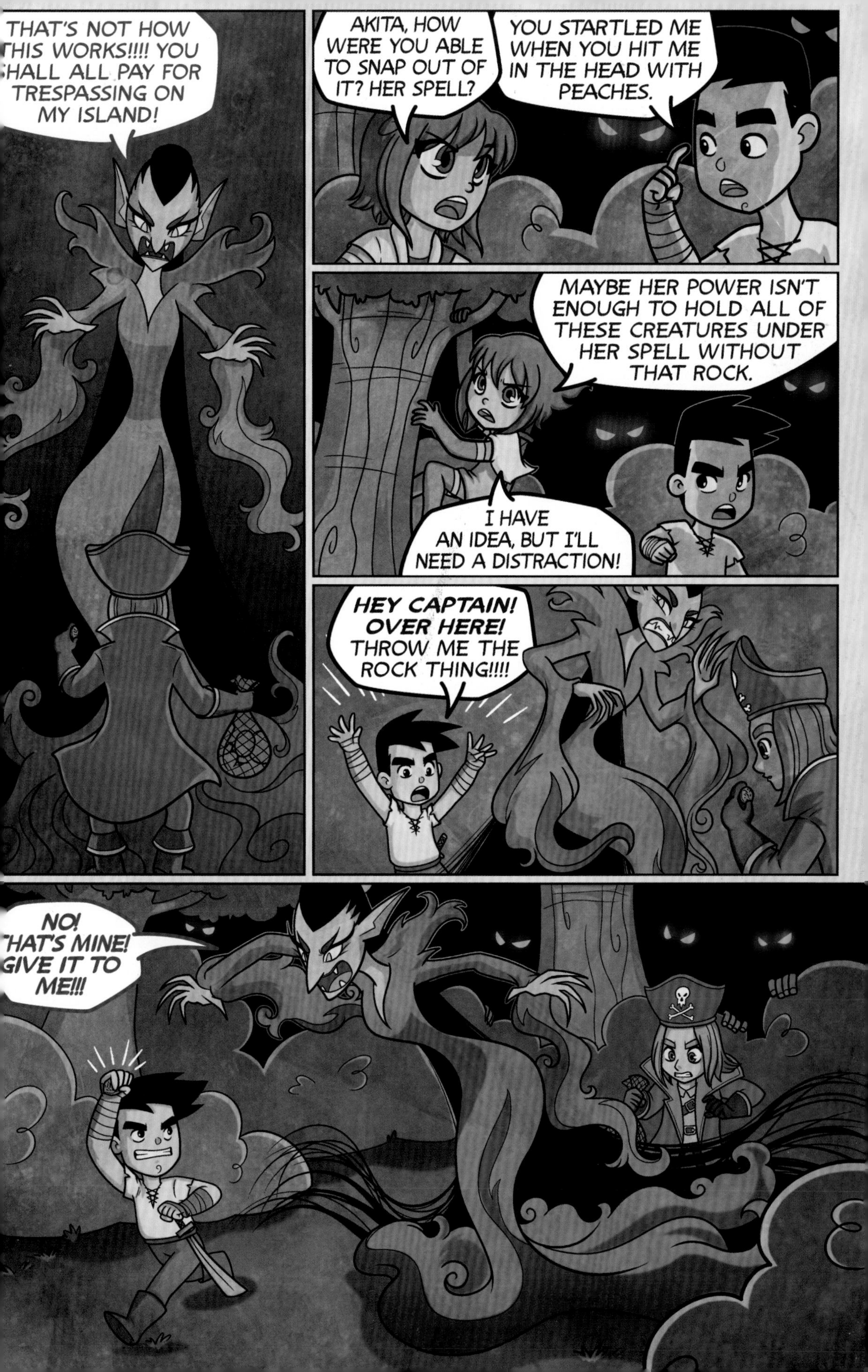
THAT'S NOT HOW THIS WORKS!!!! YOU SHALL ALL PAY FOR TRESPASSING ON MY ISLAND!
AKITA, HOW WERE YOU ABLE TO SNAP OUT OF IT? HER SPELL?
YOU STARTLED ME WHEN YOU HIT ME IN THE HEAD WITH PEACHES.
MAYBE HER POWER ISN'T ENOUGH TO HOLD ALL OF THESE CREATURES UNDER HER SPELL WITHOUT THAT ROCK.
I HAVE AN IDEA, BUT I'LL NEED A DISTRACTION!
HEY CAPTAIN! OVER HERE! THROW ME THE ROCK THING!!!!
NO! THAT'S MINE! GIVE IT TO ME!!!

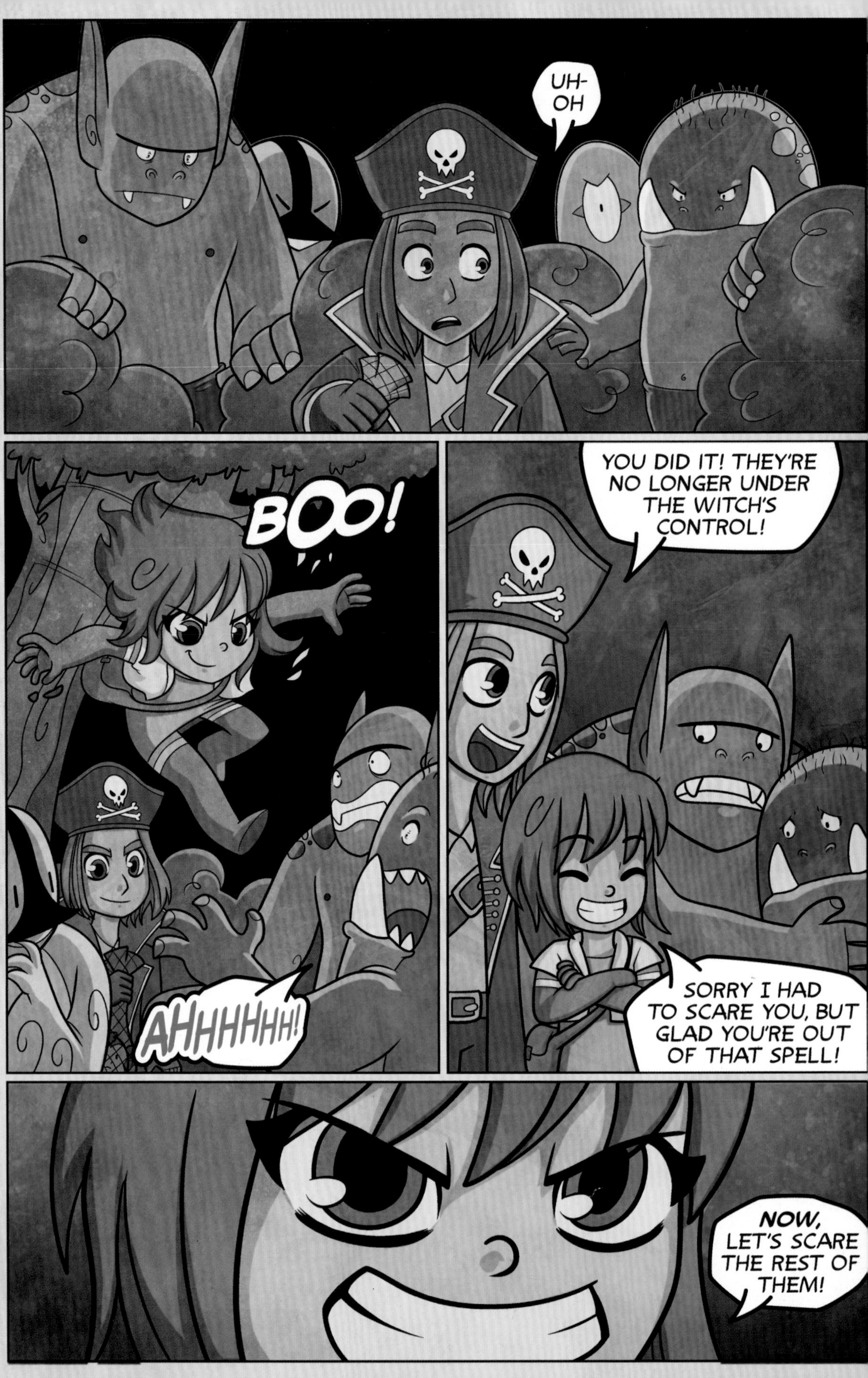
UH-OH
BOO!
AHHHHHH!
YOU DID IT! THEY'RE NO LONGER UNDER THE WITCH'S CONTROL!
SORRY I HAD TO SCARE YOU, BUT GLAD YOU'RE OUT OF THAT SPELL!
NOW, LET'S SCARE THE REST OF THEM!

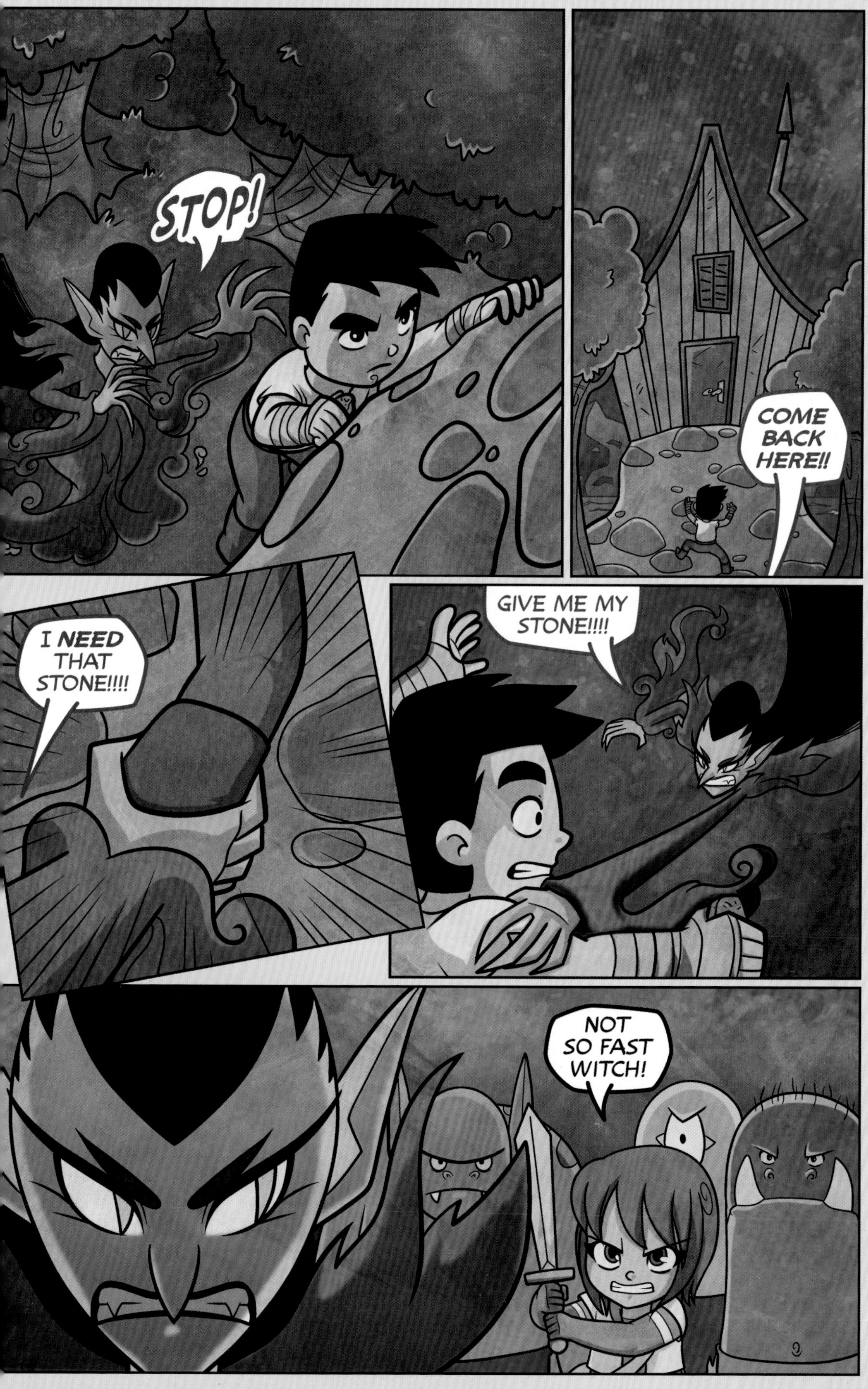
STOP!
COME BACK HERE!!
I NEED THAT STONE!!!!
GIVE ME MY STONE!!!!
NOT SO FAST WITCH!

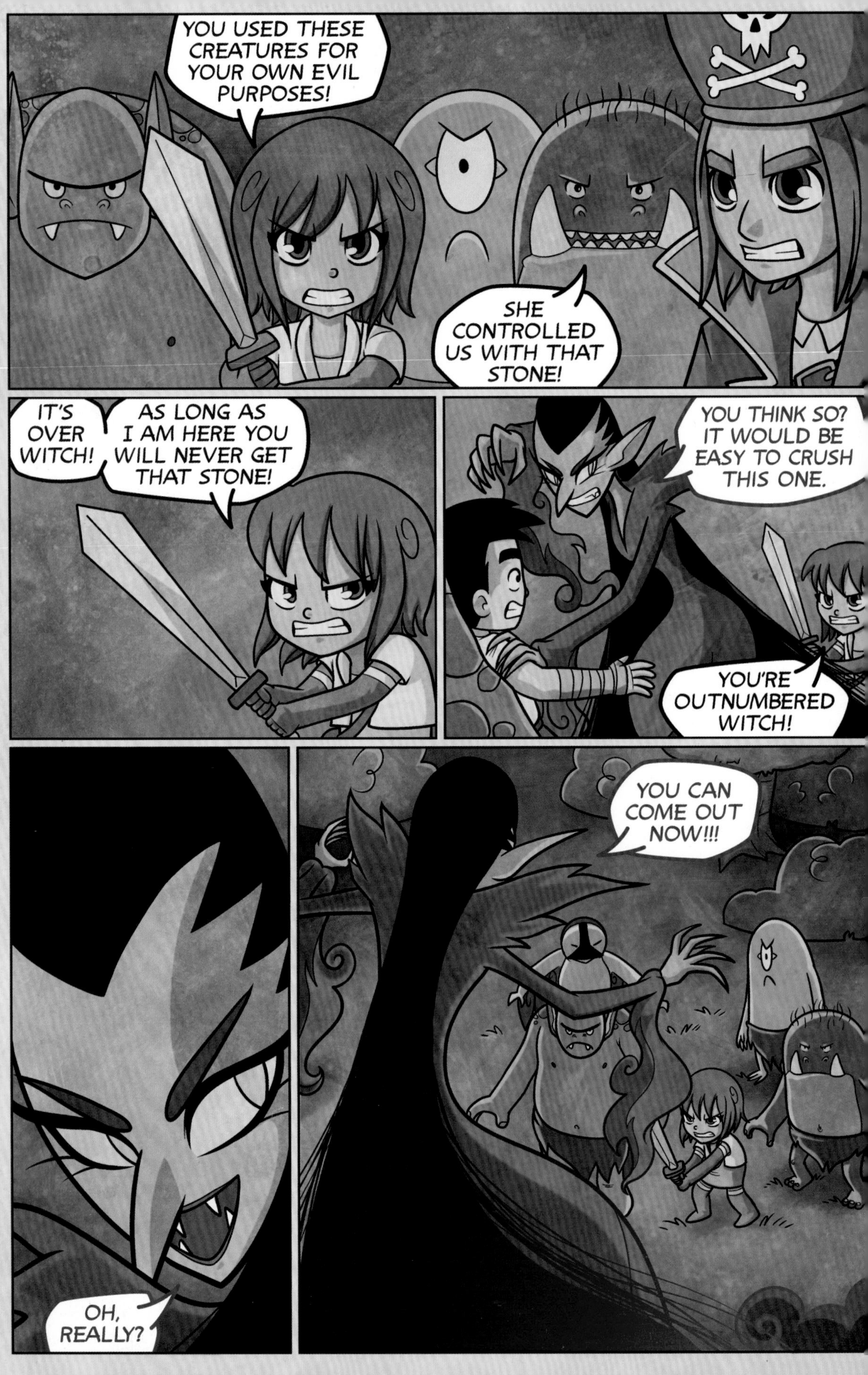
YOU USED THESE CREATURES FOR YOUR OWN EVIL PURPOSES!
SHE CONTROLLED US WITH THAT STONE!
IT'S OVER WITCH!
AS LONG AS I AM HERE YOU WILL NEVER GET THAT STONE!
YOU THINK SO? IT WOULD BE EASY TO CRUSH THIS ONE.
YOU'RE OUTNUMBERED WITCH!
OH, REALLY?
YOU CAN COME OUT NOW!!!

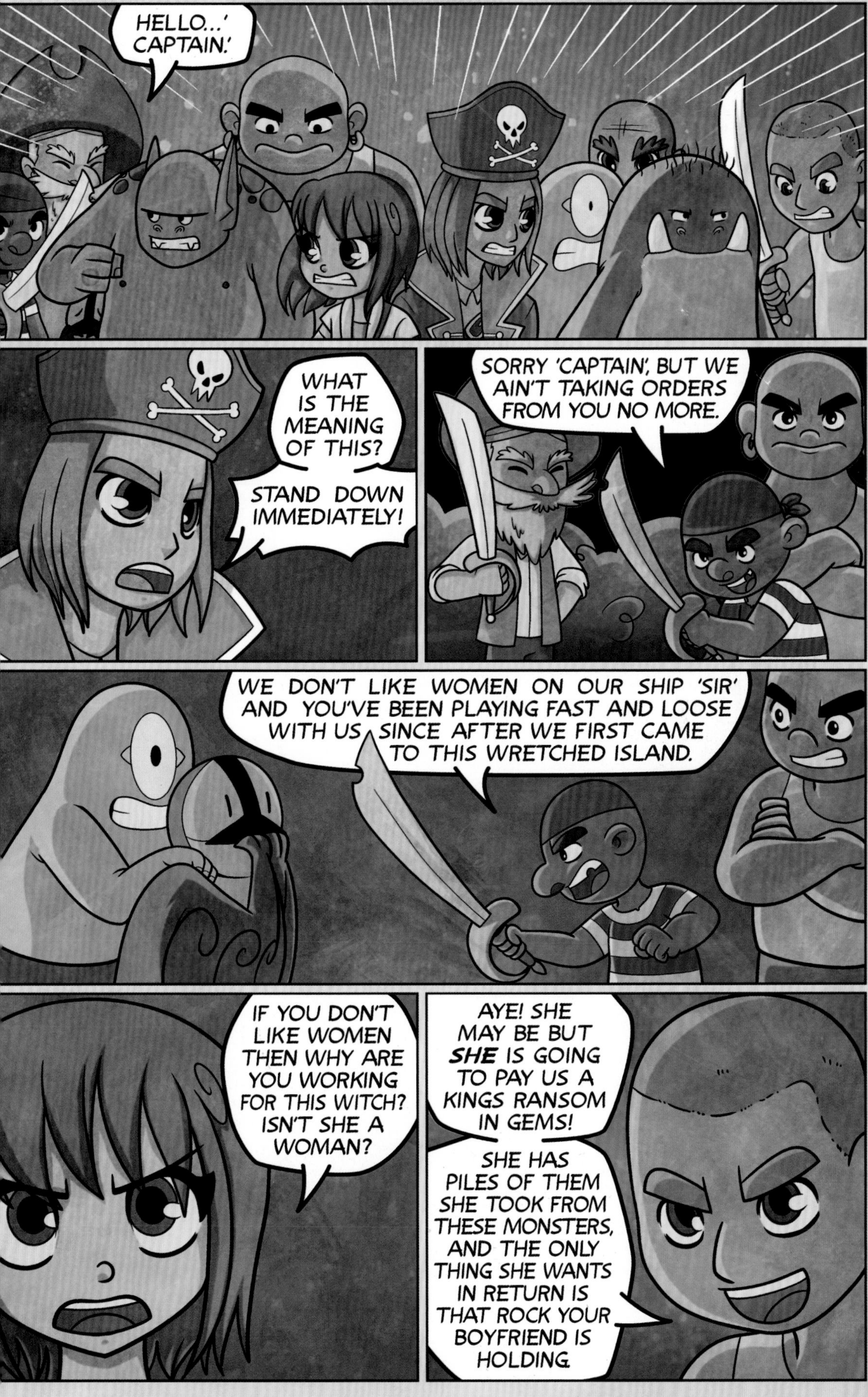
HELLO...' CAPTAIN.'
WHAT IS THE MEANING OF THIS?
STAND DOWN IMMEDIATELY!
SORRY 'CAPTAIN', BUT WE AIN'T TAKING ORDERS FROM YOU NO MORE.
WE DON'T LIKE WOMEN ON OUR SHIP 'SIR' AND YOU'VE BEEN PLAYING FAST AND LOOSE WITH US SINCE AFTER WE FIRST CAME TO THIS WRETCHED ISLAND.
IF YOU DON'T LIKE WOMEN THEN WHY ARE YOU WORKING FOR THIS WITCH? ISN'T SHE A WOMAN?
AYE! SHE MAY BE BUT ***SHE*** IS GOING TO PAY US A KINGS RANSOM IN GEMS!
SHE HAS PILES OF THEM SHE TOOK FROM THESE MONSTERS, AND THE ONLY THING SHE WANTS IN RETURN IS THAT ROCK YOUR BOYFRIEND IS HOLDING.

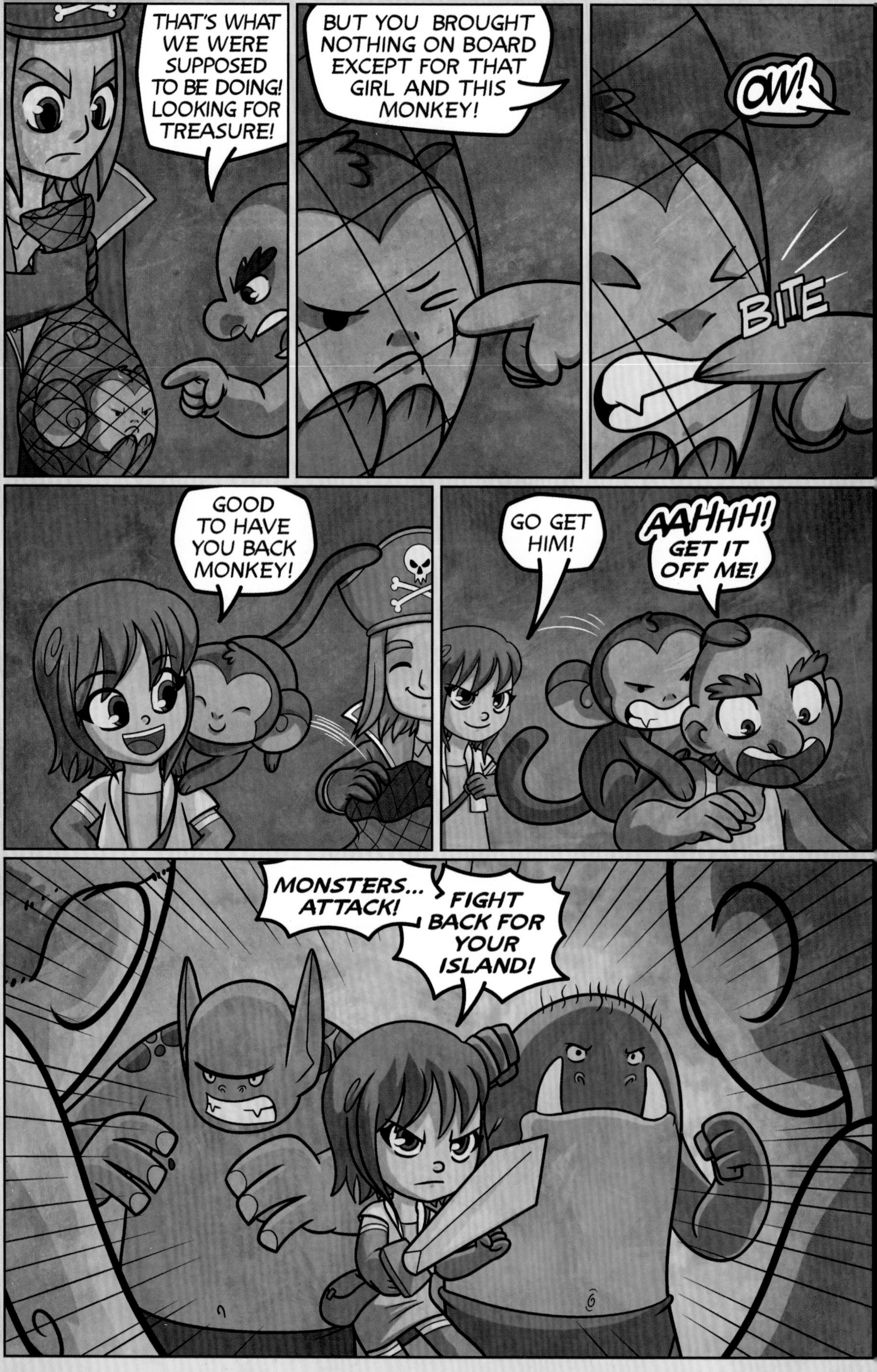
THAT'S WHAT WE WERE SUPPOSED TO BE DOING! LOOKING FOR TREASURE!
BUT YOU BROUGHT NOTHING ON BOARD EXCEPT FOR THAT GIRL AND THIS MONKEY!
OW!
BITE
GOOD TO HAVE YOU BACK MONKEY!
GO GET HIM!
AAHHH! GET IT OFF ME!
MONSTERS... ATTACK!
FIGHT BACK FOR YOUR ISLAND!

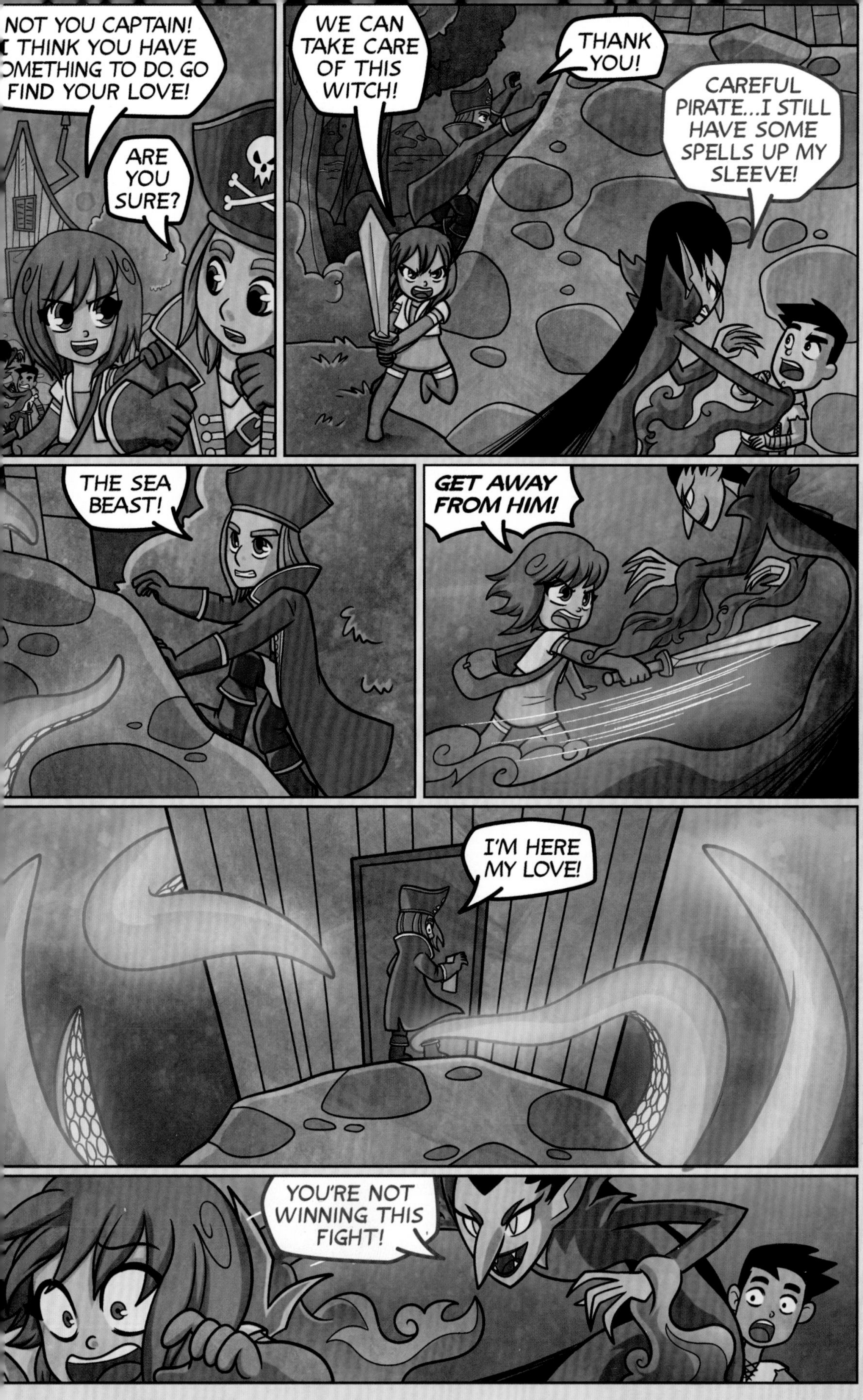

NOT YOU CAPTAIN! I THINK YOU HAVE OMETHING TO DO. GO FIND YOUR LOVE!
ARE YOU SURE?
WE CAN TAKE CARE OF THIS WITCH!
THANK YOU!
CAREFUL PIRATE...I STILL HAVE SOME SPELLS UP MY SLEEVE!
THE SEA BEAST!
GET AWAY FROM HIM!
I'M HERE MY LOVE!
YOU'RE NOT WINNING THIS FIGHT!

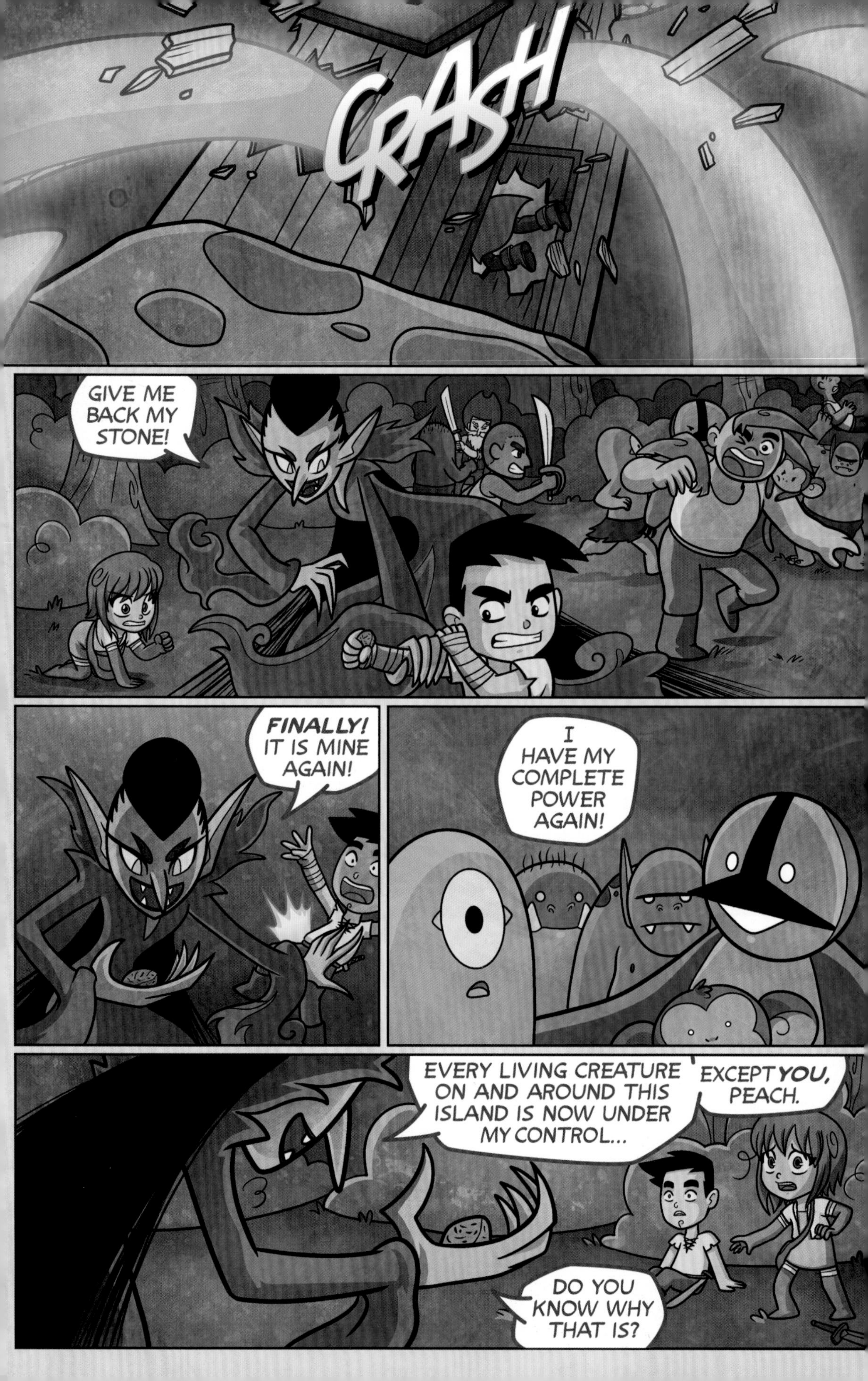
CRASH
GIVE ME BACK MY STONE!
FINALLY! IT IS MINE AGAIN!
I HAVE MY COMPLETE POWER AGAIN!
EVERY LIVING CREATURE ON AND AROUND THIS ISLAND IS NOW UNDER MY CONTROL...
EXCEPT YOU, PEACH.
DO YOU KNOW WHY THAT IS?

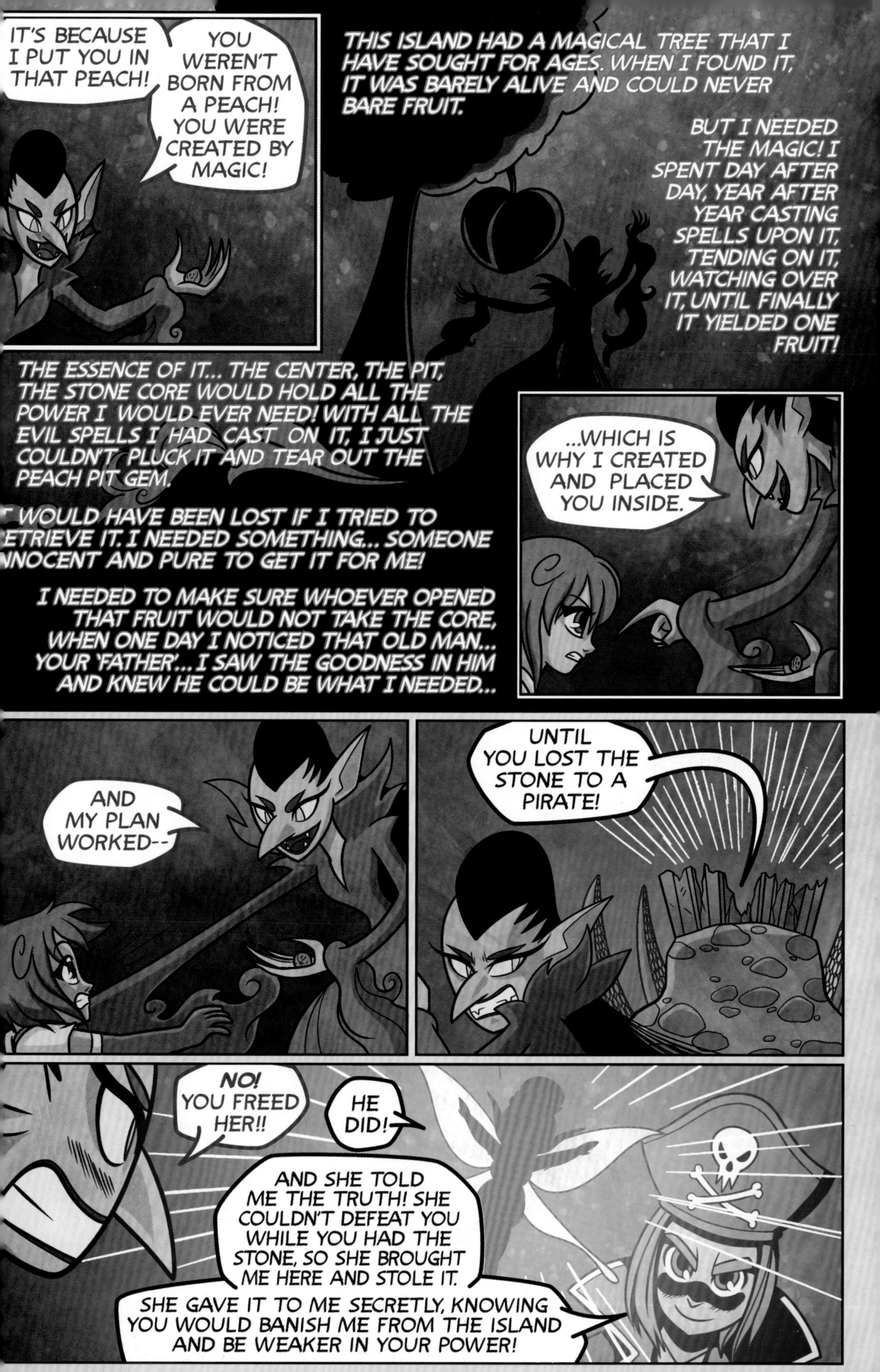
IT'S BECAUSE I PUT YOU IN THAT PEACH!
YOU WEREN'T BORN FROM A PEACH! YOU WERE CREATED BY MAGIC!
THIS ISLAND HAD A MAGICAL TREE THAT I HAVE SOUGHT FOR AGES. WHEN I FOUND IT, IT WAS BARELY ALIVE AND COULD NEVER BARE FRUIT.
BUT I NEEDED THE MAGIC! I SPENT DAY AFTER DAY, YEAR AFTER YEAR CASTING SPELLS UPON IT, TENDING ON IT, WATCHING OVER IT, UNTIL FINALLY IT YIELDED ONE FRUIT!
THE ESSENCE OF IT... THE CENTER, THE PIT, THE STONE CORE WOULD HOLD ALL THE POWER I WOULD EVER NEED! WITH ALL THE EVIL SPELLS I HAD CAST ON IT, I JUST COULDN'T PLUCK IT AND TEAR OUT THE PEACH PIT GEM.
WOULD HAVE BEEN LOST IF I TRIED TO ETRIEVE IT. I NEEDED SOMETHING... SOMEONE NNOCENT AND PURE TO GET IT FOR ME!
I NEEDED TO MAKE SURE WHOEVER OPENED THAT FRUIT WOULD NOT TAKE THE CORE, WHEN ONE DAY I NOTICED THAT OLD MAN... YOUR 'FATHER'... I SAW THE GOODNESS IN HIM AND KNEW HE COULD BE WHAT I NEEDED...
...WHICH IS WHY I CREATED AND PLACED YOU INSIDE.
AND MY PLAN WORKED--
UNTIL YOU LOST THE STONE TO A PIRATE!
NO! YOU FREED HER!!
HE DID!
AND SHE TOLD ME THE TRUTH! SHE COULDN'T DEFEAT YOU WHILE YOU HAD THE STONE, SO SHE BROUGHT ME HERE AND STOLE IT.
SHE GAVE IT TO ME SECRETLY, KNOWING YOU WOULD BANISH ME FROM THE ISLAND AND BE WEAKER IN YOUR POWER!

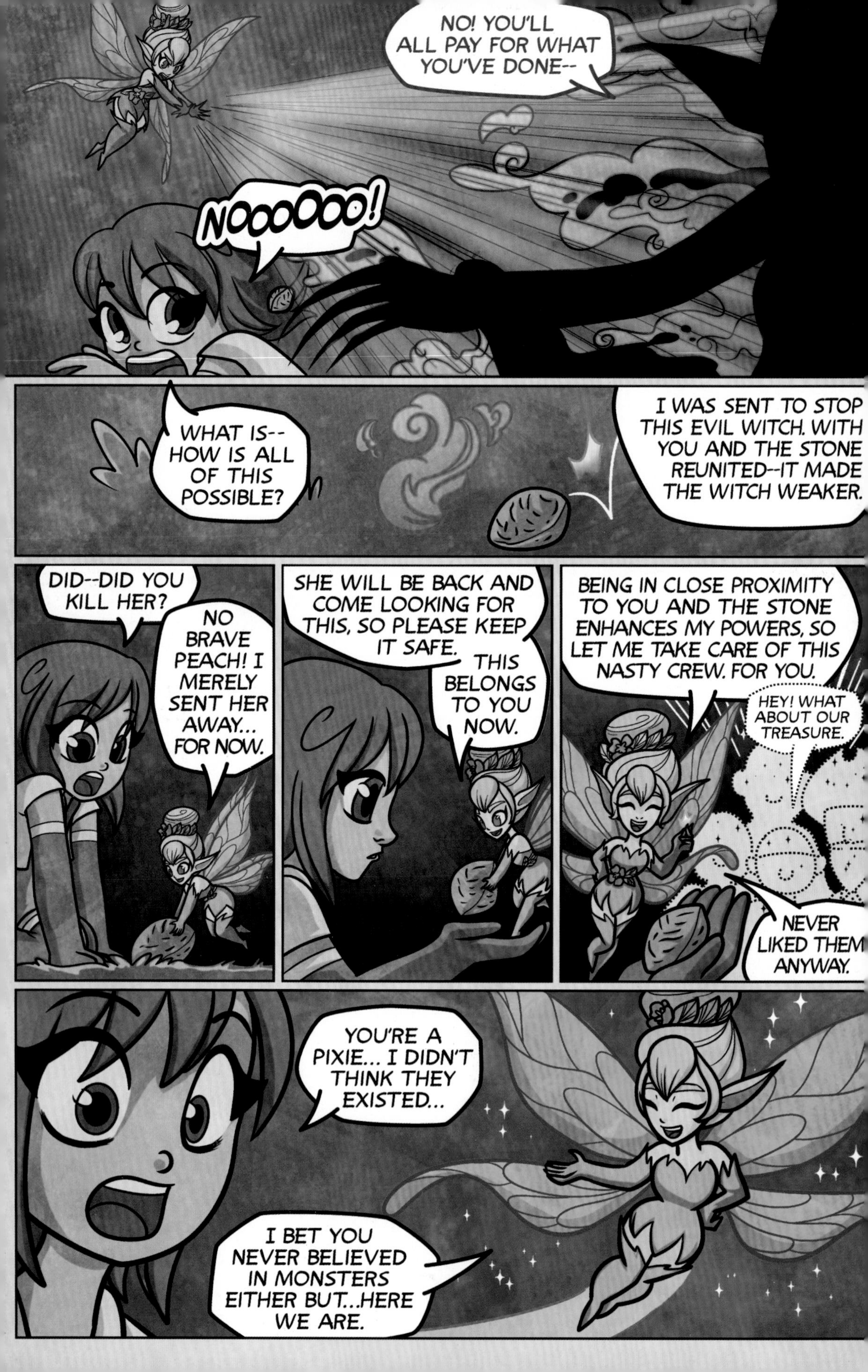
NO! YOU'LL ALL PAY FOR WHAT YOU'VE DONE--
NOOOOOO!
WHAT IS-- HOW IS ALL OF THIS POSSIBLE?
I WAS SENT TO STOP THIS EVIL WITCH. WITH YOU AND THE STONE REUNITED--IT MADE THE WITCH WEAKER.
DID--DID YOU KILL HER?
NO BRAVE PEACH! I MERELY SENT HER AWAY... FOR NOW.
SHE WILL BE BACK AND COME LOOKING FOR THIS, SO PLEASE KEEP IT SAFE.
THIS BELONGS TO YOU NOW.
BEING IN CLOSE PROXIMITY TO YOU AND THE STONE ENHANCES MY POWERS, SO LET ME TAKE CARE OF THIS NASTY CREW. FOR YOU.
HEY! WHAT ABOUT OUR TREASURE.
NEVER LIKED THEM ANYWAY.
YOU'RE A PIXIE... I DIDN'T THINK THEY EXISTED...
I BET YOU NEVER BELIEVED IN MONSTERS EITHER BUT...HERE WE ARE.

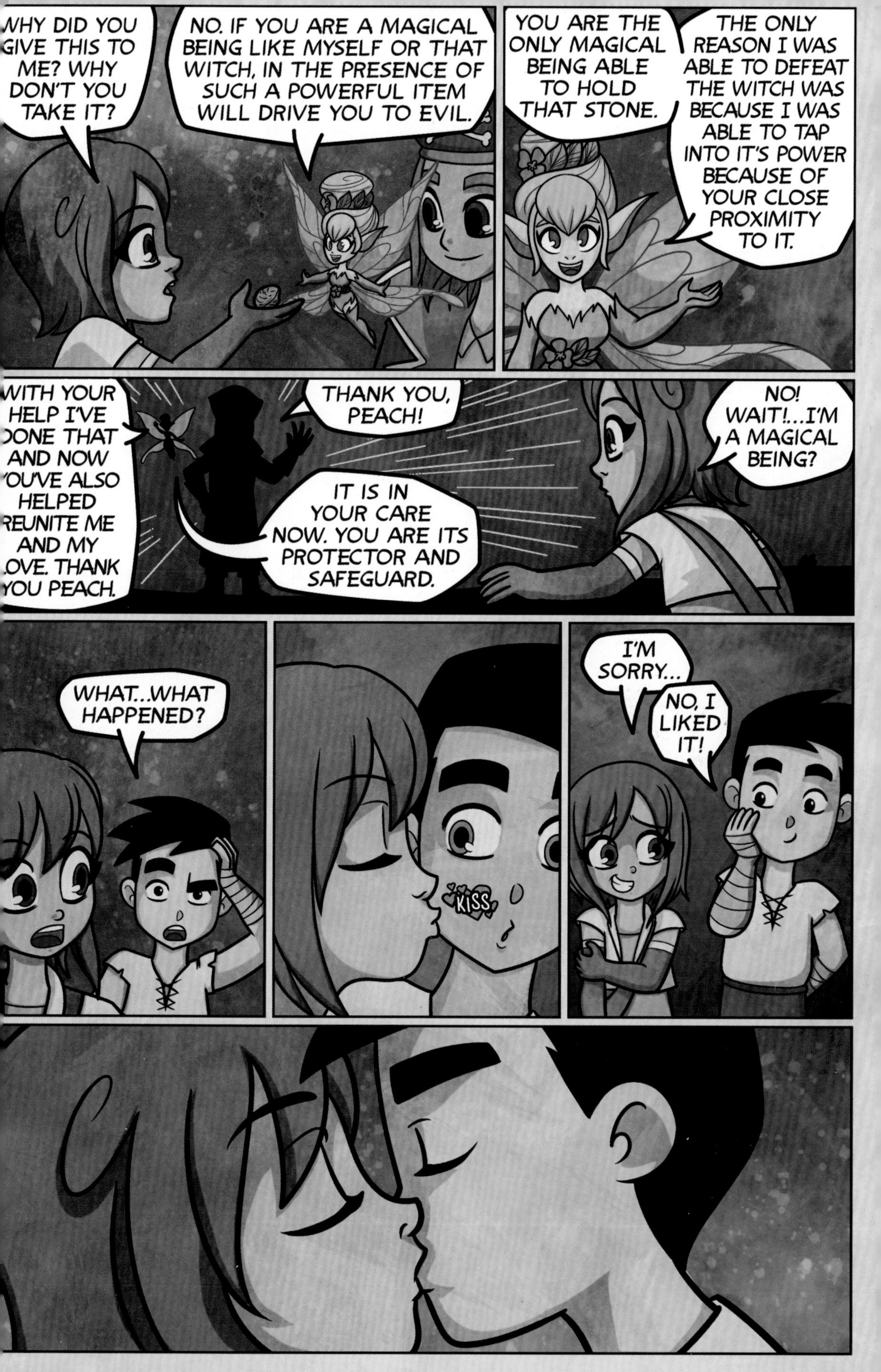
WHY DID YOU GIVE THIS TO ME? WHY DON'T YOU TAKE IT?
NO. IF YOU ARE A MAGICAL BEING LIKE MYSELF OR THAT WITCH, IN THE PRESENCE OF SUCH A POWERFUL ITEM WILL DRIVE YOU TO EVIL.
YOU ARE THE ONLY MAGICAL BEING ABLE TO HOLD THAT STONE.
THE ONLY REASON I WAS ABLE TO DEFEAT THE WITCH WAS BECAUSE I WAS ABLE TO TAP INTO IT'S POWER BECAUSE OF YOUR CLOSE PROXIMITY TO IT.
WITH YOUR HELP I'VE DONE THAT AND NOW YOU'VE ALSO HELPED REUNITE ME AND MY LOVE. THANK YOU PEACH.
THANK YOU, PEACH!
IT IS IN YOUR CARE NOW. YOU ARE ITS PROTECTOR AND SAFEGUARD.
NO! WAIT!...I'M A MAGICAL BEING?
WHAT...WHAT HAPPENED?
KISS
I'M SORRY...
NO, I LIKED IT!

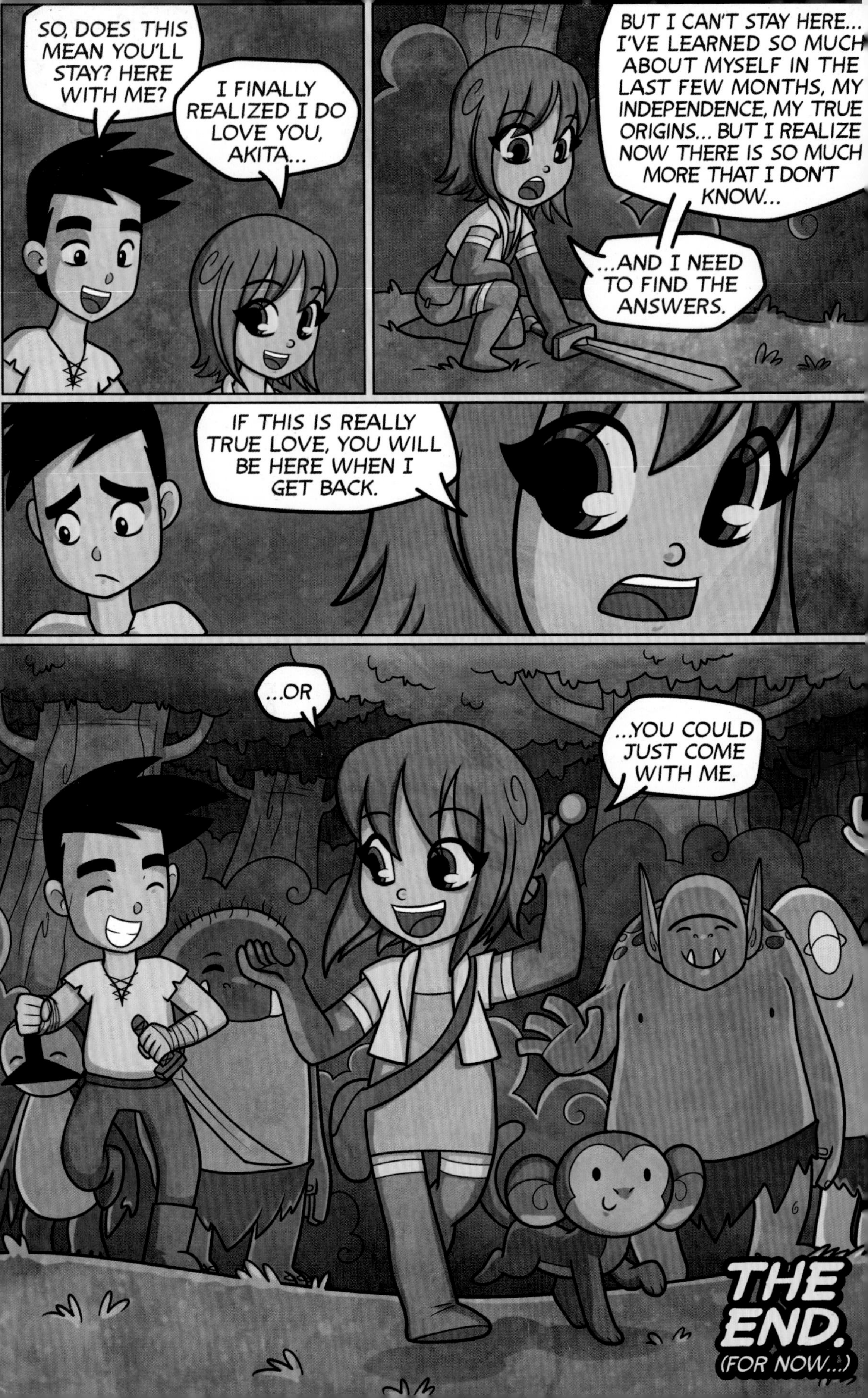
SO, DOES THIS MEAN YOU'LL STAY? HERE WITH ME?
I FINALLY REALIZED I DO LOVE YOU, AKITA...
BUT I CAN'T STAY HERE... I'VE LEARNED SO MUCH ABOUT MYSELF IN THE LAST FEW MONTHS, MY INDEPENDENCE, MY TRUE ORIGINS... BUT I REALIZE NOW THERE IS SO MUCH MORE THAT I DON'T KNOW...
...AND I NEED TO FIND THE ANSWERS.
IF THIS IS REALLY TRUE LOVE, YOU WILL BE HERE WHEN I GET BACK.
...OR
...YOU COULD JUST COME WITH ME.
THE END.
(FOR NOW...)